CW00765763

HOW DO I TELL YOU?

NICOLA MAY

Storm

Ebook ISBN: 978-1-80508-949-0
Paperback ISBN: 978-1-80508-950-6

Cover design: Jo Thomson
Cover images: Shutterstock

Published by Storm Publishing.
For further information, visit:
www.stormpublishing.co

ALSO BY NICOLA MAY

The Women of Wimbledon Common

Cockleberry Bay
The Corner Shop in Cockleberry Bay
Meet Me in Cockleberry Bay
The Gift of Cockleberry Bay
Christmas in Cockleberry Bay

Ferry Lane Market
Welcome to Ferry Lane Market
Starry Skies in Ferry Lane Market
Rainbows End in Ferry Lane Market
A Holiday Romance in Ferry Lane Market

Ruby Matthews
Working it Out
Let Love Win

Star Fish
The School Gates
Better Together
Love Me Tinder
Christmas Evie
Escape to Futtingbrook Farm

'HIV does not make people dangerous to know, so you can shake their hands and give them a hug: heaven knows they need it.'

Diana, Princess of Wales

To Kia – for good times, bad times, fun times and sad times.
HERE X

ONE

WINDSOR

The Family Home

October 2005

Victoria Sharpe sighed at the sight of the puddle that greeted her in the hallway as she entered her mother's house. Back-kicking shut the front door, the weary brunette removed her black puffer jacket and threw it with her overnight bag onto the stairs.

'Vic? Is that you, love? Let Chandler out, can you?' As the familiar voice drifted through from the lounge, a cute Border terrier appeared in the hallway, cocked his head to one side and whimpered.

Victoria lifted the pooch into her arms and kissed his scratchy forehead. 'It's a bit late for that, isn't it, lovely? Come on.'

After mopping the hallway, and with Chandler running free in the back garden, Victoria peered through the crack in the living room door. The same ache of disappointment that she had experienced through much of her adult life shrouded her like a heavy cloak. For there was her mother, slouched on the faded couch in complete darkness apart from the eerie glow of the television. Ten empty miniature bottles of vodka lay like fallen soldiers on the dusty coffee table in front of her.

Kath Sharpe glanced up at her daughter, her gaze unfocused. Her salt-and-pepper shoulder-length hair was all over the place. 'Sweetheart,' she slurred, attempting a half-smile that failed to reach her bloodshot eyes. 'You should have told me you were coming.'

As she flicked on the light and turned off the television, a fizzing anger caused Victoria's voice to tremble. 'I did, Mum, and you rang only yesterday to tell me you were making us lasagne for dinner.' She walked over to the front bay window, pulled shut the faded patterned curtains, turned on a couple of lamps and started to clear the empty bottles into an old carrier bag that was lying at her mother's feet.

'Don't throw that big orange one away, will you? I'll reuse it.'

'For goodness' sake, it's only seven o'clock, and look at you.' Victoria sighed. 'And you might as well buy a litre bottle. It must be costing you a fortune this way.'

'Oh, shut up, Miss Prissy Pants. I've been trying. *This* way means I'm trying.'

Victoria decided not to try and argue with that particular bit of addict's logic. 'I thought you were usually at the Overton-Hattons' on a Friday anyway?'

'It's half-term next week, so Connie asked if I could do a double clean once the kids have ransacked the place.'

'So I guess you've sat here all day, drinking.'

'We're all entitled to a day off, Vic. Just because you work all hours, doesn't mean everyone has to.'

Vic's 'I love my job' went completely ignored. She righted her mother's upturned slippers and placed them neatly by the sofa.

'And as for Chandler, the poor little mutt, maybe I should just take him home with me when I'm back from the hen weekend, before somebody reports you for not looking after him properly.'

Kath tutted. 'Don't be so over-dramatic. I love that dog. And he's not going to London. You don't even have a garden, do you?'

'If you ever bothered to visit me, Mum, you would know,' Vic huffed.

'It's just been a bit cold to leave the back door open, that's all,' Kath snapped. 'And over my dead body you'll take my boy anywhere!'

'If you keep on drinking like you are, Mother, then that could well be the case.'

Kath Sharpe screwed up her face and mimicked, 'If you keep on drinking like that... Anway, what hen weekend? Who's getting married now?'

'Oh, Mum. How many times! Mandy's getting married. We're going to Brighton next weekend.'

'Oh yes. Always the bridesmaid, never the bride.'

Not wanting to fuel her mother's drunken vitriol, Victoria ground her teeth and grabbed the dog's lead from the side.

Kath shifted her large bottom on the sofa. 'It's not a big deal, is it, love? The lasagne, I mean. There's a pizza in the freezer, or the new neighbour dropped in a bag of fresh samosas earlier. She's moved down from Edinburgh, she tells me. Jody, I think she said her name was.'

Victoria raised her voice. 'I don't want frozen pizza or bloody samosas. Come on, Chandler, walkies!'

'Have you heard from your brother lately?' Kath added as Chandler came flying in, jumped onto her lap and started licking her face all over.

Vic grimaced. 'Ew! Mum, don't let him do that – it's disgusting.'

'Aww, my little treasure, my little darling.' Kath ruffled the dog's ears. 'So, did you hear from Albie or not?'

'No, I left him a message on his birthday, but nothing. You?'

'Who'd have thought my precious little boy was thirty already? Looks even more like his father when he was that age, now, too.'

'Lucky him,' Vic said dismissively.

'That's not fair. Your father was many things, but his heart was always in the right place.'

'Just a shame his dick never was.'

'Victoria! Stop that talk. And yes, Albie popped in yesterday. He comes in most weeks, now. He needed fifty quid for his electric this time. I'd already given him twenty for his birthday. I really don't know what that boy does with his money.'

'All hail the prodigal son,' Vic replied with an eyeroll. 'And wake up, Mother, that money will be going straight into William Hill's pocket. You're not helping him – you know that.'

Kath Sharpe reached for the remote. '*He* walks the dog.'

'*He* plays you like a fiddle, Mum.'

'Don't be like that. He's a good lad.'

Vic shook her head. 'With a very bad habit.' She clipped on Chandler's lead. 'I'm going. I'll pick up fish and chips on the way back.'

'Get us a bottle of wine too, will you, love?'

Vic didn't reply as she picked up her bag and headed out. A woman was reversing her car onto next door's drive as Vic closed the front door behind her and Chandler let out a little bark of approval at his unexpected freedom. The window of the blue Golf slid down.

'Evening! You must be Kath's daughter. Vicki, isn't it?'

Victoria cringed inwardly at the woman's use of the pet name she really disliked. She stopped, put on her best faux smile, and nodded.

'Your mum said she was delighted that you were making the effort to come today.' The neighbour smiled warmly.

'Oh, really?'

'And thank heavens for that brother of yours. It sounds like she would be very lonely without him.' The woman got out of her car.

Victoria had already started walking on but, unable to hold her anger in any longer, turned around. 'Jody, isn't it?' Vic noticed under the outside light that the woman had long shiny black hair. Her deep brown eyes were beautifully framed by soft, dark lashes. She was a similar height and age to her.

'Joti with a t, Joti Johns... I mean Adams.' The woman had one of those mixed accents that people who had travelled to various countries seemed to pick up, the kind you could spend hours trying to decipher to work out where they were from and still be none the wiser. She held out her hand, but Vic frowned and refused to take it.

Chandler started to circle for a poo on the tiny patch of grass in front of the neighbour's bay window. Joti's face held an expression of horror at the realisation of what was about to happen to her precious piece of lawn.

Completely ignoring Chandler's intentions, Vic said, 'I appreciate your observations on my family, Mrs – or is it Miss Ad...?'

'Very much Miss... I er... I got divorced.' The woman's voice wobbled slightly.

'Oh.' Vic faltered. 'I am sorry to hear that, *Miss* Adams... but can I ask you politely to mind your own fucking business... because you know nothing about mine – or the rest of my family's, for that matter.'

With a harrumph, Joti put her head down, went inside and slammed the door shut.

A barking Chandler gleefully scrabbled at the lawn with his

back paws, causing grass and bits of *his* business to fly everywhere.

With all its riverside beauty, plentiful history and stunning architecture, Windsor held a special place in Vic's heart. She had been born Victoria Ann Sharpe in the bedroom of the house her parents had bought back in the sixties for just two thousand pounds, where her mother still lived on benefits, with a top-up from her cleaning jobs. She was named Victoria because Windsor housed one huge castle still inhabited by the royal family. And not Elizabeth, because that was her auntie's name and, in Kath Sharpe's words, 'it would just have caused too much confusion'.

Victoria's memories of living at number 28, Simpson Crescent, were neither good nor bad – up until she reached five, that was, when her brother Albie had come along, and her philandering father had upped and left, saying that he couldn't cope with the lack of sleep from another newborn. A baby he had openly declared he had never wanted. A baby who, despite being his absolute ringer as he grew, he had even cruelly insinuated wasn't his.

Her mother, who had relied on her husband's plumbing wage for everything, fell apart. To give Barry Sharpe his due, he had long paid off the mortgage with both his father's inheritance and guilt, but with no other income coming in, besides the family allowance, Kath had turned to cleaning when Albie was just two months old. That, and the various other stresses being a single parent entailed, had made her turn to the bottle.

A shivering Victoria pulled her scarf tightly to her neck as she and Chandler made their way towards the river and its long pathway.

The streets of Windsor were already beginning to fill with Friday night revellers, including squaddies from the local barracks. The town, with all its royal pageantry, was very much a tourist destination, where historic sites were visited by a plethora of nationalities. Sites including neighbouring Eton, famous for its college, whose hallowed halls had been graced by princes and prime ministers.

It was a particularly freezing October night when Victoria reached the river path.

Feeling her shoulders drop at being able to be silent with her thoughts at last, she let out a little sigh of relief. The patchy mist that had formed and floated spookily just above the water of the Thames, in combination with the sporadic cries and calls of water birds, plus creaking tree branches, made for an eerie atmosphere. Lights shining out from various yachts and narrowboats moored along the water's edge illuminated her way. You could tell the ones that were genuinely loved, with their shiny new paintwork, plant pots and twinkly fairy lights. A couple of tatty older vessels sat in complete darkness, awaiting their fair-weather owners.

Growing up, she had always loved making up stories about who lived in each boat and why – whether it be a grand tale of escape by the young couple who lived on *Pastures New*, or a city banker's weekend show-off yacht, aptly named *Fortune Afloat*. Many boats had come and gone during the years that Vic had walked this path, but there was one that had been in the same spot for as long as she could remember.

Lazy Daze, a red-and-black narrowboat that was always laden with tubs of seasonal flowers, was firmly in the 'beautifully kept' category. It was a standout vessel along the river path and inhabited by the enigmatic Jake Turner.

A voice filtered through the gloom, and Vic nearly jumped out of her skin.

'If it isn't Kath's eldest, and that little terror of a terrier. Long time no see, young lady.' Huge white plumes of smoke mixed with the chilly night air accompanied the man's posh

voice. A distinguished-looking gentleman with a white beard
and weather-wrinkled eyes sat quietly at the front of this boat,
with a thick grey blanket wrapped around him, smoking a roll-
up. His Jack Russell appeared behind him, chasing its tail and
yapping, making Chandler bark loudly in response.

'Hell, Jake, you made me jump. But good to see you.' Vic
smiled. 'Bit cold in there tonight, though, I expect?'

'God, no. Toasty as anything. A misconception of all you
naïve house-dwellers.'

'Don't knock it until you've tried it, and all that, I guess.' Vic
suddenly thought of Nate, her free-spirited other half, and how
he would be in his element living on a houseboat.

'Exactly.' Jake took a large drag from his cigarette. His little
dog ran around his feet, yapping. 'Norman, will you shut up?'
He ushered the dog inside and shut the door on him. Chandler
carried on sniffing around the path. 'From what I can see of you
in this light, you're looking well. Everything OK? Still
painting?'

Vic nodded. 'Yes, illustrating mainly... At the same place in
Putney.'

'That's years now you've been there, isn't it? I thought you'd
have your own gallery by now.'

'In my dreams, Jake.'

'When you were knee high to a grasshopper you had those
dreams, and wasn't it Van Gogh who said, "I dream of painting,
then I paint my dream"? Always keep the dream alive, young
Victoria. Promise me that?'

Vic smiled through her shiver, surprised that he had remembered her love of drawing when she had been a little girl. 'One
day, Jake, maybe. Who knows?'

'Come in for a hot chocolate and warm up.'

'That sounds so lovely, but I'm picking up fish and chips for
me and Mum.' Vic lengthened Chandler's lead to stop him
pulling. 'So, have you been on any travels lately, then?'

'Not for a while, no. I'm the old wanderer who's never wandered far.' Jake gave a throaty laugh. 'Thirty-seven years, I've been moored here now. My needs are small. And how many people can say they live in the same town as the Queen, eh? Speaking of which, how's your mum these days?' He grinned a slightly crooked grin. 'I haven't seen her or this old boy for a while.' He nodded towards Chandler, who was now busying himself sniffing a mooring post.

Victoria's face fell. 'You know – up and down.'

'The best thing I ever did was give up the demon drink, but you've got to either have a wake-up call or really want to do it.'

'It's tough for her, I know. But Jake, I just want my mum back.' Victoria's voice wobbled.

Jake's voice softened. 'You and me both, sweet girl.' He leant down to put his cigarette butt in an ashtray at his feet. 'Are you sure you don't want come in for a chat?' he offered kindly.

'No.' Vic sighed, thinking how lovely it would actually be to just sit for a while with this calm, intelligent man and not have to think about life and all its trials and tribulations. 'No thanks, Jake. I'd better get back. Next time.'

'Well, it's good to see you looking so well. And tell Kath I asked after her, will you? My Norman is always up for a play date with young Chandler on the Brocas.' He pointed his arm in the direction of the opposite riverbank. 'You tell her that too, will you?'

'Yes. I will. Definitely.' She paused for a second. 'And thank you, Jake. Thank you. That means a lot.'

Victoria's eyes stung with unexpected tears as Jake made his way back inside his floating home.

'Good boy.' Vic stopped as Chandler cocked his leg on the wall. Despite the now-dark stretch along the river pathway, she could make out two swans, silently swimming alongside them as if paddling along to her inner thoughts.

'Hello, you two,' she said aloud, and with Chandler now

happily sniffing ahead of her, her thoughts turned back to her mother. For as much as Vic tried to remain calm, it hurt her massively that Kath continued to choose drunken escape over sober reality. Especially on the weekends Vic came down from London to spend time with her.

As she walked on and the chilly night air began to clear her head further, she also began to feel a slight guilt that the new neighbour had taken the brunt of her anger this evening. If a dog had shat on her lawn and the owner hadn't cleared it up, she would be raging.

Jake noticing that her mum hadn't been walking down the path so often recently had also made Vic feel sad. Kath's deterioration was evident, and Vic wasn't sure what to do. Where was the rule book when it came to your parents making bad life decisions?

It was only recently that she had started thinking about her past and future in any kind of detail. Before, she had always lived in the moment, which involved beavering away at Glovers, the design agency where she worked as a permanent designer and illustrator, and meandering through the relationship motions with Nate, her partner of six years, without a definitive thought for the next day, let alone the next few years.

Vic had been delighted when her oldest schoolfriend, Mandy, had made the move from Windsor to London with her partner's job change, but it had also surprised her how shocked she was when said friend had announced that she was getting married.

It horrified Vic to think that in five years' time, she would be forty, and that meant thirty-five years of her life had already gone. Thirty-five years in which she couldn't recall anything of any real merit that she had achieved. The thought of this had made her not only sit up and smell the coffee, but also feel the next decade approaching at a sensational rate of knots.

Remembering the main purpose for her outing, Vic arrived

at the fish-and-chip shop, to see a young woman with a pushchair flying out of the door, causing a delicious waft of frying batter and the cries of a screaming toddler to fill the freezing air.

Thirty-five had also set off a trigger in Vic's mind about having a family of her own. Before that, she had never felt even the twinge of a maternal pull and still wasn't sure if the thought had arisen because she should be doing it or because she wanted to do it. Without discussion, she and Nate generally picked child-free hotels when they went away. Was that a sign of what was to come? And if she did decide to go down the family route, what kind of support could she expect? Her mother could hardly be relied on as the doting grandmother. Nate would be the most fun dad a child could ever wish for, but as much as she loved him, he couldn't be classed as financially or emotionally secure. Her brother lived in his own world and his gambling was a worry. And if she didn't contact her father – who was currently living with a woman twenty years his junior – on birthdays and at Christmas, she wouldn't ever hear from him. Logic told her to just let him go. But despite Barry Sharpe not being a constant in her life, she didn't want to break that bond completely. Especially now that her mum seemed to be there for her only in body, most of the time.

Hard as it was, she had to get real and accept that her life would never be like the movies, and her family were – and always would be – dysfunctional. Her father would never be that special someone she could go to for life advice; her mother would never resemble that sweet little old lady knitting baby clothes; her brother would forever be fighting his own demons. And as for her resembling the angelic daughter – well... that would never be the case, either.

She had always wished that life would throw her some kind of magical future, that her love life would start representing a heartwarming romcom, that her illustration skills would be

sought after by a famous author, or her existing painting portfolio by a huge collector. Or that she would have an art gallery
with her name above the door.

Mandy cementing her future was the wake-up call Vic had
needed. For nobody was coming to save her, and if she wanted
all these things, she realised that the only person who could set
the ball rolling on this magical mystery tour called life was her!
Maybe this was what a mid-life crisis felt like? Her mother had
told her that Sidney West, chairman of the Simpson Crescent
neighbourhood watch, had had one recently, but he was fifty
and it would take more than a two-seater sports car and a
piercing through her nose to satisfy hers.

Vic shortened Chandler's lead and headed for her favourite
bench at the leisure-centre end of the river path. When the
beloved pooch gave a tiny bark, she swept him up and snuggled
him into her for warmth.

'If only we could look into a crystal ball, hey, fella?' Or
maybe not, Victoria thought. As well as the good, you'd see all
the bad things to come – what a terrifying prospect.

She knew that to get where she wanted in life, she would
have to put a plan in place – but that would mean making big
life decisions, and she wasn't particularly good at those.

And how on earth could anyone be expected to ride ahead
into a happy future if they were always pulling the reins back
on it themselves?

Eleven-year-old Chandler could no longer be said to be in the
prime of life, and with his short legs tired, and tiny paws cold
after the walk, he whimpered to get in the front door when they
arrived back at her mum's place. Vic let him in, deposited the
fish suppers and wine on the hall table, and stealthily headed
back out to clear up the dog's mess from next door's lawn.

Just as she was bending down in front of the bay window,

the front door opened and Joti screamed loudly, causing Vic to drop to her knees and scream even louder. Vic then saw the funny side. 'I'm so sorry I startled you,' she said through her laughter. 'I was just—'

'I sorted it already,' Joti replied tightly. She was clearly in no mood for laughing back. 'Excuse me, I must get to work.'

'Work? At this time?'

'Yes, work at this time.' The attractive woman headed towards her Golf, her face deadpan. 'And anyway, I didn't think you liked nosy neighbours.'

'Touché.' Vic stood up and bit her lip. 'Look, I'm sorry I was so rude earlier. You really didn't deserve the way I spoke to you, and certainly not Chandler's untimely defecation. It was just—'

'You're right, I didn't,' Joti cut in. She got in the car and slammed the door, but then the window slid down, and she regarded Vic thoughtfully. 'When I have a little tantrum like that,' she said, her voice softer now, 'I usually take stock and ask myself what's really the matter.'

As Chandler whined for attention through a crack in the front door, Victoria stood for a second, taking in Joti's wise words. Then she burst into tears.

TWO

LONDON

The Boyfriend

'Jesus, Nate.'

Victoria put down her overnight bag, threw her coat on a chair and reached to turn down the radio, from which the Pussycat Dolls were blaring out at full volume. The kitchen sink was overflowing with unwashed glasses, dishes and pans. The draining board was empty, apart from an ashtray that was bulging with cigarette butts.

At just five feet two, with a petite frame, soulful blue eyes, neat appearance, and hair that cascaded like a waterfall of mahogany waves down her back, Victoria was the antithesis of her tall, gangly partner, who, with messy chestnut hair and full lips, had appeared in the doorway yawning loudly, wearing only a pair of snug black boxers.

Victoria tutted. 'It's three o'clock. Don't tell me you've just got up.'

'Give me a break, Vic. I haven't had a weekend off in months, and I'm on a straight seven after today.' Nathaniel Carlisle's usually light Cumbrian accent strengthened.

Embracing her, he leant down to kiss the head of his girl. 'So, how was Katherine?'

'Katherine was pissed.'

'The whole time?'

'Yep.' Vic sighed heavily. 'My fault on Friday, though, as I felt I had to drink wine to get through it myself.'

'Oh, dear.' Nate held her tightly.

'Tell me about it. I'm not sure how I managed to stay the two nights, but the place was in a mess, as usual, so I cleared up and took Chandler on a couple of decent walks to the river. It's just so depressing that she won't help herself.'

He lowered his head to kiss her. Vic quickly pulled away. 'Ew, Nate! You stink of beer, sweat and cigarettes.'

'Hmm. A desirable combination.' He grinned boyishly. 'And I did tell you to stay home. We're like ships that pass in the night, lately.'

Vic smiled back at him apologetically. 'I wish I had. I fell for the guilt trip. She sounded sober when I last spoke to her. Promised me she was off it. And when I got there, she proceeded to be vile and tell me that I was always the bridesmaid.' Vic made a little groaning noise. 'She's like Jekyll and Hyde when she's drinking.'

'I'm sorry it was so awful.' Nate squeezed her arm, then went to the fridge. 'When's Mandy's hen do, anyway?'

'Next weekend. I could do with it being the week after. I haven't arranged any sort of surprises yet and, being head bridesmaid, that's my job, evidently.'

'So I'll be home all alone again,' Nate said dramatically, levering the top off his Budweiser and pulling a piteous face. 'Although I'll be working for most of it.'

'Exactly.' Vic shook her head at him. 'And it was you who chose to take on the most anti-social job in the world.'

'Yes, and I'm still not sure if it's what I want to do. I feel caged. It's a cool restaurant, but when I'm out the back in that steaming kitchen, I could be at a Michelin star place or at Nando's. It makes no difference to me. And I can't see me becoming a head chef anytime soon. The money's shite for the hours I do, too.'

'Oh, Nate.' Vic started to busy herself by clearing the washing-up bowl.

'What does "Oh, Nate" mean? Please don't start on me. And leave that – it's my mess. I'll sort it later.'

Feeling a twinge of guilt for laying into Nate, who despite working ridiculously long hours did usually pull his weight in the flat, Vic turned off the hot tap and squeezed his arm. 'I'm sorry, Boo. I'm just agitated after the weekend I had. I looked at Mum before I left. She's sixty-one now, which isn't in any way old, and I can't see her ever giving up the booze. I reckon she'll continue the same old routine, doing the same cleaning jobs until she's so unfit she can't. She'll sit on the same old sofa, poisoning herself and watching the same crap TV for the rest of her life. It's such a waste. What if I end up like her?'

'What the fuck, Vic? Listen to me. You're the one who tells me that we're all in charge of our own destiny. You're doing well in your job, you have great friends, and most importantly, you have me.' Nate's eyes smiled at her. 'I do love you, you know.'

'I know, but we're thirty-five and still live in a one-bedroom rented flat in Wandsworth.'

'Oh, Vic. Not this again. Most couples our age are in exactly the same situation.'

As Vic emptied the filthy ashtray into the bin, her subconscious spoke up without warning. 'It's not just that, is it?'

'What is it then, baby girl? Talk to me.'

Vic let out a funny little anguished groan. 'I'm too tired to do anything now. And you will remember to ask for the weekend off for Mandy's wedding, won't you?'

'What date is it again?'

'Nate! I've told you so many times.' Vic tutted. 'And what

happened here?' She picked up her art easel, which was lying on the floor, and propped it against the kitchen wall in its rightful place. Nate shrugged. 'And it's next month, the nineteenth of November. The wedding, that is.'

Nate screwed up his face. 'Weird time of year to be getting married, isn't it?'

'I know. Her brother's flying over from New York, and it was the only time he could fit in around his work, or something.'

'I'll try and get it off but no promises, all right?'

She rounded on him. 'Really?! It's my best mate's wedding, for Christ's sake.'

Nate took a slurp of beer and laughed. 'I'm teasing you, little one.' As he kissed the back of her neck, Vic wriggled, giggled, then pulled away. 'I'll be there. But for now, how about I have a shower and then me and my moody little Sharpie can make some much needed lurve.'

Vic groaned. As much as she still did fancy him, she really wasn't in the mood for sex. In fact, she had been so stressed about her mother and worrying about the future, she hadn't been in the mood for it a lot lately. Realising that she was beginning to run out of excuses, she frantically thought back to when she'd last been menstruating. 'I've got my period, Nate. Sorry.'

'*Quelle surprise.*' Nate turned up the radio. Victoria's jaw clenched as he began singing along to the Arctic Monkeys, then he stopped, and said, 'No betting required here, I *know* you look good on the dance floor. Ruthie at work said she thought I looked a bit like a more rugged version of Alex Turner, too. I'll take that.' He started dancing around her. 'Love this track!' Nate gently smacked his girlfriend's bottom, headed for the bathroom and shouted back, 'At least come and join me in the shower.'

Who the fuck is Ruthie – or Alex Turner, for that matter? Vic thought as she turned off the radio and resumed washing up.

· · ·

It would be six years this Christmas since she had first met her quirky boyfriend in the queue at McDonald's in Waterloo station. They were both drunk, had simultaneously ordered a Big Mac meal with 'fat Coke' and then proceeded to chat about the joy that was McDonald's after a bender and the hell that was families at Christmas. He had insisted that she write her number on a serviette, which she had thrown back at him as she sprinted for the platform to find the train that would take her home to Windsor. And the rest was history.

She had been twenty-nine then, and had just moved back in with her mum after breaking up with Steady Stuart, an accountant five years her senior, who created spreadsheets to back up spreadsheets and who had insisted they had sex on the same days at the same time every week. They also had a weekly meal planner stuck on the fridge. Initially, she had liked having spaghetti bolognese every Monday and doggy style on a Saturday, for it created the order that she had never had growing up. And it helped that Stuart was extremely good-looking and hung like a racehorse. But after two years, she realised that she had just been desperate to make it work. That the magic had never been there, and as much as she craved order, order had never really craved her. And that as much as size did matter, spreadsheets did not.

Prior to that, her love life had mainly been drunken flings followed by prolonged periods of being single where she would flit on and off match.com, not really knowing what she wanted apart from occasional no-strings sex.

The spontaneity of Nate had been just the tonic she had needed after Steady Stuart. They were opposites in every way. Nate had been working at a call centre when she had first met him, then went on to be a garage forecourt attendant, a delivery man and recently a pot washer promoted to sous-chef at a restaurant in Putney. He paid his way – well, a two-thirds-to-one-third ratio on the rent, as she earned more than him. Their once-regular holidays together now consisted of Nate going away on some kind of annual mountain-biking holiday with his mates, whilst she'd have a spa break with the girls. Then, as Nate respected that his girl preferred sitting on a quiet quay or beach and painting to partaking in the more energetic pursuits that he enjoyed, together they would have the odd weekend or week somewhere picturesque and hot. So, with compromise, everything had been ticking along nicely. Until Mandy had announced her upcoming nuptials, that was.

Vic got into bed and plumped up her top pillow. Nate was already in and fiddling about with his iPod. He didn't move or look at her as he spoke. 'We used to always have a shower together on a Sunday night.'

Vic snuggled into his side and kissed him on the cheek. 'I know. I'm sorry I've been so preoccupied lately.'

'I do sometimes wonder if you still love me,' Nate replied solemnly.

Vic sat up abruptly and propped herself up on her elbow. 'Where's all this come from?'

Nate continued with his music search. Victoria put her hand over the screen, and he batted away her hand, frowning. 'Vic, stop it.'

'Boo, look at me.' Victoria's voice had softened.

Nate turned to face her and gave one of his sexy lopsided smiles that still made her heart skip a beat. 'What's up, my little Sharpie?'

She gave him a quick peck on the lips. 'It's not that I don't love you, Boo. You know I do.'

'Are you trying to convince yourself of that, or me?' Vic stayed silent as he continued. 'I tell you what, let's promise that after Mandy's hen weekend, we make more time for us. OK?'

Vic nodded.

'A date night at least once a month, and we start having our Sunday showers again.' He began to tickle her. 'Or how about we cut out the middleman and have a Sunday shag right now?'

Vic squealed and wriggled away from him. 'Oh, baby. I told you. I'm knackered and it's day one of coming on and…'

'It's OK, I can wait.' Nate kissed her nose. 'But be warned: it'll be the longest shower you've ever had. Or saying that, maybe the quickest.' He laughed aloud. 'Come on, let's get some sleep.'

Vic snuggled back down under the covers and held Nate tightly to her, covering his back with butterfly kisses as she did so. There was no doubt she loved him – but in what capacity? She realised too that on top of worrying about her relationship and family troubles, she couldn't shake the niggling discontent that her conversation with Jake about not fulfilling her potential as an artist had fuelled. And she had no idea how she was going to address any of it.

THREE

BRIGHTON

The Hen

Mandy Burgess waved frantically at Vic from the train window as it pulled into Clapham Junction station. Once Vic and her wheelie case were successfully bundled on, they sat opposite each other, grinning.

'You look lovely,' Vic said. Mandy's long, black velvet coat accentuated her voluptuous curves. Vic reached forward and touched her friend's tonged blonde locks. 'And did you curl this yourself? Impressive.'

'I did indeed. And lovely maybe, but I'm so bloody fat. Every time I think I really must try and diet before the wedding, I seem to cram more in my mouth because of the nerves. The dress has had to be taken OUT two inches already. You should have seen the seamstress's face at the wedding shop. She was like, "Well, this is rare – very rare indeed."'

Vic grinned. 'Stupid cow.'

'Yes, that she was. Thank goodness my Steve loves me just the way I am.'

Vic giggled. 'We all love you just the way you are. And

imagine if you were too skinny – how disproportionate would those tremendous breasts look on you?'

'Yes, I'd probably keep losing my balance and falling on my face, and that really isn't a good look, is it?' They laughed aloud.

'Saying that, I'd rather your curves than my washboard look.'

'Oh, Vic. You can wear anything and look good in it. And you have the hair of a Greek goddess.'

'We women are never happy, are we?' Vic sniffed. 'I have the metabolism of a marathon runner so can eat more or less what I want, but these bits of bone sticking out, around my shoulders... they just look...'

Mandy gave her friend a stern look.

'OK... I'm shutting up now. Saying that, I do wonder if when I get older and it all slows down, I'll become short and fat like a little piglet.'

'I thought you were shutting up,' Mandy replied dryly, and they both laughed. The frosty-looking man on the row of seats next to them got up and moved down to the next carriage. Trying not to laugh again, the two women raised their eyebrows at each other.

Mandy grinned. 'I'm so excited. A night away with my besties – what's not to like! Orla is running late, so is meeting us at the hotel. There's a story to her tardiness, apparently.'

'Of course there is.' Vic had a flashback to the day she had met the feisty Irishwoman who had arranged a hospitality event for some of Glovers' customers when she had first joined the company. 'Ending with the words, "He was quite the ride," no doubt.' Grinning, Vic pulled two miniature bottles of Chardonnay and some plastic glasses from her bag. 'Let's start as we mean to go on, shall we?'

Mandy waited for the train to pull out of the station, then carefully filled her glass. 'The best news is that my future mother-in-law and sister-in-law have bad colds, so they're not coming. Well, that's what they said, anyway.'

'What about your mum?'

'Sore point. Church has taken over – again! Said it's not worth her coming for one night as she's got to be there on Sunday as she forgot it's her turn to do the flowers. So, it's just me, you and Orla. I really couldn't face inviting anyone from work.'

Vic laughed. 'Sing Hosannah!'

'Don't, I'm already coming out in hives, as Mother's only gone and put me up for the "Silent Night" solo at the annual carol service.' Mandy put her hand to her forehead in mock horror. 'I might get my Steve to extend the honeymoon, so we miss the whole shebang.'

'Don't remind me about Christmas.' Vic sighed. 'I'm dreading this year, to be honest. Mum's on one at the moment. It sounds like Albie's gambling is out of control and I won't even have Nate to pacify me, as he's off up to the Lakes to spend it with his dad and brother.'

'Oh, Vic. I'm sorry.'

'Nothing to be sorry about. The facts are that my dear mother is an alcoholic and won't get any help, and my brother is bleeding her dry. Nothing's changed. Or maybe I have?'

Mandy tutted. 'Poor Kath. And what do you mean, you've changed?'

'It's just you getting married all of a sudden has made me look at myself and what I want out of life.'

'Oh, Vic. It's hardly sudden, is it? I've been with Steve for ten years, so we're practically married anyway.'

'I know, but...'

'Is everything OK with you and Nate?'

Vic bit her lip. 'We're just ticking along as usual, but I suddenly feel like I do want to do so much more with my life. It's a weird dichotomy because I reckon I could take my art further, but I also think I want kids – but I don't know if that's because society makes me think I *should* have kids. And if I don't have them, would I feel I've missed out on something? Or maybe I want them just because I don't want to be alone when I'm old.'

'Wow, that's cheery – and a lot to take in.' Mandy raised her eyebrows.

'I'm just trying to keep it real.' Vic shrugged. 'But it's a fact, our bodies have a best-before date when it comes to babies. I'm thirty-five, Mand, and stupidly assumed that things would work out on their own, that life would work out without any prompting, but it doesn't, and it hasn't yet... And I'm at a bit of a cross-roads, if I'm honest.'

'Hmm. I've been feeling similarly,' Mandy acknowledged. 'Kids has always been our next step and I want them to have the same surname, hence the big day.'

Vic laughed. 'Who says romance is dead, eh?'

'Joking aside, mate, have you spoken to Nate about how you're feeling?'

Vic groaned. 'His idea of the perfect life would be not working and living in a tent, foraging in the middle of the Outer Hebrides. Don't get me wrong, I do love him, and I do love the freeness of him.' She giggled. 'Remember when we first met and he convinced me that wild camping in the Lake District would be amazing? I was too scared to go outside the tent in the middle of the night to wee, so I had to crouch over a bucket in the corner of the tiniest tent on earth.'

Mandy laughed. 'Yes, and the walk you did on the South-West Coast Path where he had to literally drag you up the steep bits by the waistband of your jeans as you're so scared of heights.'

'I did do some amazing paintings on those holidays, though, and I really did try to follow his passions at the start.' Vic sighed deeply. 'Aww, bless Nate. I'm being so spiky with him lately.

He's done nothing wrong apart from being him. And... well...
we haven't had sex for ages either.'

'Oh. Does he still want it?' Mandy looked concerned.

'Yes. It's me who doesn't. He wants it all the time, which
makes me feel worse. He's been really understanding. I don't
know what's wrong. Is it the beginning of the end?' Victoria
groaned. 'He's all I've known for so long, Mand, but...' She put
her hand to her head. 'I don't know what's going on with me.'

'Well. If you *can* sort it between you, that will involve
communication, Vic...'

Vic screwed up her face. 'I know. I know.'

'Well, then, it could be a positive. If you do decide to go
down the kids route, maybe he can be the house husband. He
doesn't like working... and you're so talented, Vic, and your
earning power could be huge if you went for it, so you *could*
work from a tent in the middle of a field. Have the best of all
worlds. The successful career and kids running around with
bare feet being home-schooled. Then everyone would be happy.
But you just need to communicate that to him. Men aren't
mind-readers, mate. They need to be spoon-fed.'

Vic stuck out her bottom lip and touched her friend's knee.
'You're right there. Although I think you're just being nice
about my art.'

'I'm not – you really *are* talented. Ray knows that, too –
that's why he's looked after you so well for so many years.'

'I know. Ten years in one job – that's unheard of these days.
But you're right, Ray is a great boss and with Nate being so
flaky with his work, I need that stability.'

'I understand that,' Mandy added. 'But what do you mean
about taking your art further? Can you not do that as well as
work at Glovers?'

Vic sighed. 'I guess I want to promote it to a wider audience.
Take more time to do my own pieces and sell them privately.
My dream is a gallery of my own, but that costs and I need a

guaranteed income to pay for life and all its trappings, and well... I'm not sure I'm even good enough. And I'm definitely not brave enough to take that step.'

'That Mrs Imposter Syndrome is a right bitch, isn't she?' Mandy tutted. 'I just wish I had an ounce of your ambition.'

'It's clearly not combined with drive, though, is it?' Vic drained her drink.

The train pulled into another station and an elderly couple took the seats adjacent to them. Mandy cleared her throat. 'A happy marriage, kids and a little part-time job has always been the extent of my future wants and needs. And the only reason I chose to be a teacher wasn't for the love of it – it was for the steadiness of it all and knowing my exact holiday dates. But as soon as I have a kid, that's it, I'm out of there. It's far harder than I ever bargained for.'

'And being a mum won't be?' Vic raised her eyebrows. 'Steve knows of this cunning plan, does he?'

'I'm off the pill already, so hopefully he will do soon.' Mandy grinned and took another sip of wine. 'And as for you, darling, there will be a solution. There always is. Just after my dad died, Mum said to me that life is what happens to you when you are busy making other plans. Remember, they had a luxury cruise around the world all booked and paid for – but Dad's heart had other ideas.'

Vic reached out and squeezed her best friend's hand. 'Yes, that was so tragic. He'd be so proud of you, you know?'

'Thanks, hun.' Mandy sniffed back a tear.

'Anyway, this weekend is not about me, my lovely lady. It is about Miss Mandy Burgess, soon to be Mrs Mandy Taylor.' Vic reached into her bag and pulled out two bright pink straws and handed her friend one. 'Ooh, look! Plastic willies!' she exclaimed, causing the old couple nearby to laugh. 'Where did they come from? Suck on this, lady, and let's be as tacky as hell.'

Mandy raised her glass in the air. 'And what goes on in Brighton, stays in Brighton. OK?'

'Sorry, sorry, I know, I'll be late for my own fecking funeral, so I will.' Orla O'Malley's loud Dublin accent reverberated around the Brighton hotel lobby as she sped across to where Vic and Mandy were tucking into cocktails and thick chips, her unruly black curls flying everywhere. Her long, red faux-fur coat was done up on the wrong buttons, allowing a glimpse of one of her perfectly pert fake boobs, housed in a black lacy bra.

Vic immediately handed her eccentric half-Irish, half-Nigerian friend the cocktail menu as Orla continued. 'I dripped the whole yolk from a bacon and egg butty *all* down my posh new top. Went to the disgusting train bog, tried to rub it with a paper towel, got blue fluff all down it, so took it off, threw it in the bin, and put my coat back on. So I need to go shopping in The Lanes before we go out tonight. Where are we going, anyway?'

'And breathe... and sit down,' Mandy replied calmly.

'After you've put your tit away, that is,' Vic added.

Orla dealt with her stray boob, completely unabashed. 'So, what are we doing, Vic?'

'Umm. OK, so a cocktail and light lunch here, and as it's sunny, maybe head to the pier? Or a bit of retail therapy, now madam here needs a new top, get ready, then dinner and a nightclub of everyone's choosing. There's a twenty-four-hour café on the front so we can stuff our faces into the early hours with unnecessary carbs and hate ourselves for the rest of the week.'

'So, in short, you haven't planned anything specific, have you?' Orla chipped in, then summoning the waiter with a wink, swiftly ordered a Sex on the Beach.

'And what exactly have *you* brought to the party, Miss Shag O'Malley?' Mandy drained her glass and let out a little burp.

Orla assumed a posh British accent. 'I'll have you know, dear friends, that I *am* the fucking party.'

'Well, at least we have plastic willies to start,' Vic laughed, handing Orla one. 'And our dear little hen – or should I say, this old bantam here – said she didn't want to dress up or have a fuss made of her.'

'Jesus, Vic, we all love a fuss.' Orla went to undo her coat then, remembering she only had a bra on underneath, stopped herself.

'It's all good, Vic.' Mandy slurped her cocktail through a straw. 'Let's just go with the flow, ladies. We haven't all been together for what seems like ages.' She looked at Orla. 'And where were you last night, anyway, you dirty harlot?'

Orla grinned. 'I woke up next to the most delicious-looking creature in East Finchley. On the bed, there was a book of Byron's poetry and one of those weird cats with no hair staring back at me. Scared the fecking life out of me. The cat, not the man. Anyway, I was so rattled that I remembered neither being serenaded nor shagged, so for fear of getting scratched – or worse – by the hairless beast – again, the cat, not the man – he did have a full old nest of chest hair – I just upped and left.'

An already tipsy Vic descended into fits of laughter, but Mandy was serious. 'Does it not bother or worry you that you constantly wake up with strangers?'

'He wasn't a stranger, I chatted to him for a while in the bar the night before. I know his name – well, his first name, anyway – and it was fun at the time, I think.'

Mandy shook her head. 'It may be a bit dull sometimes, but it makes me realise how happy I am that I just have Steve to wake up to. At least I know where I am.'

'What's happening here? Do I smell judgement?' Orla gave

the young waiter a big grin as he placed the colourful cocktail down in front of her.

'No,' Vic replied bluntly. 'Just jealousy.'

The rhythmic pulse of heavy bass echoed through the still night as Victoria stepped out of the buzzing nightclub onto the Brighton beachfront. With a sense of liberation, she inhaled deeply, letting the cold, salty air fill her lungs. A lethal combination of cocktails and too much wine had left her feeling heady.

She plonked herself down on a bench overlooking the sea, and decided to call Nate.

'Hello.' The shrill voice of a woman answered his mobile. Loud music blared out in the background.

'Erm, can I speak to Nate, please?' Vic's drunk mind wasn't even sure why she had called him in the first place now.

'Sure, who wants him?' The woman was shouting.

Vic felt her heart beating faster. 'It's Vic... his girlfriend.'

'Oh, I thought he was a single Pringle.' Vic moved her ear as the woman shouted. 'Nate! It's your *girlfriend*!'

'Hey, it's me.' Vic tried to keep upbeat.

'Sharpie! You having fun, baby girl?' Nate sounded off his face.

'Who was that?'

'Just a girl I work with. We all decided to go back to hers after shift. Shit... my battery is about to d—'

Vic glared at the screen. She was so used to Nate either being at work or home chilling when not at the restaurant, that the fact that he was out partying and had allowed a woman to pick up his phone had completely thrown her. Who was she? And where was this house they were all at? And was it 'all' of them or just him and her? And he clearly hadn't conveyed to whoever had just picked up his phone that he had a girlfriend. Also, how dare he moan about always working and not getting any weekend downtime. It sounded just like how they used to party, together. Hedonistically, without a care in the world. Maybe they *were* just stuck in a rut of boring monotony now. She tried to call him back, but his battery had clearly gone. 'Fuck you, Nate Carlisle,' Vic drunkenly uttered under her breath.

'Talking to yourself is the first sign of madness. Mind if I join you?' a man's voice asked, a hint of hesitation in his voice. Vic peered up at him blurrily. He was late thirties, she guessed, with cropped blond hair. His straight nose housed a single diamond stud.

Victoria gestured to the empty space beside her. 'You'll catch hypothermia out here.' He took off his jacket, put it over her shoulders, then reached for a pocket and pulled out a cigarette. 'I'm Danny, by the way.'

Vic hiccupped. 'I'm drunk, by the way.'

'What a pretty name. Is that Gaelic? Or maybe Celtic?'

Vic giggled. 'Victoria Sharpe.'

'How very posh.' Danny smirked.

Vic laughed. 'Hardly.' She held out her hand to him and assumed a plum-in-the-mouth accent. 'Pleased to make your acquaintance, kind sir, and thanks for the *very* trendy jacket.'

'See, you *are* posh.' He punched her arm playfully.

'I do come from Windsor and because everyone thinks you have to be loaded to live there, I quite often randomly get asked if I ride horses.'

'Hmm. That is random. Let me guess, you're down here on a hen weekend?'

'Yes, and I love my mates dearly, but I've hit a wall and rather than jump about raving, I either want to sit here and cry like a baby or go back to the uncomfortable single bed in my hotel room and sleep like one.'

'Choices, choices.' Danny lit the ready-rolled cigarette. 'If I told you that my partner had just told me they've been seeing someone else for three months and wondered if I'd consider an open relationship in order not to lose me, would that make you feel any better?'

'Shit, I'm sorry, Danny. That sucks.' Realising that her new companion's cigarette was full of far more than tobacco, she took it from his hands. 'Can I?'

Vic inhaled the fragrant smoke deeply and when she had stopped coughing, announced to the air, 'God! Why can't things be easy?'

'Hell, lady. I'm the one who's heartbroken.'

'Yes, you are. Sorry, how selfish of me.' Vic hiccupped again. 'So, you're not considering it, then? The open bit, I mean.'

'No way. The trust has been broken already.'

Victoria turned to look at him. The distant thump of the nightclub's music gave their conversation a rhythmic backdrop that was almost hypnotic. The copious drinks she had consumed turned her inhibition switch to green. 'For what it's worth, I think you're a very handsome man, Danny, and your partner is a fool.'

Danny's forehead wrinkled. 'Didn't someone once say, never kiss a fool or let a fool kiss you?'

'Whoever that someone was, well, they were pretty smart.' Vic furrowed her brow. 'And who said anything about kissing?' Putting her tongue inside her cheek, she started to laugh.

'Nobody.' Danny blew a plume of smoke into the sky. 'But, if it's time for unadulterated complimenting, you're not so shabby yourself, Victoria Sharpe. Great dress, and love these shoes.' He lifted Vic's bare leg to take a closer look at her strappy heels, and began throwing exaggerated kisses up her thigh, making her screech with laughter. 'Jesus! I've heard quieter seagulls.' He took another toke of the sweet-smelling tobacco. 'But now we're both honorary members of the Brighton Beach Mutual Appreciation Society, why don't you tell me why it is you want to cry like a baby?'

Suddenly, Vic heard a shout of 'Sharpie!' from the front of the nightclub and saw Mandy waving at her. 'You all right, mate?'

'Yes, fine,' Vic called back. 'I'll be in in a minute. Just nabbing a fag off a handsome stranger.'

'OK. See you in a bit.' Mandy disappeared back inside.

'Good mate you've got there.'

'The best.' Vic took another, much smaller drag of the joint, then blurted, 'My mum's an alcoholic. I feel I'm not following my passion, and I don't even know if I want to have kids but if I don't decide soon it will be too late. I've just found out my boyfriend is at another woman's house, and for the first time ever in our relationship, I'm not sure if I trust him or not.'

'Wow, right. Just the few things, then. Doesn't trump me being cheated on, though.' Danny took another long, slow drag and held it down for a few seconds.

'You clearly didn't major in empathy, did you?' Vic put on an expression of fake disdain. 'What do you do, anyway?'

Danny blew a plume of smoke skywards. 'I have a gallery in The Lanes.'

Vic gasped. 'Shut the fuck up! No way. That's so cool. I'm a graphic designer, but my passion is illustrating, and I do the odd watercolour. Do you paint yourself?'

'Yeah, mainly abstract, but I make most of my money from exhibiting and selling other local artists' work,' Danny replied proudly.

Vic's face lit up. 'Isn't it just the best feeling when that urge to paint takes over and you find yourself creating something from way down inside you? I love it. I forget everything else that's happening around me.'

'Yes, I hear you totally' – Danny nodded – 'and when I've finished, I sometimes look back at what I've done and can't believe it was me that it came out of.'

Vic opened her eyes and mouth wide. 'Exactly! Exactly

that!' She felt exhilarated at just the thought of it. 'It's great that you support other artists, too. I'd really love to come and have a nosy at your place. Are you open tomorrow?'

'We only open Tuesday to Saturday in the winter. Here.' He retrieved his wallet and handed her a card.

'Danny Miller Arts,' Vic read aloud. 'That's so cool. You really are living my dream.'

'Then you must come down and show me your work. If you're any good, I'll exhibit it for you.'

'Any good? You cheeky...' It was her turn to punch him gently on the arm and they laughed together. Vic felt a sudden appreciation of the immediate connection between them. As they continued to pass the joint back and forth, their conversation meandered seamlessly through a myriad of topics, from childhood memories to dreams of the future. To relationships, and heartbreak and then to...

'So,' Danny said, his words slightly slurred, 'what's the most adventurous thing you've ever done sexually, then?'

Vic grinned. 'Well, there was this one time on a beach...' She leapt up. 'Come on!' She lifted his coat from her shoulders and threw it at him, then put her bag over her shoulder. 'I'm high as a kite and hot as a... what can I be as hot as?' she giggled.

'You're just hot as fuck,' Danny laughed and hoisted her up on his back. He piggybacked a screaming Vic over the stony beach. When he threatened to throw her in the ocean, she kicked off her shoes and squealed as the icy water hit her toes. He went to steady her as she wobbled and then, without warning, he leant in, and their lips met in a short but tender kiss.

When they broke apart, he looked stricken. 'I'm sorry, Vic. It kind of just...'

Victoria looked right into his eyes. 'I'm not.' She grabbed him back towards her and found his lips again. Their eyes remained open, fixated on each other with a fierce hunger for whatever lay ahead. A drunk and stoned collision of bodies driven by lust; an exploration of physical desires unencumbered by the weight of emotional entanglements.

A lone seagull screeched above.

Rudely awoken by her bladder, Vic began to recollect the goings on of the night before and groaned softly. She was thankful the en-suite light was on so that she could easily gather her clothes from the floor of Danny's stylish apartment and hastily dress in there. Not knowing what one-night-stand etiquette was these days, she was just searching in her bag for a pen to leave a note for him when he stirred.

'Hey.' He smiled.

'Hey.' Vic smiled tentatively back.

'Doing a runner, were you? I don't blame you. I have terrible morning breath.'

'It's just...' Vic sighed.

'It's OK,' Danny replied sleepily. 'I really do hope you work everything out, and I mean that.'

'You too,' Vic whispered, a whole gamut of emotions swirling through her.

'And do pop to my gallery if you ever find yourself in Brighton again.'

Vic picked up her bag. 'I'm not sure, I...'

'Only regret the things you don't do in this life, Vic. Be kind to yourself, eh?'

Blowing him a kiss, Vic made her way down the stairs that she couldn't even remember climbing just hours before. Thankfully it was early and, hoping the streets would be empty, she stepped out onto the street. Mortified to be greeted not only by a chilly breeze, which sent her thin silver dress whooshing up over her thighs, but also the beeping and cheering from two builders in the cab of a white van, she did a deep curtsy and stuck two fingers up at them.

Vic suddenly felt desperate for the toilet. This walk of shame, right along the front of Brighton's promenade, was going to be not only cold but long. With a pounding head and feeling sicker by the minute for having cheated on Nate – and with the lesser worry that the girls might have forgotten to get her jacket from the nightclub cloakroom – she began to strut as fast as her strappy heels would allow her.

Taking in the pier and the grey, angry-looking sea, she thought not only what a magnificent painting it would make, but also that her familiar memories of Brighton and its land-marks would now most definitely bear a different weight. Namely, getting off her face and having the most amazing sex with a handsome artist called Danny Miller.

She was approaching the road that led down to their hotel when the sound of laughter and excitable chatter reached her ears. She was about to put her head down and march on past when she noticed that there, sitting outside the twenty-four-hour café, wearing their thick winter coats and being kept warm by the outdoor heaters, were Orla and Mandy, stuffing their faces with full English breakfasts.

'Well, well. Looks like someone had quite the night. Don't tell me you got the ride, too?' Orla teased, her grin widening. 'Here.' She handed Vic her coat, which Vic put on hurriedly. 'After you messaged us, we luckily remembered to get this for you, 'cos clearly that was the last thing on your mind when you went off with young blondie there.'

'I guess that's who you've been with?' Mandy said, almost apologetically. 'He was cute, I'll give you that.'

Vic could feel the group on the table next to theirs pricking up their ears and felt herself flush with embarrassment. Mandy pulled out a chair and put her hand on top of her friend's as she sat herself back down. Vic took a huge glug of Orla's orange juice, let out an exaggerated breath and shook her head.

'I'm so sorry for leaving you on your hen night, Mand.'

'Don't be silly. The two of us ended up dancing on the beach like silly buggers and then coming here, where the action was still happening.' Mandy hiccupped. 'But when either of you two decide to get married, please make sure it's not in the autumn or winter, because if it is, we are flying to the Caribbean for the hen weekend.'

'I'm *never* getting married, but I've had the best craic,' Orla said. 'Without a fecking man in sight, as well – see, I can do it!' she laughed. 'Anyways, tell us everything, Sharpie, and it better be good.' Orla looked at her phone. 'Your message said, and I quote: "I'm off my face and talking art with a real cutey. See you later." So, come on, tell us. Did Vic get some dick?'

Vic grimaced. 'I feel so bloody guilty, but before I go into the sordid detail, I really must pee!'

As Vic let herself into the flat that night, the relief she felt when she could hear Nate snoring was immense. Getting into bed as quietly as she could, she pulled the covers up to her neck and turned over to face the wall. From what she could remember, she'd had great fun with Danny. He had seemed like a decent and genuine guy, and he was as hot as they come. But that wasn't the issue here, for it was guilt that was now lying heavy on her heart. Because, for all his faults, Nate Carlisle was a good man, and she had been unfaithful to him.

And it wasn't that she didn't like him or despised him in any way. Quite the opposite. He had done nothing wrong and when they were getting on, they did have great fun together. She had always considered herself to be loyal and honest and had never cheated on *anyone* before. She thought back to Joti's comment. So, what, really, was the matter?

With feelings of self-loathing and confusion, Victoria Sharpe fell into a fretful slumber.

FOUR

LONDON

The Workplace

'Bloody hell, Vic, you look like death warmed up.' Ray Glover, the impeccably groomed, exuberant forty-five-year-old boss of Glovers Design, stopped at her desk on his way through to the kitchen of his design studio office. 'Oh yes, of course, Brighton this weekend. How was it? I have to say, me and my Marcus were a tad jealous. We just stayed in with a Waitrose risotto and perved on Ian Waite's arse on *Strictly*.' He waved his hand camply in the air. 'Coffee, darling?'

'Yes, two sugars, please.' Even to her own ears, Vic sounded groggy.

He placed the coffee mug on her desk. 'It was two-spoonfuls good, eh?'

'Erm, yes.'

'Victoria Sharpe, is there something you're not telling me?' Then, in full Elaine Paige musical belt, he burst into song: 'I know you so well.'

'Ray, I love you, but not now, OK?'

Since *that* night, Vic's infidelity had sat heavy on her chest like a lingering heartburn, and even thinking about it was more uncomfortable than she ever could have imagined, let alone talking about it.

'OK, OK, Grumporia.' Ray raised his eyebrows. 'But, whilst I remember, we need to get the final rebrand carton designs off to Krispy Wheats today.'

'Really?' Victoria sighed. It wasn't that she didn't enjoy working at Glovers, because she really did. But the nine-to-five had been getting her down lately, especially when all she wanted to do was spread her artistic wings and have a break from the monotony of it all. Plus, Glovers seemed to be getting a name for carton design, and that was so far removed from the freehand creativity she loved. But rent and bills weren't going to get paid on uncertainty, and Nate's salary couldn't be relied upon to support them both if she did decide to go out and get herself established in her own right. One of her biggest regrets had been not saving. But with the expense of living in a big city, anyone who lived in London on a regular wage and claimed to save was either a liar or a hermit.

Ray headed for his office, then turned back. 'And, oh yes, Jerico Flint called earlier. He wants to talk to you.'

Vic grimaced. Jerico was her favourite client but she didn't have the energy right now. 'Can't Penny find out what he wants, and I'll speak to him tomorrow? He's a lot to deal with when I haven't got a lot in the tank.'

'Penny's off on her half-term gallivant, darling, and you know how Jerico loves you.' He put his hands in the air. 'Why oh why I only employ women beggars belief. They're either moody, pregnant, menopausal or on school holidays. You're not up the duff, are you?'

'Ray! You can't say or ask that.'

'I just did.' He gently closed the door of his glass office shut and blew her a kiss, leaving behind a lingering whiff of the most gorgeous cologne.

Vic turned on the shiny new iMac G5 that Ray had recently bought for the office. Then, tentatively sipping her coffee, she checked her watch, logged into her email, and texted Mandy.

> Emergency Maccy D's, Marl Road at 12.30?

Mandy's reply was instant.

> Abso fucking lutely!

Taking a deep breath, Vic searched for the last email from Jerico Flint, got his phone number off his signature and reached for her desk phone.

'Jerico Flint, at your service.' Vic smiled at the man's deep and sultry telephone voice, which would soon go to whatever voice or accent he wanted to use, depending on his mood or inclination.

'Hi, Jerico. It's Victoria from Glovers.'

'He missed a trick not calling it Glovers Covers, didn't he?'

Vic forgot her woes for a minute. 'Like I said before, Jerico, we don't just do book covers here, we do all kinds of design. So, how did *Mr Pigeons and the Glasgow Kiss* fare in the big wide world of publishing?'

Vic fingered the first in his detective novel series that she had illustrated for him, and which had sat on her desk unread for the past six months. Realising who she must be on the phone to, Ray put his thumb up to her through his glass office and showed off his perfect white teeth in an exaggerated grin.

'I got to seven thousand in *Detective Tales* on the Amazon paperback chart, and number two hundred and two in *Scottish Mystery Fiction*, but I'll take that. The whole project has so far made a significant loss, but on I go. It's about the art, not the money, anyway, isn't it?'

'That's what us creatives are trained to say, but most of us are either lying, or it makes us feel less shit about ourselves if we are not getting the success we feel we deserve.' Vic let out a large sigh.

It was Jerico's turn to laugh. 'Ha, yes. To make my fortune writing full-time, give up the day job and run off to St Lucia with Gillian Anderson. Just imagine!'

'Gillian Anderson, from *The X-Files*?'

'The one and only! I find her both alluring and terrifying, all at the same time. Quite a magnificent combination. And if you've never been to St Lucia, Vic, then you have to go. It's got so much soul.' Jerico left a thoughtful pause. 'Hmm, Maybe Mr Pigeons could go there and set up a donkey sanctuary or similar, but I was thinking I'd set the next one in London. I mean, I haven't even been to Glasgow, so I was kind of winging my research by just using Mr Google anyway.' Jerico stalled, his voice now softer. 'And dare I ask why the big sigh, Queen Victoria?'

'A bit too much fun at the weekend, I'm afraid.'

There was a smile in his voice as he said, 'Ah, one can never have too much fun, little lady, and do you know what the best cure for a hangover is?'

'Go on. I'll take anything today.'

'Being under twenty-five.'

Vic burst out laughing, and she suddenly felt a little better. He was a lot, but a good lot, and she had forgotten how hilarious he was.

'So, the new one is called *Mr Pigeons and the Waterloo Clock*.' He paused for a second. 'I said clock, Victoria. Don't be smutty, now.'

Vic shook her head at the craziness of the effervescent man at the end of the phone. 'So I was thinking along the lines – illustration-wise for the cover of *Mr Pigeons*, that is – and he looks like me, as you know – actually, you don't know that, as you've never seen me,' Jerico enthused without taking a breath. 'So, anyway, he could don a different-coloured trilby from last time, and he could be running for a train, and we could feature the Waterloo clock face, somehow, maybe just a huge softer image behind. Oh, I don't know. You're the drawing brains of this outfit.'

'Well, that saves me having to think too hard, I guess.' Vic's lips pursed in thought. 'But I'll do some preliminary sketches for you with some different options.'

'Good stuff! Same price as before, please. I'll pay you on the dot once you deliver the goods,' Jerico replied firmly.

'Of course. I'll send over a quote for approval. When do you need the finished drawing?'

'I'm publishing the book myself again and want to get it out there whilst the few who bought it still remember his Glasgow adventure so, yesterday, darling, yesterday. We really must try and meet in person. Always good to put a face to a name, don't you think? You were at lunch last time I came in to approve the illustration. Oh, shit, that's the doorbell. Can we say Friday for preliminary sketches? Thank you, wonderful girl. Toodlepip.'

And he was gone.

The golden arches, twelve thirty, and Vic and Mandy found a table, sat down, and got ready to tuck into their Big Mac and Quarter Pounder with cheese meals, respectively.

'Why on earth did we decide yesterday that hair-of-the-dog at lunchtime after literally no sleep was the right thing to do?' Mandy stuffed in five of her thin, salty chips in one go. 'I'm so happy it's half-term and Steve is working away. I'm having this, going straight back to bed, and staying there until Wednesday. I'm supposed to be searching for wedding favours. My mother-in-law's on about having sugared almonds. I mean, has anybody even eaten a sugared almond since the eighties?'

Vic smiled. 'A chocolate lolly embossed with both your smug faces on will do me. I'm so jealous. I want my bed so bad. Although I don't want to see Nate. I won't be able to look him in the eye.'

'I take it you said nothing last night?'

'Thankfully, he was sparko when I got in and he'd gone out for a run when I woke up. Which is so out of character for him. He just left me a note by the kettle, saying he loved me and he'd see me later.'

'What are you going to do, Vic? Are you going to tell him?'

'I really don't think I can. How do people cheat and just get on with their lives as if all is OK?' Vic took a huge bite of burger, and a blob of cheese oozed down her chin.

'Maybe they just pretend it didn't happen. Could you do that? I mean, you aren't intending to see Blondie again, are you?'

'God, no. Don't get me wrong. He was a really nice bloke, but he's got his own relationship issues, and it was just what it was. A one-nighter. Sex. Nothing more, nothing less.' Vic reached for a serviette. 'I haven't smoked gear for so long and it turned me into a raging nymphomaniac. Maybe open relationships *are* the answer – it would be easier in one sense.'

'Where has that come from?' Mandy was wide-eyed.

'Oh, just Danny's partner – that's Blondie's name, by the way – or maybe now ex-partner – I forget – had suggested it.'

'I am so vanilla. Steve thinks it's his birthday if I get on all fours.' Mandy was now attempting to open her ketchup packet. On the third pull she got it. 'I take it you used a condom?'

'Yes, of course.'

'Well, that's something.' Mandy proceeded to pull out her gherkins and put them on top of Vic's chips. 'And you did say you were shit-faced.'

'Thankfully, he insisted. He and his flat were exceptionally clean, which was a bonus.'

'Hark at Monica,' Mandy laughed.

'There was a reason we called Chandler "Chandler" you know. If the little munchkin had been a girl she would most certainly have taken Monica as her moniker.'

Mandy's face lit up. 'Very good.'

'Sharpe by name, sharp by nature, and all that.' Vic grinned, sliding her friend's unwanted gherkins into her Big Mac.

Mandy continued punching her chips down. 'Anyway, I do need to know as soon as possible if you are splitting up or not, as I'll take Nate off the wedding list. The venue we've chosen isn't cheap, you know.'

'Jesus, Mand, you're ruthless,' Vic laughed. 'I'm not going to tell him before Christmas. I can't. In fact, I might never tell him. It wasn't anything to do with Nate. He'd done nothing wrong. It's me. So why hurt him? And on a practical note, there's too much going on with your wedding and with Mum.' Vic bit her lip. 'I just keep hoping that I can erase what happened from my mind and carry on as usual, in ignorant bliss.'

'Wow.' Mandy was wide-eyed. 'You call me ruthless.'

'It's not that I don't feel guilty, Mand. It's the opposite. Nate doesn't deserve what I did. I was the one turning the poor sod down for sex and then one toke of a joint, and I drop my knickers for someone else.'

Mandy winced. 'You and Orla do get yourselves into such bloody scrapes.'

'So, go on, then, tell me what would you do in this situation, Miss Vanilla Pants?' Vic felt suddenly agitated.

'I'm not walking in your shoes and, without wanting to sound like Mother Teresa – although I clearly do – a good Catholic girl like me wouldn't have shagged some random on a night out, would I?'

'That's so helpful.' Vic sighed deeply. 'And don't make it sound like I've done it before. I think you'll find that's Ms O'Malley you're thinking of.'

'Sorry, sorry.' Mandy's face twitched.

'I've got a lot to sort out in my head, Mand.' Vic wiped her mouth with a serviette. 'Nothing is ever black and white, is it? Especially in relationships. Whether that be with friends, family, or lovers.' She blew out noisily. 'Poor Nate. But what happened doesn't warrant the explosion I know revealing it would cause.'

'Have you spoken to Orla?'

'Just quickly on the phone last night.'

'I dread to hear her worldly advice on infidelity.' Mandy sucked her Coke noisily through a straw.

'It was surprisingly useful, actually. She said if you don't know what to do, do nothing, say nothing and the answer will just come to you when you're ready.' Vic screwed up the dirtied serviette and put it down on the tray. 'So, the decision is made. I don't know what to do yet, so I'm saying nothing. Not sure how I'll live with the guilt, but I'm going to have to. And whilst I'm dealing with that, I need to have a good think about my future.'

'We've made some of our best decisions under the watchful eye of Ronald McDonald, haven't we?' Mandy reminisced, looking at the life-size cut-out of the man in the corner.

Vic was thoughtful. 'Hmm. Not sure about that corkscrew perm you had back in 1988, though.'

FIVE

OXFORDSHIRE

The Wedding

November 2005

October turned into November. Vic and Nate continued to pass like ships in the night. Their Sunday showers didn't happen, and Nate didn't even ask for them anymore. Conversations were short. After the first flush, Vic felt surprisingly little guilt. Nate didn't seem to notice any difference in her. And then Mandy and Steve's wedding was upon them, in a beautiful hotel in the Cotswolds. And as the happy couple shared their vows, Vic couldn't help but feel a twinge of grief for the passion she and Nate had once shared. The absence of physical intimacy between them had created a quiet tension, a longing that hung in the air like unspoken words. She had managed to push the night with Danny right to the back of her mind. In fact, she was actually quite scared how easily her guilt had waned. Her justification for not saying anything was that it had been fun, a physical act of pleasure devoid of all emotion, and what good would it do to tell Nate and hurt him? Did that make her a coward?

Her decision to do nothing and say nothing, had *changed* nothing. Because an answer hadn't come to her yet, and she was still in the same state of flux she had been in prior to her infidelity. Maybe her cheating had in fact highlighted that, despite her confusion, she did see a future with Nate. Because if she had wanted to end it, then telling him she'd slept with another man for fun, after turning Nate down for sex on many an occasion, would be a sure-fire way to get him to leave her. Or maybe it was just that she was too scared to make a decision, because of the practicalities it would throw up. But that was no way to live.

The only decision she'd made was that Christmas – the ultimate buffer for wants, dreams and major life events – would mark the end of her procrastination. And as soon as the festivities were over, she would attempt to hatch a life plan.

The wedding service itself was beautiful. During the plethora of after-dinner speeches, including the best man, the mother of the bride, the father of the bride, the husband, *the* bride, and the second cousin of Aunt Fanny (when did just the best man's speech become not enough?), Vic and Nate necked champagne like they had never tasted it before. Then, as the ballroom was being turned into a dance floor for the evening reception, Nate grabbed a half-full bottle of white wine and a couple of glasses from a table and led Victoria to a quiet corner.

'Vic,' Nate said as he poured them each a glass of chilled French Sauvignon.

'Even the way you said my name sounded ominous then. What's up?' She took the offered glass.

'We need to talk. We need to talk about us, Vic. Cheers.' They clinked glasses. 'It's been so long since we... well, you know. Got jiggy. Played hide the sausage.' He let out a weird noise, something between laughter and despair.

Vic's face remained straight. 'Can you ever be serious?'

'That's what you fell in love with, wasn't it? The buffoon in me.'

'There's a lot more to you than that.' Vic felt tears sting her eyes. 'I'm so glad you've said something.'

'I miss it, Vic. I miss us. I miss the closeness we used to have. If you don't want to be with me, then just tell me. I'm a big boy, you know. I can take it.'

'Can you ever see yourself marrying me, Nate?'

'Wow! Sharpie! What the fuck?' Nate took a huge slug of wine. 'You can do better than that for a proposal, though, can't you?' He smirked.

'Stop diverting. I want to know.' Vic didn't smile. 'Do you want to spend the rest of your life with me?'

'Well... the whole marriage thing... erm... not yet. This entire day must have cost a fortune. We need money to do that, and your mum and my dad are hardly rolling in it, are they? And we have zero savings, don't we? And I kind of don't believe in it, really.'

An unexpected dart of relief ran through her. 'And how about having kids? Is that even on your radar?'

'Whoa, Vic. What's happening here?' Nate took another huge glug of wine.

Tears started to run slowly down Vic's face. 'It's just... with Mandy getting married, I kind of thought that might be the next step for us. And look... Nate.' Her 'say nothing, do nothing until the time was right' plan suddenly fell into swing. The time had come. 'I love you, Nate, but I'm not sure we are travelling in the same direction anymore.'

'I love you, too, Vic. A bit of paper won't change anything. And as for kids, never say never. Let's talk about it. If it's what you want, we can make it work.'

'That's the thing – I don't even know if I want kids. And you're hardly stable where jobs are concerned. I don't want to struggle like my mum has all her life. And if I'm honest, after the turmoil I faced growing up, I'd worry so much about being a good enough mum.'

'So, you're prepared to give us up to go and find some rich geezer to give you the life you want. Is that what you're saying?'

'Don't be silly. That's not what I want. I don't need to be looked after.' Fuelled by alcohol, Vic's subconscious began to do its usual job of rearing its head. 'It makes me so angry that we've never had an open and honest conversation about what we want out of life. As long as I've known you, we've just skipped around, *playing* at life.'

'No, we have been living it, Vic. Like everybody else. Getting through and making the best of it. So come on, then, let's talk now. I didn't even know you were thinking like this. Which makes you as much to blame here as me with this one. I would happily continue as we are forever. Bloody society setting its two-point-two-kid ratio, and women having to be married by a certain age, and the importance placed on owning a house. It's all bullshit!'

'And there lies the problem.' Vic took a drink. 'I want to do more with my life. With my art. And as women, we *do* have a countdown with regards to a family.'

'Make your mind up, Vic. What is it – marriage? Kids? Work? Are you not happy with anything in your life?'

'This is it. I'm so confused. I don't actually know what will make me happy. There, I said it. And... maybe us women, we can't have it all?' Victoria paused and sighed. 'And I don't even know if I want it all or...' Another pause. 'Or maybe running away and living off the land *is* the right answer.'

'Living off the land? What the hell are you on about?' He put his hand on top of hers. 'I've never stopped you doing anything, Vic, ever. In my humble opinion, you are stopping yourself.' Nate became animated. 'You have the talent, and you *have* the balls. I am in awe of your creativity. A little bit jealous, in fact. You know what you are good at! Follow your dreams,

Vic. There is nothing that would make me happier. And as for you having a baby, if you decide that's what you want, then let's worry about it when it happens. Stop overthinking everything.'

He took her hand and squeezed it. 'Any kid would be lucky to call you its mum.'

'You mean that?' Vic's voice was childlike.

Nate nodded. 'Of course I do.'

'And have I really got the talent?'

Nate sighed deeply. 'For fuck's sake, Vic, you make things so hard for yourself.' He downed his wine and suddenly looked serious. 'And I don't think you realise quite how hard it is loving someone who clearly doesn't love herself.'

Nate's hand reached for Vic's, their fingers gently squeezing and then, in their drunken haze, in the dark corner of a noisy wedding, they were kissing. A tender kiss that conveyed a multitude of unspoken emotions. The familiarity of each other's searching lips rekindling a flame that had been dimmed, but not extinguished.

Back in their hotel room, their lovemaking went from fast and furious to loving and tender. Passionate yet a little angry. Intimate yet defiant. Nate, ever the considerate and compassionate lover, ensuring Vic was sated before he came, too. As he did he burst into tears. Vic had never seen Nate cry.

'Darling, what's wrong?' Vic kissed his forehead.

'If we are going to be open and honest with each other, then I have to tell you something. Something really bad.' Biting his lip, he turned his head away.

'You're scaring me now. What is it?' Vic sat up in bed. Nate got up, went to the bathroom, and put on the soft, white hotel robe, which looked comically short on his long body. 'Just tell me!' Vic urged.

'You know the weekend you went to Brighton?'

'Yes.' Vic's voice shook, the drink escalating her anger.

'I slept with someone else.'

'I see.' Vic's voice came out oddly calm. 'Let me guess. Ruthie, was it?' She said the other woman's name in a babyish voice.

'How the fuck did you—?'

'Call it women's intuition. You mentioned her in the kitchen once when I came back from Mum's. And the night of the hen, I rang you and a woman answered your phone and said she didn't know you had a girlfriend. Who works with someone, and doesn't know if they have a partner or not?'

'I'm so sorry, Vic.' Nate came to sit on the bed. 'Why didn't you say anything before?'

'I had a moment of doubt, then brushed the phone call away as I thought maybe I was just being paranoid. You've always had girls as friends, so I didn't really think anything of it until now.'

'Vic, I'm so fucking sorry.' He went to hold her hand and she pulled it away.

'Just a one-off, was it?' Vic felt tears threatening to break free. Nate was silent for far too long. 'That's a no, then. You just told me you loved me, and you'll have kids if I want them.'

'You're different, Vic. That was different.'

Vic's voice lowered. 'When else?'

Nate remained mute.

'When else?' Vic shouted again.

Nate faltered. 'That weekend you were at your mum's.'

'See. I knew it!' Victoria felt sick as the tears started to flow. 'You tried to fuck *me* that night too! What is wrong with you?'

'Me and you weren't having sex, Vic. The girl put it on a plate. She's left work now. She wanted more from me, but I said there was no way I was leaving you, that it's you I love. It was just lust with her – it meant nothing! And I'm so, so sorry. You mean everything to me.'

'So why tell me now?'

'Because it's been eating me up inside, Vic.'

Amidst the anger and pain, Vic felt a sudden rush of relief: the burden of being the cheater somewhat lifted. This would be the ideal time to throw her own infidelity hat into the ring. To say, *I understand exactly what you are saying because I've done exactly the same, too. And I'm sorry. Really fucking sorry.* But two wrongs didn't make a right and she clearly *was* a coward. Nate laying himself bare had weirdly made her respect him more than ever. But could she forgive him? Because knowing he had slept with someone else was hurting her a whole lot more than she had expected. She got off the bed and started frantically getting dressed.

'What are you doing? Come here.' Nate tried to pull her into an embrace.

'I want to go home.' Vic's voice wobbled.

Nate sighed. 'It's late, we're both pissed, and you'll never get a train back to London at this time.'

'Then I'll find Orla and stay in her room.'

Nate blocked her escape route. 'This can't be the end of us. Please, Vic. It honestly meant nothing. I love you. I properly love you. I will do anything to make it up to you.'

Vic put her hand to her head, her face pained. 'I just need time to think. OK? I'm so bloody confused. About everything.'

'OK, but travel home with me tomorrow, please. We can talk. I just had to tell you. I respect you too much.'

Vic shut the door behind her and rang down to the hotel reception. 'Hi there. I'm staying in room 205 with Orla O'Malley and I've mislaid my key. Could you send someone up to let me in, please?'

Vic awoke alone in a king-size bed. Her head was pounding. Groaning, she reached for her phone and checked her messages.

Nothing from Nate, but a late-night reply from Orla saying that she had pulled 'a live wire' and would come straight back to the room as soon as she was up.

Vic took in the fancy hotel bedroom – the headboard, crafted from reclaimed wood, adding a connection to the surrounding countryside. She had been so distracted when she had got there that she hadn't bothered to shut the heavy red curtains, so long decadent windows let in natural light and allowed for views of the rolling hills and lush gardens that surrounded the charming Cotswold-stone listed building.

She was just about to make herself a cup of tea when Orla came tearing in, slammed the door shut dramatically and flopped down on the love seat in the window alcove. Her smudged smoky-eye make-up made her look like a panda, and her hair had settled itself into a gloriously huge afro. 'Jaysus, Vic, I'm so sorry I gave a cock more importance than you. I didn't see your message until *so* late.'

'Honestly, it's fine. I was so pissed I crashed out.' Vic took in her mate's unkempt appearance. 'Orla, just look at the state of you!'

'I know! Who'd have thought it of the quiet, unassuming Mr Winkler?'

'Nooo! The head from Mandy's school Mr Winkler, you mean?' Vic was wide-eyed. 'I thought he was married.'

'I didn't ask but he was obviously ready for some kind of action, so he was, as he had a cane in his bag and didn't spare the horses when he used it on me, I can tell you. He kept shouting, "Give the head some head." Hilarious! What a night! I need coffee and some soothing antiseptic ointment delicately applied to the welts on my arse.' Vic screwed up her face. 'Anyways, what the feck *are* you doing in here? What's going on with you and Nate?'

Vic handed her mate a coffee. 'Oh, Orla, I really don't know what to do. And for goodness' sake don't say "do nothing" this time. It's too big for that now.' She passed Orla a milk sachet.

'Will you just fecking tell me? I'm dying here.' Orla took a sip of her drink, screwed up her face and reached for the sugar.

'Nate slept with some girl from the restaurant. *Twice.*'

'Oh. Did you say, "Touché, darling – I bet my Brighton boy was hotter?"' On realising that Vic wasn't finding her the remotest bit funny, Orla got up and moved to sit next to her friend on the bed, and placed a hand on her knee. 'I'm sorry, mate. How are you feeling?'

'It's just a mess, isn't it? How can I possibly be angry, when I've done the same? Although him doing it twice means that only the first time it probably wasn't planned, so you could say he's the worse of the two of us.'

'Blimey, that's a lot to get my head around at this time of the morning. So, did you tell him about Blondie?'

'No!'

'Are you going to?'

'No.' Vic groaned. 'Maybe I should, now. I don't even know what to feel anymore.'

'OK, so my advice, for what it's worth, mate, is for you to have a break from Nate. Get your head straight. You can then maybe tell him about Blondie once you've had the break if you want to, so you are both on a clear and honest footing. Being honest, if it was me, I wouldn't say a word. You can act the spurned woman with Nate and dine out on it for years to come. And, whilst you're apart, work out what it is you really want. See if you do miss him.'

'It has really pissed me off, him sleeping with someone else.'

'Is that because it obviously would do, or because you really do care about the bloke?'

'Hmm. OK. I hear you. Your "time apart" idea is a good one.'

'Yeah, 'cos even if you don't realise it, you're clearly both unhappy. And I know I'm the queen of the one-night stands, but I do believe that if you genuinely love someone, you don't cheat on them.'

'But life isn't always that clear cut, Orla, is it?' Vic sighed deeply. 'I so don't want to go back to Mum's – being there alone would depress me, even without having to do the London commute every day as well.'

'You can stay with me.' Orla took a sip of coffee.

'Oh, Orla, I dunno. Your sofa bed is like a rock.'

'Hark at the princess and the pea here. It's fine. Aletta has already gone home to Amsterdam for an extended Christmas break. She won't be in London again until mid-January. You can have her room. She's cleared most of it out, anyways.'

'Well... if you're sure. You're nearer to work, too, so that's perfect, and I'd much rather be away from our flat so that I can think properly, on neutral ground.' Vic kissed Orla's cheek. 'Thanks, mate.' She reached for her phone. 'I'd better ring a taxi to take me to the train station. Nate wanted me to travel home with him, but I just couldn't face talking to him, so I lied and said I was coming back with you in the car.'

Orla grimaced. 'I feel bad. I'm stopping off to stay at my sister's now, or I really could have driven you back.'

'Don't be silly. You have a life too, and it's not your fault my relationship is in tatters. I will go home, pack a bag, and tell Nate that I'm moving out for a while.'

'How do you think he'll take it?' Orla winced as she shifted on the bed.

'At this precise moment, I don't actually care.' Vic poked her head in the mini-bar and made a gagging noise. 'Even looking at the wine makes me feel a bit sick. I'll take a couple of Cokes for the journey, OK?'

'Go for it.' Orla waved her hand nonchalantly.

Vic placed the cans into her handbag.

'So, I'll see you back in London tomorrow night. Here, take

my key – and no wild parties in the flat without me, OK?' Orla grinned.

Vic put the key in her bag. 'I do love an after-wedding breakfast, but I can't face anyone this morning, and I don't want Mandy to have to get involved in this so soon after her wedding. So, can you just tell her that I felt so awful I had to head straight home? That's not even a lie.'

'Of course. But what was it Marilyn Monroe said? "If you can't take me at my worst, then you sure as hell don't deserve me at my best." Me, you and Mand – we're friends forever, you know that.'

'Let's give her a break today of all days, though, eh? Love you, mate, and thanks so much for having me at yours.' Vic leant down to kiss the top of Orla's wild black hair.

'Love you back, and Sharpie, it'll all work out just grand. Don't you worry.'

SIX

LONDON

The Flu

A loud banging and somebody shouting her name awoke Victoria from a vivid dream where she was in a wedding dress, but it was Nate who was getting married – to somebody else, whose face she couldn't make out because it was covered with a really thick black veil. In fact, the last two nights since Mandy's wedding, she'd had anxiety dreams about being on her own and Nate not being in her life. But as distressing as they were, they still hadn't compelled her to rush back to him to sort everything out. Right now she felt too unwell to consider it. And despite her own infidelity, she was still angry with him and also cross with herself for not having the courage to be upfront with him about what had happened in Brighton. There was clearly something amiss in their relationship, but facing it would mean decisions would need to be made – and what if she made the wrong one?

Realising she was wet with sweat, she slowly put on her dressing gown and almost crawled to the front door. Seeing it was Orla, she raised her hand feebly then headed straight back to bed with her friend in hot pursuit.

'Feck me, Vic, you look dreadful. What's wrong with you?'

Vic whispered, 'I feel so awful. In fact, I wasn't this ill when I had what I thought was proper flu two Christmases ago. I'm burning up and my throat feels like it's got razor blades down it.'

'Oh, Vic. I've got chicken soup in the cupboard. Let me get you some of that.'

'God, no. Could you just get me a pint of water, please? And if you go to the shop, some paracetamol and anything else that may ease this throat.'

'You poor darling. Let me get the window open to let some fresh air in. It smells like fecking death in here.' Orla got hold of the duvet and shook it down to make it more comfortable. 'There's loads going around at the moment. It's that time of year, isn't it? And I'll go now and get you whatever you need. Are you sure you don't fancy anything? How about some soft ice cream to ease that throat of yours, or a nice cup of tea? Oh, Vic, poor you.'

'Honestly, I'm good, Orla. I think water, paracetamol and sleep will be the answer. I've got some kind of rash, too – must be a heat rash, as I'm literally burning up. I'll have to buy new bedding for Aletta, as I'm sweating through. I found an under-sheet of yours in the airing cupboard, so hopefully I won't stain the mattress.'

Orla's face was full of concern as she headed for the kitchen. 'Don't you be worrying about those kinds of things,' she shouted back. 'Do you think you need to talk to a doctor?'

'No,' Vic groaned. 'If you don't mind getting me that stuff, I just need to rest up and get better.'

As Vic rested her head back on the pillow, her phone rang. When she saw it was Nate, she groaned and ignored it. He rang again and, sighing, she reached for the phone. 'Nate,' she croaked.

'Oh my God, Sharpie, you sound fucking terrible. Getting pissed isn't going to solve anything, you know.'

'I'm not drunk, I've got the flu, I think. I feel dreadful.'

'Oh no, baby girl. Do you need anything? I can run anything by Orla's that you need.'

'No, it's fine. I'll be in touch when I'm better. OK?'

'I miss you,' Nate added quietly.

'We'll talk properly when I'm better.' Victoria hung up.

The following Sunday, Vic appeared from her bedroom. Orla was lying on the sofa catching up on *Strictly Come Dancing*. She smiled at a much brighter-looking Vic. 'Here she is. How you feeling today, darling?' Orla paused the TiVo.

'I can't tell you how happy I am that I feel *so* much better. I'm just so pleased you didn't get it. I honestly can't believe how ill I've been.'

'Well, it's good to see you looking better. You had me worried there for a bit, so you did. You look like you've lost weight, though.'

'And I've hardly got that to lose.' Vic put her hands to her tiny waist. 'It's a good excuse to eat all I want over Christmas now, though, I guess.'

'Bitch.' Orla gently threw a cushion at her. 'You never have to worry anyways.'

But there was something else on her mind and she hesitated for a second before telling her friend. 'The only thing is... I've got a discharge from my bits. Without being too graphic, it's kind of fishy-smelling. And now I'm paranoid I've got something wrong down there, too.'

'Nice!' Orla screwed her face up. 'Maybe it's thrush? Your body's been fighting to get you well, so it kind of makes sense that it could be.'

'I forget what it feels like. I haven't had it for so long.'

'Well, if you're worried, there's a brilliant sexual health clinic connected to the Chelsea and Westminster. I still go there and get free condoms sometimes. The staff are so lovely. Just get checked out, mate, there's no shame in it, and it's quicker and easier than going to the doctor, for something like this. If it is something dodgy, everything can be cleared up with antibiotics these days, so don't worry. Being honest, I've had a course from there myself a few years back. It did wise me up, though. Condom city all the way now!'

'I'll pop down there tomorrow.' Victoria joined Orla on the sofa. 'To be honest, after getting through this flu, I can deal with anything. But woe betide Nate if he's given me some kind of STI. It must have come from him – Danny and I used a condom.'

'Talking of Nate, you haven't mentioned him much.'

Vic sighed. 'He called the night you got back. I told him I was ill, so he's sent a few texts asking how I am and saying he's missing me, but that's it.'

'And how are you feeling about everything?'

'I don't know, Orla. I feel so confused. Something's clearly not right in our relationship but I can't seem to imagine a life without him. What would you do?'

'Aww, mate. It's a tough one, and as much as I can say what I think, whatever happens, ultimately you have to do what's right for you.' Orla spun the remote control around in her hand.

Vic groaned. 'It's such a mess.' She took a deep breath. 'But you're right, it's time to pull my big girl's pants on and start making some decisions. I've been drifting along with Nate – and Glovers, if I'm honest with myself. And I don't want to wake up when I'm fifty and realise that I'm stagnant, like a ship that's been in the same bloody harbour all its life.'

Orla raised her eyebrows. 'That's very profound, love. Anyways, you know where I am if you need to chat anything through, eh?' Yawning loudly, she added, 'Talking of Glovers, I guess you'll be going back to work tomorrow, now you're better, will you?'

'I told Ray I'll be back on Tuesday, so I might as well take the extra day. Then just two weeks of work and it'll be Christmas. This year has flown.'

'Yes, I can't wait for the long break. It's been a crazy old year.' Orla dipped her hand into the tub of Quality Street that was sitting open on the coffee table, already half empty.

'When are you flying back to Dingle?'

'I've just got to get a huge project plan finished for an event I'm managing in January, then I'll head there. Mammy is already beside herself. I'll be back here for New Year, though, that's for sure. There's only so much Guinness and small-town gossip a gal can take in one hit.'

Vic grinned. 'OK, so who's going to win *Strictly* this year, then?'

Orla pressed play. 'It's got to be Darren Gough, surely; he's been brilliant from what I've watched so far.'

'Ray wants Zoe Ball, but only because he lusts over Ian Waite,' Vic added, then, after five minutes of watching, she stood up. 'Right, enough of the spangles for me. I'm going to have a hot shower and head to Oxford Street for Christmas shopping. Fancy coming?'

'I'd rather dance naked in the snow than face those crowds.' Orla stretched out on the sofa and yawned. 'But I'm so glad you're feeling better.'

SEVEN

LONDON

The Sexual Health Clinic

The next day Victoria Sharpe found herself knickers off, lying on a hard black plastic-coated bed in the sexual health clinic that Orla had directed her to.

'BV?' Vic repeated as she lay looking up at the grey-haired sexual health nurse, her voice hollow.

'Yes. Bacterial vaginosis.' The efficient woman took off her gloves and binned them. 'But a course of antibiotics will get you sorted in no time.'

As she sat herself up on the bed, Vic felt herself reddening. 'How mortifying.'

'Don't be silly. It's quite common and it's not sexually transmitted, but having it can increase your risk of getting other sexually transmitted infections.'

'Ah, OK.' Vic smiled, her relief palpable.

'So, how about whilst you're here we give you a full service down there? You can go into the new year fresh and ready for action.'

'OK, let's do it. I've never been to a clinic like this before.' She'd always thought of them as taboo places. Vic laughed at her own naivety. 'I'm glad it's been so easy.'

'Why wouldn't it be?' The nurse looked slightly peeved. 'Sexual health is as important as any other kind of health. We all do it. Have sex, I mean. And it's confidential here, of course.' The nurse smiled as she washed her hands in the corner sink. 'Are you on the pill?'

Vic nodded.

'Do you use condoms too?'

'Umm. I've been with my partner for six years, so I haven't been.' What was it about doctors and nurses that made you feel safe enough to blurt your life story? 'I did have sex with someone else recently, but we used a condom.'

'Good. That's what I like to hear. About the condom, I mean.' The nurse busied herself getting items ready for testing.

'Saying that, I found out my boyfriend cheated, too.'

'Did he use a condom?'

'Funnily enough, it wasn't the first thing on my mind to ask.' Vic sighed deeply. Somehow saying it aloud brought all the mess of the situation back. She tutted. 'Jesus. The way I'm talking, anyone would think I was a teenager.'

'So, this is a really sensible idea to get fully checked out.' The nurse headed over to a unit to start placing some further swabs and tubes on a tray. 'And there's no judgement here.' She relayed, with her back to Victoria, 'I've heard about more affairs than a Relate counsellor, and you've done the right thing seeing us today. I'll need to take some more swabs, and how about we get you tested for HIV whilst we are at it, if that's OK with you? A full minge-monty, I call it.'

'Er... sure. OK.' Victoria laughed at this slip in professionalism.

'And is it OK to text you the results to the mobile you gave us on the form?'

'Yes, no problem. That's fine.'

And as the nurse pulled on a fresh pair of disposable gloves, Victoria lay back on the bed and, in line with the Victorian saying, thought of England.

EIGHT
LONDON

The Author

19 December 2005

Two weeks later, Vic was relieved that it was nearly time for the long Christmas break. Her BV infection had thankfully long cleared up and she was feeling so much better. Now that the agreed amount of time had passed without conversation with Nate, she was beginning to feel clearer about both infidelities.

She had just arrived at the outside door of Glovers when her mobile rang. Seeing it was Nate, she took a huge breath.

'Hey, Sharpie. How's it going?'

'Hey, Boo.' Her beloved nickname for Nate suddenly felt alien to her tongue. 'It's going OK, thanks. Just arrived at work.'

'I know you're missing me.' There was a hopeful lilt to Nate's voice.

'So much so, if I was an animal, I'd be a pine marten,' Vic joked.

'Sharpie, sharp as a tack, as always,' Nate laughed. 'Anyway, I know we said we'd meet and talk after Christmas but...'

'It's good to hear your voice,' Vic intercepted – and meant it.

'Aww,' Nate cooed, then, 'Shit, I'm late.' He started to talk really quickly. 'I just wanted to say that just in case you did need to reach me, I'm not going to be ignoring you but work is properly manic this week, what with office parties every lunch and dinner. Then I travel up to the Lakes with Tim for a few days, and you know what me and the brother are like when we get together.'

'It's fine. Go! Have fun.'

'Vic?' Nate's voice softened. 'We're going to be OK, aren't we?' Vic then heard what sounded like a bicycle bell and Nate shouting 'Hello' to a work mate. 'Vic, I gotta go, sorry. Laters.'

The bell in this instance had most definitely been a saving grace, for as much as Vic had missed Nate, living without him hadn't been as terrible as she had thought it would be. Maybe that was because they had only spent a short time apart, and she had Orla for company. In reality, she hadn't had the chance to feel alone with herself, or even her thoughts, for that matter.

She was glad to be spending Christmas in Windsor with her mum, without the routine of work or the frenetic backdrop of London town. She was also very much looking forward to sketching some winter river scenes and actually having the headspace to think about her job and her art too. She needed to work out exactly what would make her happy.

Letting herself into the office, she put her handbag down on the side in the kitchen and reached into the cupboard for a coffee cup.

'Morning, morning. Hurrah for it being my last day until January the third.'

The cropped-haired blonde with a bright red trout-pout and black statement glasses came sauntering in, grabbed herself a mug and poured a coffee from the jug.

'Morning, Penny.' Vic grinned. 'You do make me laugh. You

only work three days a week – and that's when you bother to show up at all.'

'Three days plus two children equals a lifetime of hard graft and misery. Well, eighteen years of that guaranteed, anyway.' A smirking Penny shimmied to get milk from the fridge.

'*Bonjour, bonjour. Joyeux Noël.*' Ray Glover came flouncing in, blowing air kisses. 'Please note, I made the coffee this morning and also, I have a surprise for you today, Victoria Sharpe.'

'Oh no. That sounds ominous.'

'Not at all.' Ray rinsed his mug under the tap. 'I spoke to Jerico Flint last night, and he was insistent he came in to meet you before he heads off on his Christmas holidays.'

'Ah, OK. I can't believe I still haven't met him in the flesh, to be honest.'

'He's a complete hottie, so you won't be disappointed.' Ray grinned.

'Really? He did like the new cover, didn't he?' Vic enquired pensively. 'Because he didn't seem his overly effusive self last time we spoke.'

'Well, his novel is out already, so he must do. Right. I'm off to the accountant's this morning. I'd better check what books need cooking before I leave.' Ray poured himself a fresh coffee.

'I need to get cracking too.' Penny picked up her drink from the side. 'The terrible twins have a dentist appointment at two thirty – ha, "tooth hurty", funny. So I need to leave early, I'm afraid.'

Giving Vic a knowing look, Ray headed to his office and shut the door.

'Victoria Sharpe, the pleasure is all mine.'

Vic laughed as Jerico Flint doffed his trilby at her. 'Hi. Great to meet you, and you are so not how I imagined you to look.' She grimaced. 'Shit. Sorry! I literally just said something I was thinking out loud.'

'Oh, I do love it when one's psyche has a moment of unwanted external revelation.' Jerico looked over his over-sized horn-rimmed spectacles at her.

'Mine has a habit of doing that,' Vic laughed.

'You imagined an unkempt, white-haired mad-professor-type, wearing ill-fitting chinos and smoking a pipe, didn't you?'

Vic didn't answer. Instead she took in the man in front of her. His appearance and sardonic, affable persona reminded her a bit of Vince Vaughn, the American actor whom she had loved in the hit summer romcom *Wedding Crashers*.

Jerico Flint was around six foot, Vic reckoned. She had always liked a tall man, with both Nate and Steady Stuart fitting that mould. He was broader than Nate, though, with shoulder-length hair, raven black, and olive skin. He was around forty, she guessed. But it was his eyes that truly captivated her. They were a vivid green, surrounded by delicate crinkles. His indigo jeans were complemented by a vintage velvet blazer in a rich shade of burgundy, paired with a paisley shirt in hues of blue and gold.

Ray had come out of his office and was loitering to speak with Jerico, and Penny waved at the author from her desk.

Ray shook Jerico's hand and winked at Victoria. 'Ignore this one being so rude – you just can't get the staff these days. I'm off to a meeting, but I wanted to wish you an incredibly happy Christmas.' He handed Jerico a bottle-shaped gift bag.

Jerico recognised the neck of an expensive bottle of brandy inside. 'How very kind.'

Ray headed back to his office and Vic chimed in. 'So, where were we? Yes... I have to confess I imagined you were older. I love your jacket, by the way.'

'Oh, this old thing.' He laughed with his eyes as he handed Vic a book. '*Mr Pigeons and the Waterloo Clock*, signed, sealed and delivered. A gift for its jacket designer extraordinaire.'

Vic took it and grinned.

'Everyone is loving this cover. I mean, people say don't judge a book by one, and all that, but thank you. It's going down a storm.' He reached into his bag and took out a beautifully wrapped present. He handed it to her and, as if he knew her trait of never patiently waiting to open anything that was given to her, added, 'Save it until Christmas – if you can.' He winked. 'It's been so lovely to meet you, Queen Victoria.' Then, with a pretend bow, he reached for her hand and held it a little longer than necessary.

'You too,' Victoria giggled.

As soon as the office door shut behind him, Penny shouted over from her desk. 'Whoa there! Get a room, you two. I could feel that spark from here, lady.'

'Don't be stupid.' Vic was blushing, as she too had felt an energy between them that had really lifted her mood. Ray hadn't been lying either; Jerico Flint sure was a striking-looking man.

'Well, you're both creative, so you have something in common, at least. Talking of which, how *is* the gorgeous Nate? Did he manage to escape the dreaded lurgy?'

Ouch! Vic recoiled inwardly. 'Surprisingly, yes.' She sighed, not wanting her judgemental colleague to know anything further. For despite working with Penny Clayton for the past three years, there had never been closeness enough between them to trust Penny with anything more than surface-level chatter.

She would tell Ray about Nate, but not before Christmas. It was all too much to relive what had been happening, and the new year might bring a whole new story anyway.

As she sat back at her desk, she heard a text ping into her phone. It was the sexual health clinic asking her to come back in for a face-to-face appointment at four p.m. the next day. A feeling of panic enveloped her.

Ray, who was heading off to see the accountant, caught a glimpse of her expression. 'You all right, Vic? You've gone a bit pale.'

'Fine, fine. But I did forget to tell you I need to leave at three thirty tomorrow, as umm...' She dropped her voice to a whisper. 'As, umm... I've got a smear test.'

'Honestly!' Ray grimaced. 'Give me strength!' Throwing both arms in the air as he strode towards the door, he shouted back to her. 'And that's it, you can chuck the discrimination book at me. I don't care. I *am* employing only men – and handsome ones at that – forthwith!'

NINE

LONDON

The Diagnosis

Victoria could confidently say December the twentieth, 2005, was the longest day in her whole thirty-five years on the planet.

With a feeling of dread in her stomach, heavy and dense as a block of lead, she got off the bus and followed the same steps she had taken just two weeks before. That morning, she had tried to concentrate on creating a mailshot for an ice-cream company but had ended up just drinking back-to-back cups of coffee and staring at her computer screen. What she had found out the night before, and what was worrying her the most, was that chlamydia could remain asymptomatic, and there was a chance, if that were the case, that it could affect a woman's fertility.

Vic felt a sense of relief at the familiarity of seeing the same grey-haired nurse who had examined her sitting behind the glass-fronted reception desk.

'Hi, I'm Victoria Sharpe. I got a text about an appointment today.'

'Oh, Victoria, hello.' Muttering something to her colleague, the woman came out from behind the desk. 'This way, please.'

With a pounding heart, Vic followed her into a small treatment room. As well as an examination bed and sink, a table flanked by two chairs housed a variety of leaflets and a box of tissues.

The nurse ushered Vic to sit down, then joined her at the table. 'I'm Sandra Bellows, and I'm one of the sexual health practitioners here. We didn't get the chance to share full introductions before.'

'No – just some bodily fluids,' Vic joked, then blew out a huge breath. 'I know why I'm here. It's chlamydia, isn't it?'

The nurse closed her eyes for a second and took a deep breath. 'I'm not sugar-coating this in any way, Victoria. All of your tests have come back, and you are showing as HIV-positive.'

Victoria felt the blood drain from every single part of her body.

'Sorry. What did you say?' Her voice wobbled. 'I think you must have made a terrible mistake.'

'I'm afraid not,' the nurse said, her expression concerned and kind.

'HIV? No!' Vic put her hand over her mouth in horror, then burst into tears.

Sandra put one hand on her shoulder and passed her a tissue with the other.

'No! You're wrong. It's gay men who mainly get it, isn't it? Or people in Africa? Name me one woman who has it!' Vic pulled at her hair. 'Oh my God, oh my God, does this mean I'm going to die? Oh my God.' She stood up and started pacing around. 'Oh fuck! How? Does this mean I'll get AIDS?' She sat down again.

When she had quietened down, Sandra spoke in a calm and deliberate voice. 'You will get the best treatment there is at the

Chelsea and Westminster. I can promise you that. We are going to look after you. OK?'

Vic was inconsolable. 'How can I have HIV, though? I've had the same boyfriend for six years.' She shut her eyes for a second and her thoughts turned to Danny. But they had used a condom, so it was impossible that he could have given it to her, surely.

'Your assigned consultant will be able to answer all your questions,' the nurse replied in a soothing tone.

Victoria sniffed loudly, feeling sick to her stomach and desperately wishing for this not to be real. 'Am I going to die, Sandra? I'm so scared.' She gripped the woman's hand. 'I just can't believe this is happening to me.'

'Would you like to call somebody?' Sandra's voice was as soft as it was strong. 'It's fine, I can leave the room if you want to do that.'

'No, no. I'm fine,' Vic blubbered. 'What happens now?'

'OK, so we need to take some more bloods and a urine sample, and I have to ask you a few questions.'

Vic's mind was racing and she started to ramble to herself. 'Fuck! Oh my God. Nate must have got it off that stupid bitch from work, or someone else for that matter, and given it to me.'

'Like I said before, there will never be any judgement here.' The nurse took Vic's hand and squeezed it again. 'And the important thing is to get you sorted. Can I ask if you can remember having any flu-type illness recently or in the past few years?'

Vic stared at her, remembering how ill she had felt at Orla's. 'Yes! Just recently.'

'Did you notice a rash at all?'

'Yes, I did.'

'OK.' Sandra nodded knowingly. 'Exactly which dates was that?'

Vic took out her diary with shaking hands and relayed the

dates to Sandra. 'Is that connected, then? The rash. I have to say it's the most ill I've ever felt in my entire life.'

'I'm sure it was. And yes, it's a good thing if it is connected because it means we're diagnosing you early,' Sandra replied matter-of-factly.

'Is... is there a cure, or one on the horizon?'

'Not yet. But the research going on around the virus is massive and the drug treatments we have available enable people to live a long and healthy life now. It's not a death sentence like it used to be, Victoria. I promise you that.'

Vic tried to think straight about what to do next. Her voice was now a whisper. 'How do I tell Nate? How do I tell him? Or maybe he knows already! I take it having unprotected sex is how I would have got it?'

'You're not a drug user, are you?'

Vic shook her head. 'The odd toke of weed if it's on offer.'

'You don't inject yourself with anything?'

Vic screwed her face up. 'No way!'

'Sorry, I have to ask,' Sandra replied sympathetically. 'Then yes, I would say you got it via sexual contact.' She scribbled down some words on a pad in front of her. 'We can contact anyone you've been in sexual contact with if you'd like us to, as it's very important they are tested too.'

'I fucking hate him!' Vic wailed. 'I want to talk to him first – is that OK?'

'Yes, of course. The sooner the better, really.'

'I can't take it in.' Victoria sniffed. 'It's like I'm going to wake up in a minute and it's all been the worst nightmare I've ever had in my life.'

'You're going to need support through this, and don't be frightened to take it. And make sure to ask as many questions as you need to. Here are some information leaflets.'

Victoria put them straight in her bag without looking at them.

'So, will I need to take some form of medication now?'

'We have an appointment for you back here with Dr Anna Raglan tomorrow at four, if that's OK.'

'Yes, yes, of course.' Vic shook her head manically.

'Let me scribble that on here, so you don't forget.' Sandra wrote the appointment details on the top of a leaflet and handed it to her.

'This leaflet is for the Terrence Higgins Trust. They are the leading HIV charity and have a direct number to call for emotional support, advice and any information you may need. They will also be able to set you up with a counsellor if you'd like one. There are various support groups you will be able to attend – if you want to, that is. If you feel that you desperately need to speak to anyone outside of their opening hours, Samaritans are available twenty-four seven as well.' She jotted their number down too and stood up. 'We will get you sorted, I promise you.'

'Thank you.' Victoria sniffed, her face streaked with tears. Nausea suddenly enveloped her.

'Here.' Sandra handed her a wad of tissues that she had wetted with warm water. 'Wipe your face, and would you like a drink of water before we continue?'

Vic shook her head. 'No... thank you. Let's just get on with it.'

TEN

The Aftermath

That evening, as the train slipped its way out of the city on its way to the more suburban landscape of Windsor and Eton Riverside, Vic felt an anguish and despair she had never experienced before in her whole life. She wanted to crawl out of herself to escape what was happening to her. It wasn't that she didn't want to be alive anymore, but she just didn't know where she wanted to be. She had always loved catching a glimpse of the London Eye on the city's skyline, especially at Christmas time, when it was all lit up. She also delighted in staring into the various offices and flats which looked out over the busy tracks outside Waterloo station. But today these small joys eluded her.

Sipping discreetly from the first of the three miniature bottles of wine she had bought on her way to the station, Victoria stared out of the window, her eyes blurring with tears she blinked away, in complete and utter shock. The tipsy chatter that surrounded her from those who'd been for an after-work Christmas drink soon became white noise as she imagined how Nate – and everyone else she loved, for that matter –

would react on her telling them that she was now a woman living with HIV. But if she had it, Nate would have it! Maybe he knew already and just couldn't tell her. Maybe that was why he had stopped pestering her for sex after Brighton. But no, if he knew, they surely wouldn't have slept together at the wedding. He would never do that to her. Or, shit, maybe that was when she had contracted it. Vic's face screwed up in anguish. None of this was making sense in her head now.

People talking far too loudly on their phones about their day, or communicating about what time they were getting to a particular station for their lift home, were really beginning to annoy her. Opposite her, a good-looking guy in a long, smart black coat was listening quietly to an iPod with his earphones, nodding his head away to whatever tune was taking his fancy. Taking in his chiselled features made Vic suddenly realise that if she and Nate were to split, she would be single for the rest of her life, because who in their right mind would want to sleep with someone with a metaphorical grenade up their fanny?

All these commuters carrying on with their normal lives, not having any clue what was going on within her mind – or body, for that matter – made her want to scream out loud, 'Do you realise what's happening to me?!' 'Do you care?!' But on the other hand, she felt so dead inside she wanted to keep everything in, to not let anyone know what was going on. Because if she were to let out her emotions, or the fact that she had HIV, the reactions of others would be too intense for her own shattered self to cope.

The sexual health nurse could not have been nicer, but she had also been very matter-of-fact, leaving Vic under no illusion that she had a serious health condition and that life as she knew it had changed forever.

As if taking comfort from mother's milk, and not caring what anyone thought of her, she kept her lips around the tiny necks of the wine bottles, downing them one by one until all three were empty.

Vic felt wobbly as she got up and made her way along the platform and to the public toilet at Windsor and Eton Riverside station. After peeing like a horse, she emerged in a complete daze. She loved the fact that it was cold and the wind in her face was biting. It was as if enduring the Arctic temperature was punishment for the mess she had got herself into.

She headed straight for the river and began to walk the path she had trodden so many times – times when the problems she had been facing had seemed so great. But now that her health was affected, she realised that without your health you had nothing. She had wasted so much time sweating over so much small stuff, all of which had had a clear solution. Solutions that she had been too much of a coward to carry through.

In a haze of alcohol and foreboding, she walked and thought. She passed Jake's boat. It looked so warm and welcoming with its fairy lights and the cosy orange glow coming from the tiny windows. A bright red poinsettia sat on one sill, a miniature Christmas tree on another. A sudden childhood memory of long summer holidays, when Jake would allow her and Albie to run wild on deck, whilst he and her mother sat chatting in the sun, flitted across her mind. The recollection of such simple, beautiful times now felt like a different lifetime.

Knowing she wasn't in the right frame of mind to speak to the old family friend, she sped up. She couldn't see or tell anyone – not today, for this was her day of reckoning. Of processing what was happening inside her, and thinking about what her future may hold. Of punishing herself for being so stupid as to trust the one man she had thought would never fail her.

It wasn't until she reached her favourite bench that she

stopped. Looking around to check that she was alone, she finally allowed herself to cry, and the crying became so intense and powerful that her whole body shook from head to toe. An explosion of anger, resentment, disbelief – but mainly fear: terrible fear. When she felt like her body was empty of everything, she reached into her handbag for a tissue and her hand fell on the leaflets that Sandra had given her. Scrabbling for the miniature torch that had fallen out of the posh crackers her brother had probably nicked from somewhere last Christmas, and which had remained in the detritus at the bottom of her bag ever since, she began to read from one of them. If she focused on the words she could ignore the pain in her heart that threatened to consume her. But as she read that Terrence Lionel Seymour Higgins was one of the first people known to die of an AIDS-related illness, at just thirty-seven years old in 1982, the tears took over again. Soon she, too, would be that age, and it was so young.

When she had cried herself out, she wiped her face and forced herself to carry on reading. Born in Wales, Higgins felt alienated because of his sexuality. He moved to London, worked in the House of Commons by day and as a bartender and DJ by night. Higgins collapsed at the iconic Heaven nightclub and was admitted to hospital, where he died. The Terry Higgins Trust was formed in 1982 by a concerned group of community members and Terry's friends. It was named after him to personalise and humanise the issue of AIDS. It was formalised in August 1983, when it adopted a constitution and opened a bank account, and the name of the trust was changed (*Terrence* rather than *Terry*) to sound more formal. They offered support, understanding and information – all of which Vic sorely needed, right now.

She took out her phone. Shaking as she dialled the number, she was greeted by the soft, kind voice of a man. 'Hello, THT Direct. How can I help you?'

She began to blurt, 'Hello, I'm Victoria. I found out today that I have HIV. I'm a bit drunk. Sorry.' Vic let out another massive sob.

'Today, you say. Well, I'm so glad you have called us, Victoria. My name is Brian and I'm here to listen. Feel free to talk or rant to me, I'm not going anywhere. You can ask me anything you like. It's totally confidential here.'

His friendly, casual manner was a balm to Vic's torn and battered soul.

'It's just so frightening,' Vic wailed. 'I haven't told anyone yet and I don't know how to, and I think my boyfriend has given it to me, which means he has it too. It's just such a mess.' She let out another explosive sob, and the man waited for her to settle.

'So you tested because you thought your boyfriend has the virus, is that right?'

'No.' A weird little squeak came from her throat. 'I didn't know I had it. I just had a sexual health check and I found out then. And I have slept with someone else, but that was before... I just don't know what to do.'

'I can hear that you are very upset, Victoria, and it's OK to feel that way after finding out about your diagnosis. Have you got an appointment arranged with a doctor yet?'

Vic sniffed. 'Yes, tomorrow, at the Chelsea and Westminster. Happy Christmas to me.' She let out a funny noise between a laugh and a cry. 'I'm drunk – did I mention that? I'm sorry to call you when I'm drunk.'

'Are you feeling OK at the moment?'

'Yes. I had terrible flu recently so I'm a bit knackered, but I'm OK – physically, at least.'

'That's good you're feeling OK now.' The man's understanding tone began to soothe her. 'I was diagnosed a couple of years ago. I take tablets and my viral load is stable. I have a loving partner whom I met after my diagnosis. HIV isn't the death sentence it used to be, Victoria, and research is ongoing and effective. There is hope that there will be a cure one day.'

'Really?' Vic sniffed.

'Yes, really. Do you understand what having HIV means?'

'I think so. The woman at the clinic gave me the basics, and a few leaflets, which I skimmed through. I want to understand it, though. What's on my mind right now is just how huge the stigma is. I'm guilty of it myself. I didn't even think women could get HIV.' She gave a bitter laugh. 'How ignorant is that?'

'You are not alone in that,' the man replied kindly.

The stark reality of it all was beginning to sober Vic up. 'I do remember seeing Princess Diana supporting the cause. You would have thought that she, of all people, would have been able to change people's minds about it.'

'She really did help massively, God rest her soul.' Brian's voice lifted slightly. 'The London Lighthouse was remarkably close to her heart – it was amazing when she visited and got the press on board. It might be somewhere you want to go when you feel up to it. They host meetings where you will be able to gain any information you may need about living with the virus, or you can just go along and chat in general with people who understand, and, of course, won't judge.'

Vic felt suddenly overwhelmed at this stranger's outpouring of pure kindness.

'Did you feel you could talk to people when you were diagnosed? I feel like I want to just hide away,' Vic blubbered.

'From my experience, everybody deals with it differently and it's a great start that you've called us, so well done for that. The reason I do what I do is because the charity was, and still is, a lifeline for me.'

'That's so good to hear. Did your friends and family understand?'

'Some of them. There will be people out there who can support you, Victoria, even if it is only a small community – and if not, then Terrence Higgins is always here for you. As are other charities. You don't even have to tell anyone outside those who may be at risk if you don't want to.'

Victoria started crying again. 'Thank you, thank you so much... I forgot your name. Sorry.'

'Brian. I'm Brian.'

'Brian. You've been brilliant.' Vic felt a wave of gratitude to this man just for being there. There was so much she needed to know, so much she would have to face now. 'Before I go, is there anything else I should know, or that might be helpful for me to understand. I'm going to have to work out how to tell people, and I can't even begin to think how to do that...'

'Well, you need to know that some people are still terrified of HIV. They don't understand it. They still do think it is a death sentence and they're going to catch it from you. But in reality, it is a very fragile virus that doesn't survive outside the body for long. And despite the misconceptions of so many, it *can't* be transmitted through sweat, urine or saliva.'

Vic hadn't even thought about that, but it was such a relief to hear it. 'So, I can't pass it on to my flatmate, for example if we share a cup or a towel, or have a hug?'

'No. All of those things are perfectly safe – and you'll be needing some of those hugs.'

Vic inhaled a deep breath of freezing air, which made her feel slightly giddy. She let out a little moan. 'And how on earth am I going to tell the person who gave it to me?'

'Everyone is going to react differently, Victoria, and they may not react in the way you expect. I would suggest that you are in a quiet place and have a leaflet handy about transmission. And maybe tell them how easy it was for you to get tested and suggest they go and seek medical care as soon as they can.'

'It's going to be so awful.' Vic sniffed.

'It's going to be emotional, that's for sure,' Brian replied kindly. 'And of course, you can obviously direct them to us if they need support.'

Vic shivered dramatically.

'How do you feel now we've been chatting for a while?'

She hiccupped loudly. 'Still shit, but better than I did. Thank you. Thank you so much. And happy Christmas, Brian. You're amazing, do you know that?'

'Get some rest if you can,' Brian said gently. 'Make sure to check out our website. You really are not alone. I can assure you of that. And do call us, whenever you need to.'

Arriving at her mum's, Victoria hugged Chandler like she had never hugged him before, opened the back door to let him out for a pee, cranked up the heating, then went to the kitchen sink and downed half a pint of water. She could hear the television blaring in the living room. She went in and found her mother sound asleep, head back, mouth open, snoring, a half-empty litre bottle of vodka on the coffee table. Taking a big slurp from it herself, with a grimace, Vic turned off the TV.

Then she noticed that the familiar well-worn familiar Christmas tree had been decorated, and felt a small glimmer of hope. The battered white lace-dressed angel that had been in the decorations box ever since she could remember was sitting with her silver legs hanging over the side of the mantelpiece. Two envelopes, one with her name, one with Albie's, were propped up beside it. She ripped at her own to reveal a *To My Darling Daughter*-embossed Christmas card. Inside a twenty-pound WH Smith voucher and the words: *Thought you could get some drawing bits and pieces. I only just realised the word HEART contained the word ART. No wonder you're good at it. Happy Christmas, Victoria. Love, Mum XX*

Silent tears began to fall down Victoria's cheeks. With the shield of alcohol wearing off, and feeling suddenly spent with emotion, she took off her coat, slumped down on the floor and rested her back against the sofa beside her mum's legs. Placing a throw she had pulled from the armchair around them both as if they were in some kind of cocoon, she laid her head back on her mum's knee.

Alcoholic or not, this was the only mum she would ever have, and she loved her. She loved her with all her heart. This was the mum who, when Vic had been sick as a child, would make her Heinz tomato soup and put mashed potato in it. The mum who would go straight down the shop and get her Lucozade as soon as she had a 'bug'. The mum who would put a cool flannel on her head when she had a temperature, or calamine lotion on her itchy spots when she came down with chicken pox. And boy, did those spots itch! The mum who would sing 'Bridge Over Troubled Water' to her baby girl when she or Vic were feeling sad, as it got to number one the year Vic had been born and Kath loved it. And the mum who would fight her every corner at school if for one moment she thought her precious girl was being treated unfairly.

Whether Kath Sharpe would be able to comfort her only daughter when the darkness came and pain was all around, Victoria didn't know. But what she did know was that the only person in the entire world she wanted to be with at this moment in time was her.

When Victoria awoke with a jump from a weird, unsettling dream in which she was trying to drive up a sheer mountainside in a London bus, it took her a second to work out where she was. Lying on the sofa with the throw up to her neck, it seemed, and Chandler a dead weight on her feet. For one glorious moment, she felt happy to be surrounded by such familiarity. Then it all came rushing back and reality hit. Life as she once knew it really was well and truly over.

Pleased at least that the heating had clicked on, she brought her watch close to her face and squinted at it, just about able to make out that it was seven a.m. With her mouth dry as a desert, she pulled her feet gently out from under Chandler and made her way out into the hall. As she did, she heard heavy snoring coming from the dining room. Perplexed, she poked her head around the door to make out the silhouette of her mother under a mountain of covers, on what looked like Albie's old single bed. Vic was just wondering how Kath had got up off the sofa and herself back onto it without her realising, and why her mother was now sleeping downstairs, when Chandler came tearing into the hall. Shushing him, Victoria splashed her face in the kitchen sink, put on her coat, then groaned at the thought of having to head back to London for her hospital appointment.

Wishing she hadn't been quite so rash in her need for comfort and familiarity, and hoping Kath had been so drunk that she hadn't realised that her only daughter had even been there, she reached for the dog's lead and whispered: 'Just a quick walk out the front, mister, then I must get to the station.'

ELEVEN
LONDON

The Realisation

Later that day, hungover and sitting in a sterile consulting room at the hospital, Vic played over in her mind what an HIV consultant should look like. She was pleasantly surprised when a naturally pretty woman in her early thirties, dressed in a casual navy suit with a plain white T-shirt underneath, and sporting trendy white trainers, entered the room. Her brown bob was short and sleek, her face light of make-up.

'Victoria?' The woman came towards her, holding out her hand.

Vic stood up and shook the woman's soft hand.

'So sorry to keep you waiting. I'm Dr Ragland. We are going to be seeing a lot of each other, so please do feel free to call me Anna. In fact, I insist that you do.' The doctor's face was open, her demeanour friendly and engaging.

Pushing back the tears, Vic felt her shoulders drop. She took a deep breath before whispering, 'Hi.'

'Please, take a seat. How are you feeling today?'

Vic sat down and burst into tears. 'Frightened. I just feel frightened.'

'Well, let me try and alleviate some of your fears.' The doctor handed Vic a tissue from the box on the table. 'Have you spoken to anyone yet about your diagnosis?'

Vic shook her head. 'Nobody I love. I called Terrence Higgins, though. They were amazing.'

'Yes. Good. I'm glad you've done that. And did reception confirm which address you would like your correspondence sent to?'

Victoria nodded. 'Yes. Everything is going to my mother's house.'

That morning, Vic's intention had been to head into work to take her mind off everything, but on her way back into London, she realised that she just couldn't face it. In fact, she couldn't face anyone or anything. So instead, she had left a message for Ray – a harmless lie, telling him that she was dealing with an emergency in Windsor and that she hoped it would be OK to use up her remaining annual leave and go back in the new year.

With Orla thankfully having already left for Ireland, Vic hadn't had to see her, either. And as for Nate, she was relieved that they had discussed meeting up after Christmas so that when she did have to relay the life-changing news, she would be armed with all the information and would hopefully have all her facts in order. Saying that, though, maybe he did know that he had it already, and the reason he hadn't said anything when he spoke to her was that he was also playing the same waiting game about telling her. Or maybe he didn't know anything, because if she hadn't said yes to a general sexual health check, knowing what she knew now about HIV, she could have been carrying the virus for years.

Dr Anna was looking through a stack of notes in front of her. 'So we're waiting for the results of a second test, but looking at your bloods, I think we can safely say that you do have the virus.'

'OK,' Vic whispered.

'Without blowing your mind with too much information at this stage, would you like me to give you an overview of what having HIV means?'

'Yes, yes, please.' That morning, Vic had been on the computer at Orla's, looking up every piece of information she could find on HIV, but the more she read, the more terrified she felt. 'I've been reading stuff online and—'

'Probably best you use me as your world wide web from now on,' Dr Anna said. 'Depending on who's doing the writing, some of those articles may not be as factual as us medical professionals would like. I'm afraid a lot of people have very skewed opinions on the subject.'

'Reading between the lines, I think if I had leprosy, it'd be more socially acceptable.' Vic let out a massive sigh.

'It's going to be tough, including dealing with the stigma that, sadly, is out there, but you've got this, we've got this.' Dr Anna leant forward and looked directly at Vic. 'So, just to give you a clear explanation, when someone contracts HIV, the virus begins to take over specific cells in the immune system, called CD_4 cells. When these cells replicate, the HIV cells inside them also replicate. HIV hijacks the cellular machinery of CD_4 cells to reproduce and shed more HIV, which means the viral load increases. As the HIV viral load increases, the number of healthy CD_4 cells decreases, as they are destroyed when they create HIV copies.'

Vic screwed her face up.

'Sorry, I realise that's a lot to take in, Victoria, but it is important to have the facts. In brief, though, all you need to know is that once treatment starts, our aim is for you to have a low viral load and a high CD_4 count. Then we will have your HIV under control. The good news is that your levels are such that I don't recommend we start treatment yet. Once it is started, you are on it for life and, as with all medications, there are likely to be side-effects. From now on, we will monitor you here regularly, but if you're feeling unwell at any time, you can walk straight in, and we will check out what's going on for you.'

'So, I can live a normal life until then... until the time comes that my viral load rises and CD4 count drops?'

'That's right. You must, of course, always use a condom when having sex from now on. And do your best to keep yourself healthy, eat the right foods, try not to smoke, or drink too much alcohol. Always use sunscreen, too. This leaflet is worth a read.'

Vic cast her eyes down it and began to skim-read. *HIV can be spread as follows: vaginal/frontal and anal sex without a condom, sharing drug-injecting equipment, sharing sex toys, mother-to-child transmission, during pregnancy, birth or breast-feeding and coming into contact with contaminated blood. HIV cannot be spread by kissing, hugging, shaking hands, sharing space with someone, sharing a toilet, sharing household items such as cups, plates, cutlery or bed linen, or any other general social contact.*

'I guess that makes my decision on having children or not a whole lot easier.'

'I was coming to that – I'm so sorry, Victoria. I should have waited to hand you that leaflet,' the doctor stuttered.

'I read about it online this morning and didn't allow it to register, to be honest,' Vic said. 'I've never had a burning urge to have a child. In fact, I've been in a real dilemma as to what I should do with regards to starting a family. But when you're told it's not any kind of option, that's a whole different thought process, isn't it?' Vic's voice wobbled.

'Treatments are progressing all the time,' Dr Anna replied, with a softness to her voice.

'I need to be realistic here.' Vic was suddenly matter-of-fact.

'And spinning it on its head, my decision about having children has been made for me. Maybe that's a positive out of this whole awful mess. And I'm not stupid, Anna. It's going to be difficult enough dealing with me having this bloody virus, let alone throwing trying to have a family into the mix.'

'Keep the conversation going, though, Victoria, because you may say that now, but all kinds of feelings are likely to engulf you. And I'd be lying if I said all of this is going to be plain sailing, but I will do my damned best to make sure it's as easy as I can make it from my end. And if you decide you do want a child in the future, then we will talk about that again.'

Victoria took a huge breath. 'Thank you. Thank you so much.'

'So, I will see you again early February.' Dr Anna shut Vic's file. 'You will get a letter confirming everything, but as I said, any worries, please call this number here, or if you are *really* concerned about anything at all, then just turn up and we will do our best to find somebody to see you.' Dr Anna handed Vic a card. 'Do you have any plans for Christmas?'

'I don't feel like celebrating anything, but I'm going to my mum's in Windsor. You?'

'Oh, just a quiet one for me.' Dr Anna stood up and squeezed Vic's shoulder. 'Be kind to yourself, Victoria, and I'll see you in a few weeks.'

The overground Tube rattled its way back to near Orla's flat. Just days before, Vic had not even heard of the term CD4, let alone known that cells of that name were surging around her body, protecting her from all kinds of infection.

Also, how ironic that *art*, the subject she had practised and loved all her life, was also the abbreviation for antiretroviral treatment – the drugs that would eventually keep her alive.

Exhausted from her jumping train of thought, Vic shut her

eyes. A vision of handsome, wild-haired Nate sprang to mind. She was surprised at her own self-control in not picking up the phone to him and screaming out that she had HIV and it was all his fault, but as she had thought before, once the secret was out, it was out, and it was huge, and it was hurtful, and it was terrifying. And the longer she kept it in, the easier she felt it would be.

Her brief rest was interrupted by a text from Mandy.

> Vic! Where are you? How are you? We need to talk honeymoon, it's been an age. Christmas is madness, but let's set a date for new year. Love you x

Vic hadn't even thought about how she would tell her friends. She expected Orla to not even break her stride, but dear, sweet, innocent Mandy... She had no idea how she would react. And what if they didn't support her? What if they couldn't cope with it all?

To try and turn her thoughts away from the darkness, she reached for the small art pad in her bag and began to turn the pages. Her etching of rowers on the Thames at Putney made her stop and think back to that beautiful summer's day in July, when she'd got up early and sat on a bench in complete peace, aside birds singing in a tree above her, and had sketched the relaxing river scene.

She wished she could bottle the feeling that using her creativity gave her, and take a sip of it every time she was feeling low. Maybe that was it: she should engineer doing what she loved for herself, every day. Because she was under no illusion that from now on, there were going to be good days and bad days, and sad days when the elixir of art may be her saving grace.

But now, just for a few days, and with Christmas afoot, she would pretend that everything was fine and dandy. That she didn't have a life-changing health condition, and that she didn't have an insurmountable mountain to climb, and that whatever happened, everything was going to be all right.

TWELVE
WINDSOR

Christmas Eve

Vic arrived at her mum's with a small wheelie case just as Joti was about to pull off her drive. Rolling down her window, the neighbour called out, her voice cold, 'Glad I've caught you, Vicki.'

Vic prepared herself for confrontation.

'I'd really appreciate you keeping an eye on that dog of your mum's whilst you're here. He did it again the other day. In exactly the same place. It's not on.'

Vic felt her hackles rise. But the last thing she wanted to do was to get into any kind of doorstep fracas, especially not over dog shit. She hurried to open the front door before she said something she might regret.

As if Joti had picked up on Victoria's thoughts, she added, 'And you should know that I saw your mum walking the dog up and down the road here in her dressing gown and bare feet the other night.'

To Joti's surprise, Vic stopped in her tracks and broke down in tears.

The neighbour's stony expression cracked, and her face was suddenly full of concern. 'Oh no. Sorry. I really didn't mean to upset you.'

Vic wiped her face with her jacket sleeve. 'It's fine. I'm just not feeling myself today.'

'Do you want to talk?' Joti looked up at her with honest, kind eyes, and Vic felt bad once again for how their last conversation had gone.

With tears still streaming down her face, Vic shook her head. 'No, it's OK.' She sniffed loudly, wanted to shout that nothing was OK, that she had HIV and her alcoholic mother was clearly becoming a danger to herself and she had no idea what to do about any of it. 'It's just a worry, all this, isn't it?'

'I'm on the last of a run of night shifts tonight, so if you did want a chat another time – well, you know where I am. Right, I'd better go. Happy Christmas, Vicki.'

Vic's return 'Happy Christmas' was lost on the wind. Wondering what Joti's job was, she made her way inside, propped her case up in the hallway and threw her coat on the stairs.

There was no sign anywhere of either her mother or Chandler. She was also sure that Albie should have been there by now, as he was only planning to stay that night and go back home to his girlfriend and her two kids in Reading for Christmas Day night.

Turning up the heating, Vic went through to the kitchen and, on opening the fridge was pleasantly surprised to see a small stuffed turkey in a baking tray, and some potatoes, parsnips and brussels sprouts sitting in water, ready to be cooked. On the side were her favourites: mince pies, a small Christmas cake, a bowl of satsumas and a tin of Quality Street. On top of the fridge, alongside a large pack of dry-roasted peanuts and some Pringles, were cans of beer and a few bottles of wine. All this unexpected order set Vic off again, tears spilling down her cheeks. Her plan had been to see what her mum had managed to buy and then head to the supermarket before everything had sold out, to pick up the slack. It was such a relief that her mum had had the clarity and wherewithal to go shopping herself. And also heartening that she had remembered a lot of the things that Vic and Albie enjoyed.

Putting the white wine in the fridge, Vic poured herself a glass of red, popped the tube of Pringles open and was just about to call her brother to see what time he was arriving when she heard a commotion at the front of the house. As she walked to the window to see what was going on, her mother came flying through the front door, swiftly followed by a shaking Chandler. The shouting continued outside.

'Vic, your brother's in trouble.' Kath's voice was shaking.

'OK, Mum, stay in the kitchen with Chandler.' Vic remained calm, but stern. She could hear the fear in Albie's voice as she pushed open the front door.

'I told you not to come here. I had to get my old dear to come to the cashpoint with me, as I didn't have enough. I *was* going to meet you under the arches as planned. I'm late, but I've got it. Oi, get the fuck off me. Come on, mate. Not here. Please!'

Then Vic heard a smack, then somebody falling to the floor. She ran outside to see a man, his face hidden by a black hoodie, punching her brother in the head. As she switched the outside light on and screamed for the hoodie man to stop what he was doing, he sprang up, grabbed a handful of the notes that were now flying around the drive, and took off. As he turned, he crashed into Vic, knocking her right onto the concrete, causing her elbow to split and begin to bleed profusely. She could see the flash of blue lights turning into their road.

'Get in!' she hissed at Albie. 'Get in, now! I'll handle this.'

'But, sis, I—'

'Go! Just check on Mum.'

Vic pulled off her scarf and wrapped it around her bleeding

arm. As the police car drew into the drive, she casually walked towards it. A female officer got out. Another police officer was on his radio in the driver's seat.

'Are you all right? We've had reports of some kind of disturbance at this address.'

'Yes, umm... er... It was a right to-do.' In shock at what had happened, and with blood beginning to drip down her arm, Vic began to speak really fast. 'The dog escaped, my brother ran to stop him going into the road. We both shouted and had a bit of a scuffle.' She faked a smile. 'It's Christmas and... too much to drink and... you know what siblings are like. I tripped and fell – no biggy – and that was it. I cut my arm. Mother, brother and dog are inside. No harm done. I just need to get in and sort this.' Vic pulled the scarf tightly around her arm.

'And you expect me to believe that, do you?' The police officer remained expressionless.

'Yes... I do.' Vic was now shaking with both cold and shock as the woman began to question her further.

'What's your name?'

'Victoria Sharpe.'

'Do you live here?'

'No. I'm just here for Christmas with my mum.'

'And your brother?'

'What about him?'

'Does he have a name?'

'Albert Sharpe, but we all call him Albie. And... umm, he's just visiting too.'

'Before we go on, that arm looks nasty. Let me take a look – you might need stitches.' The policewoman went to move the scarf from Vic's arm.

'No! No. Don't touch it.' Vic was surpised at her own agressiveness.

'OK. OK.' The policewoman put her hands up. 'I've got first aid in the vehicle, that's all. Let me just see if it might need stitches.' She moved forward again to move the scarf, which was now soaked with blood.

Vic burst into tears. Her voice and face now full of desperation, she repeated, 'I said, don't fucking touch it.' Her make-up was now streaked down her face. 'Please.'

The other police officer got out of the car.

'All right,' the policewoman replied calmly. 'It's OK. I won't.'

'It's not OK, though, is it?' Vic whispered through her tears. 'You shouldn't touch it because... because I've got HIV. I just found out.'

The policewoman's tone became kind and gentle. 'That is really good of you to let me know, Victoria.'

'Please don't be too nice to me. I'm only just managing to hold myself together.' Vic made a noise between a blubber and a wail.

'I'm so sorry you've had that news. I can't imagine how difficult that must be to take on board.' The police officer was sincere. 'And it must be really hard telling people.'

'You're the first person I've told, actually,' Vic whispered, noticing a curtain twitch in the neighbour's house opposite. She realised that telling a stranger had felt a much easier thing to do, compared to the enormity of having to tell those she loved dearly.

'That's sounds like a big step, so well done.' The policewoman nodded for her colleague to get back in the car. 'I've got gloves in the med box, so I can happily patch you up.'

'I think the neighbours have had enough of a show, don't you?' Vic shivered. 'I'm going to get in the warm and jump in the shower. These things always look worse than they are, but thanks for the offer.'

'So this... this family kerfuffle won't have any repercussions tonight, you don't think?' The police officer looked directly into Victoria's eyes.

'No, we're all good.' Vic nodded firmly, not quite believing that she had got away without any further questioning.

'I appreciate you telling me about the – you know. That can't have been easy. And take care of yourself, eh?'

Vic's elbow was now really throbbing. 'I will, thanks.'

As the police officer reached the car door, she turned. 'Oh, and advise your brother to stay away from those sharks. He's a minnow in a big dirty pond, and he might not get off quite as easily next time.'

When Vic appeared from the shower, Albie was sitting at the kitchen table drinking a beer, waiting for her. Her mum was right: he did look so like her dad when he was younger, with his dark, quiffed hair, dimples and sparkly blue eyes.

'Where's Mum?' Vic picked up the glass of red wine she had poured earlier.

'Catching up on the soaps.'

'Is she all right?'

'She's pissed, so I guess so. I feel so bad that I had to push her through the door before. I just didn't want her getting involved.' He motioned towards the large plaster on his sister's elbow. 'Are you OK?'

'My arm took the brunt of the fall.' Vic lifted her elbow to look at it. 'It looked worse than it actually is.'

'I'm so sorry.' He jumped up to hug her, but she pushed him away.

'Get off me. And so you should be sorry. You could have been really hurt.'

He smiled. 'I didn't realise you cared.'

She couldn't stop a grin forming. 'Nor did I.'

'Thanks, Vic. I mean it. I heard what you said to the old bill. You were brilliant.'

Vic felt a rush of anxiety fly to her stomach. 'You heard everything?'

Albie didn't look her in the eye. 'Enough to know that you got me off the hook, sis,' he stuttered.

He went to the back door. His hand visibly shaking, he lit a cigarette. 'I didn't deserve you doing that for me. Sis, you're amaz...' He blinked fast to stop the tears that had formed in his eyes.

'Yes, I saved your bacon this time, but do you owe anyone else?'

Albie shook his head.

'Is that the truth?' Vic took a slurp of wine. 'Because if it's not, I will be angrier than you've ever seen me.'

Calm again, he turned to face her. 'Angrier than when I cut your Barbie's legs off from the knee down and stuck her in the top of the rotary washing line so you couldn't reach her?'

Vic managed to keep a straight face. 'I mean it!'

'I swear.' Albie tutted and let out a huge sigh.

'And don't be huffing at me, Albie Sharpe, because this has gone beyond anything you've done before.'

'I know, I know. Leave it out now, sis.'

'How much have you had off Mum?'

'I'm going to pay it back – all of it. I promise.'

'She's not a cash cow, Alb. She gets measly benefits and her cleaning money. That's it! You can't keep doing this to her. On top of that, we've got to face the fact that she's not well.'

'I know that. Don't you think I don't worry about her, too?'

'Not enough, clearly, Albie. Not nearly enough. I'm impressed she got all the Christmas food prepped though, aren't you?' Vic replied.

'I didn't notice the prep, but I did see all the goodies. Told her she'd done good, but she said it wasn't her.'

'Oh.' Vic frowned. 'Who was it, then?'

'I didn't ask.'

Vic felt strangely put out. 'I was all set to do it, though.'

'Don't be getting all territorial, Vic. Just be grateful some-one's helping Mum when we're not around, whoever it may be.'

'It was you who helped her get your old bed downstairs, though, I take it?'

'Not me, but it was a good job, because when I turned up the other day, she had fallen down the stairs.'

'Oh no!' Vic put her hand to her forehead.

'Yeah, sis, she had a proper egg of a bump on her head. Bigger than this one.' He pointed to the large lump behind his ear. 'My Lisa told me to stay the night in case the old dear was concussed.'

'And you didn't think to call me?'

'I didn't wanna worry you, and you're miles away.'

Vic sighed. 'I'm a big girl, Albie, and I'm not that far away, really. I can make my own decision if I come or not. I can easily hop on the train, or even get a taxi if need be. So next time, I want to know. You hear me?' Albie nodded. Vic took a drink of wine. 'So is it just the gambling you're struggling with now?'

'Yeah.' Chandler came tearing in from the back garden and started gulping water noisily. Albie stubbed his cigarette out on the patio, shut the door and sat back at the table. 'That geezer works for a loan shark I met in the pub.'

'For goodness' sake, Albie!'

'Please don't shout at me, Vic. I'm fucked. I've got a problem and I don't know what to do about it.' Tears filled his eyes.

Vic sighed, her voice then pained. 'Oh, Albie. Let me see if I can find out if there any organisations that can help you.'

'No. You've got enough on your plate. I can do this. I *will* do this. I know what I need to do. It's all in the mind. Although part of me thinks rehab is the only answer to break the pattern, but it's so fucking expensive to do that, and I have to keep graft-ing. Lisa said if I miss another month's rent, she's chucking me out.'

'Where are you working at the moment?'

'Got myself a job on a site in Wokingham. The best sparky in Berkshire, me.'

Vic managed a smile. 'Does Lisa know about your gambling? Maybe you could give her money as soon as you get it so you don't have a chance to spunk it?'

'I'm not telling her, Vic. I'm thirty years old. I need to sort this myself.' Albie put his hand to his head. 'Ouch. He got me a good'un there. But at least he's got his money now. Wanker!'

'Please take care of yourself, though, Alb.'

Albie put his hand on hers. 'Are you sure you're OK, Vic?'

'Yes, yeah, of course. It'll take more than a cut on the elbow to stop me.' She quickly looked at the ceiling to suppress more tears.

Albie's eyes welled up again too. 'I so appreciate what you did out there. And I know I've been so shit lately, but I'm gonna really try, OK? And, Vic... if ever you need me, I am here for you. You hear me?'

'Blimey.' Slightly overwhelmed that she had at last managed to scratch the emotional side of her brother, Vic felt unexpectedly less alone. 'It looks like Lisa's knocked some feelings, as well as sense, into you. Have a beer, for goodness' sake.'

They sat in a comfortable silence for a while, allowing Vic to realise she hadn't thought about her HIV for at least twenty minutes. But once the thought was there again, it took her over like a runaway train. There were so many 'if onlys' running around in her head.

If she had been more loving and had had sex with Nate, maybe he wouldn't have gone elswhere and slept with someone else. And despite him being nothing but encouraging about her creative desires, if she had just upped and left and followed her dreams without him, then she wouldn't care or even know who Nate was shagging now. Not that she wanted Nate to have the virus either. But on a selfish note, if he did, at least they could now deal with it together. But like her old gran used to say, 'If ifs and ands were pots and pans, there'd be no work for tinkers' hands'.

She drained her wine and shook her head as if trying to scare away the thoughts. But the HIV wasn't going away and she had to think about it because she was living with it. And she had to think about it because after Christmas her next conversation was to be the hardest she would probably ever have to have in her whole life. Because if Nate *didn't* know, then she was the one who would be telling him that his life as he knew it was over too.

THIRTEEN

WINDSOR

Christmas Day

'Quick, kids. It's nearly three, I can't miss the Queen. And then we can do presents when she's finished,' Kath Sharpe announced, untying her apron and heading to the living room.

Albie looked to Vic as if their mother had gone completely mad.

'The Queen's speech,' Vic clarified. 'Don't worry, Liz and the corgies aren't coming round for figgy pudding.' She laughed, pulling a small chunk of turkey off the carcass and put it into the dog bowl as Chandler whined at her feet. 'Go on in, I'll clear up this mess.'

'If you're sure. 'Cos you know how much of a royalist I am.' Albie winked.

Vic flicked him with a tea towel.

'Oi! Actually, come on, Vic. Leave that. I'm going home tonight and I hardly ever get to see you.'

'I'll be five minutes.' Vic sat back at the kitchen table and poured herself another glass of white wine. After living with an alcoholic mother, she was wise enough to know that wine wasn't the cure-all answer she needed. But, momentarily, it allowed her to forget, and at this point in time that was exactly what she wanted to do.

Putting the last plate into the dishwasher, and not remembering how patchy the mobile signal at her mother's place was, Vic was startled by an array of texts beeping in all at once. She wiped her hands on a tea towel then, sitting back down, she began to read.

> Happy Christmas, darling girl. I hope everything is working out in the shires. Love Ray and Marcus xx

> Merry Christmas, Missus. Remember if you can't get over one, get under another one. Love you and can't wait for the New Year's Eve craic! Orla xxxxxx

> Mr and Mrs Taylor would like to wish you a very happy Christmas. See you in 2006! Much love Mandy and Steve xx

Her face dropped on seeing the next one.

> Dec 27 at the flat, say 6.30? I'll cook dinner. Your Nate X

Vic put her hand to her chest and stuck out her bottom lip. Oh, to be able go back in time to pre-Mandy's hen night, when she thought her worries and woes were so significant. When life consisted of living in a cosy flat in Wandsworth with a man who was handsome and kind. Where, granted, she wasn't quite sure what the future looked like, but she had a job that she liked. When it was only herself who was holding her back, nobody and nothing else.

It had taken her health being compromised for her to realise exactly what she had already, and now her whole world was going to be blown right out of the water and she wasn't sure how she was going to cope. In fact, the thought of meeting Nate in a few days absolutely terrified her.

Hearing comforting words from Albie to her mother coming from the other room, Vic abandoned the clearing up and pushed open the door to find her mother in tears.

'Mum, what's wrong?'

The Queen was just rounding off her speech: 'I hope you will all have a very happy Christmas this year and that you go into the new year with renewed hope and confidence.'

'I hope we do too, Your Majesty, and thank you,' Kath Sharpe directed at the television screen. 'Oh, look at her, Vic. She always looks so smart and just, well... beautiful. She'll be eighty this coming year, too.' She sniffled.

'I didn't realise quite how shit a year it had been until I saw this,' Albie piped up and went and sat next to his mum on the sofa. Vic sat on the armchair opposite, thinking she could make both of their years so much worse with just three letters, but it just didn't seem right, and she didn't have the energy or inclination to tell her family that she had a life-changing health condition, today of all days. Because then, not only would it be 'where were you when you told your family you had HIV?' but adding 'on Christmas Day' into the mix would make it seem ten times worse, and ruin Christmas for them all forever more.

Kath Sharpe reached up her sleeve for a tissue and blew her nose loudly. 'All those poor people who got washed away by that dreadful tsunami last Christmas, and the floods in New Orleans – and as for those bombings in London in July... I never told you how scared I was that day, Victoria. I knew our Albie was working locally, but I couldn't get hold of you on your mobile.'

'I know.' Vic thought back to that day. 'The phone signals went down – everyone was trying to call. Thankfully me and Nate had taken a random day off, and we had walked to a pub on the river in Putney so we weren't anywhere near the Tube. I did call you as soon as I could.' Vic recalled the memory, awash with both fear and sadness, but also of happier times with Nate.

'Yes, darling, you did. I do love you, you know, both of you.' Chandler jumped up onto Kath's lap in one leap.

'Mum. It's all right.' Albie blew out a huge breath. 'And I promise I will pay you back all the money I owe you. OK?'

'You have to, please, love. I'm not made of money, you know. And you also have to keep away from those greedy bookmakers. My old dad used to say that you never see one riding a bike. You're your father's son all right.' Kath Sharpe carried on in a rare moment of sobriety. 'If you need other things to do, the garden wants sorting and this old house hasn't been decorated for years. Actually, son, why don't you pay off your debt in jobs for me?'

Albie screwed up his face, and Vic kicked him discreetly. 'I think that's a brilliant idea, Mum. Don't you, Albie?'

Albie grimaced again as his mum continued. 'I found my will the other day when I was having a tidy-up. You'll be all right when I'm gone. Your dad paying for this house made sure of that.'

'Mum!' Vic tutted. 'Stop it. It's Christmas Day.'

'Yes, it is. And present time.' Kath moved Chandler to her side and reached for the envelopes on top of the fireplace. 'It's not much.'

Vic had resealed hers after opening it, and made sure to show great delight for her voucher and her mum's lovely words. Albie thanked her for his cash. Vic reached for her rucksack. 'Here you go.' She handed her mum and Albie their gifts.

Albie shuffled about on the sofa. 'I didn't... I umm... I'm sorry. I wasn't able to...'

'Next year, you will be able to,' Kath Sharpe said boldly. 'Won't you?'

'Yes, Mum.' Albie's voice was childlike for a second. 'And, what it is they say? "Your presence is better than any presents."'

'But you're not supposed to be the one who says it, if it's about you!' Kath's shoulders suddenly shook and the alien sound of laughter, rich and genuine, cut through the air of number 28, Simpson Crescent. On her mother's face was a light that Vic hadn't seen for what felt like a lifetime – a glimmer of a spark of the woman her mother used to be before the alcohol had taken hold.

Albie joined in and, through her fear and vulnerability, Vic felt a sudden flash of hope. When she was ready, she would tell them, and if she was never ready, then that was all right, too. For despite their dysfunctionality, they were all still here, still together – a family at Christmas who loved each other in their own strange and wonderful ways.

That night, Vic was getting ready for bed when she noticed an unwrapped present in her rucksack. Pulling it out, she smiled at the tag, simply written with the words *Queen Victoria* in the most perfect calligraphy. Excited that she hadn't opened it already, she ripped at the neatly wrapped gift. She wasn't surprised to see that it was a book, nor that its title reflected the eccentric author, who wasn't scared to shock or titillate. '*Lovers and Other Strangers: Paintings by Jack Vettriano,*' she read aloud and then said, 'Aww.' She had only once mentioned in passing how much she had liked the artist. Smiling as she looked at the print of *The Singing Butler* still hanging on her old bedroom wall, she opened up the book to find written in the same perfect script as the label, the words:

Keep on creating, Queen Victoria, for you are rather good at it.

Yours festively,
Jerico Flint
Christmas 2005

She had talked to Jerico Flint just a handful of times and had only met him once, but she already felt a strong alliance with him. Which she found both alarming and strangely endearing.

She was just folding up her clothes and laying them out on the tub chair in the corner when another text beeped in from Nate.

Vic?

Jolted back into reality, she felt her face contort in anguish. She began to type.

> Nate, we need to talk – and I mean properly talk. You may already know something but if you don't I have something to tell you. And it has to be face to face because

Vic stopped, groaned, deleted the text, then started to type frantically again.

> Nate, it's going to be OK, but something has happened and it's huge, but we can do this, we can get through this together

'No, no!' she said aloud, and sighed deeply. Then, after about twenty minutes of further typing and deliberation, she typed simply, *I'll be there x*

FOURTEEN

LONDON

The Confession

27 December 2005

Vic still felt physically sick as she walked into the road of her London flat. If anyone had asked if her train journey from Windsor had been busy, she would have had no idea, because she had been deep in dark and terrifying thought the whole way back. But there was no getting around it, she had to face this head on. She had gone through how she was going to start the conversation a million times in her head, but every time she said something out loud, she felt faint at the sheer horror of it. There was no easy way to say it – a bit like Sandra had done with her, she just had to come straight out with it. She could almost convince herself that if she was telling Nate he had cancer it would be easier, because at least there was a cure for some cancers out there. But with HIV, there wasn't. Yes, the virus could be managed, but the fact remained that there was no cure. What there certainly was, though, was a huge stigma around anybody having it, whether they be gay, straight, man or woman. And that would make the conversation all the more difficult.

Vic stopped at the bottom of the familiar metal stairs. What if she headed straight back to the train station, got a ticket to the depths of nowhere and went missing? Maybe that was the answer – just run away. But that's what she'd done all her life: run away from looking to the future.

With a heavy heart, she put her foot on the first step. This time last year she had been overjoyed to be getting home with Nate, when they had got out all the Christmas goodies and snuggled down to watch a cheesy film. A welcome respite after the dramatics of spending Christmas Day with her drunken mother and Boxing Day with his belligerent father, who had come down from the Lake District and insisted that he stay in a cheap hotel down the road from them.

She was scrabbling in her handbag for her key when Nate opened the door, wearing a blue paper crown and his James Bond tuxedo apron.

'Hey.'

As he took her wheelie case, he gave one of his butterfly-inducing lopsided smiles. But instead of her heart missing a beat, she thought it might actually stop in fear.

'Hey.'

Feeling sick, Vic attempted to smile back. Her mobile then started to ring.

'Bollocks!' She scrabbled in her bag again to see who it was.

'Take it if you have to.' Nate headed into the kitchen.

Not recognising the number she let it go to voicemail. 'It's fine. Whoever it is, they can wait.'

Vic and Nate stood looking at each across the kitchen table. It was as if she were seeing him for the first time. For some reason, he looked more handsome than ever before. As his big brown eyes searched hers for a clue as to what she was thinking about his betrayal, she realised just how much she had missed him. She wanted to just fall into his arms and have him hug everything better. But it would never be better. Because all this was his fault.

'Wine?' Nate went to get glasses from the cupboard.

'No, I'll just have some water, thanks.' Vic felt more awkward than on their first date six years ago.

Nate flicked the kettle on.

Vic heard the beep of a voice message on her phone.

'Do you want to see who it is? I really don't mind.'

Vic shook her head. 'No. Nate, we need to talk.'

'Yes, that's the whole reason you're here, isn't it?' Nate looked at her intently. 'I know that face, you're weirding me out. Vic, what's wrong?' He laughed, then on looking at her again, stopped. 'Fuck, it's serious, isn't it?' He half-smiled. 'Not sure I'm ready for a Christmas dumping.'

Vic leant forward and put her hands on the draining board, her face to the sink. Despite her insides swirling like an erupting volcano, her voice remained remarkably level. 'Nate, I've got HIV, which means you must have HIV. As in, I must have got it from you.'

The silence was deafening. Vic turned to face him.

He took a huge slug of his wine. 'This is a joke, right?'

'I'd be pretty sick if it was, don't you think?' Vic's voice wobbled.

'So, you're saying you have HIV?' He drank the words in as if they were a poison that he couldn't spit out. His face contorted and then he let out a roar that a threatened silverback would be proud of. 'HIV, as in the virus that leads to AIDS? Do women even get it?'

Vic burst into angry tears. 'Clearly they do, because you fucking slept with one who has given it to you. Then, as it's transmissable through *fucking* someone other than your partner, you gave it to me, Nate.'

'No, no, how can that be possible?' Nate's voice was softer now. Silent tears were running down Vic's cheeks. 'Oh God.' He went to hug her. She pushed him away. 'Fuck! Vic, what does this even mean?'

'It means we've both got a virus that affects our immune system and we will need medication for the rest of our lives to keep us alive, basically. You'll need to go to the hospital as soon as you can, to get tested.'

Nate put his hand to his head. 'I feel fine.'

'Yes, so do I. We need to get clued up, the pair of us. We will feel fine, for a while...' She paused. 'Have you had any kind of flu since you shagged her?'

Nate screwed his face up. 'No. Why? You're scaring me now, Vic. I can't have got it. It's impossible.'

'How else have I got it? We've been together six years, Nate.'

'Well, what about you? There's nothing you're not telling me? No chance you could have caught this from someone else?'

Vic bit her lip. This was the time, she had to stop being a coward. 'But...' She hesitated, then forced words out at a hundred miles an hour. 'I did sleep with someone else too. In Brighton, at the hen weekend.'

Nate's face crumpled. 'And you've given me all this shit and allowed me to feel all this pain and guilt, and you're no better than me.'

'I'm sorry.' Vic started to sob again. 'I'm so fucking sorry.'

'So how do you know Mr Brighton hasn't given it to you?'

'We used a condom, that's why.'

'So did I!' Nate shouted.'Every time. Do you really think I'd be that much of a cunt to sleep with someone behind your back without one?'

'Every time?' Vic growled. 'You said you only did it twice.

And for the record, I didn't think you were that much of a *cunt* that you'd sleep with someone else full stop!'

'Pot kettle, Vic.' Nate pulled at his hair. 'For fuck's sake. What is happening here?'

He reached for his wine glass, and in doing so caught the bottle of open wine, sending it smashing to the floor. 'Bollocks!' He grabbed his keys and headed to the front door.

'What are you doing?'

'I need some air, I need to clear my head. I need to think...' Nate grabbed his coat off the chair. 'And I need to digest exactly what is going on here. Because I feel like I'm going to explode because, whatever the outcome, you've got HIV, Vic, and I might have it too. And that's fucking serious shit and... and... despite it all, I still love you.'

The door slammed behind him.

Vic sat down, her face ravaged with pain. Nate was right: this was fucking serious shit. And despite this, he had still just declared his love for her. And the worrying thing was that she could easily have said it right back. But after time apart and too much time to think about the reality of the situation, she wasn't sure, if she said it now, that she would be saying it for the right reasons.

She jumped as her phone pinged. It was a text from her mum saying what a lovely Christmas she had had. Then, on pressing the voicemail button, all her fears rushed at her like a bull to a matador.

'Victoria, it's Danny. You know, Brighton Danny. I need to talk to you urgently, ideally face to face. I can get the train to Clapham and meet you there, or come to Brighton. Up to you. Just let me know, OK? It's really important. Call me.'

Victoria ran to the kitchen sink and promptly threw up.

FIFTEEN

BRIGHTON

The Realisation

Victoria sat on the bench where she and Danny Miller had first met, her eyes trained on the grey-skied horizon. Her thoughts turned to Nate and the fear and pain she had seen in his eyes before he had upped and left the night before. She had called him several times but in true Nate style, he didn't want to talk – he needed space to think. So she had eventually left him an emotional message telling him it was highly likely Danny had given it to her and that, from what she had read, it was less likely that Nate had it, as woman-to-man transmission was possible, but rare. Then, after clearing up the mess of the smashed wine bottle, she had booked a room in Brighton for the night and headed to the train station.

She checked her watch for the second time.

'Mind if I join you?' She looked up, to find a red-eyed Danny standing in exactly the same place he had stood back in October. She gave him a weak smile, and he bent to kiss her on the cheek, then sat down and lit a cigarette.

'If only we could rewind to that night, eh?' Vic bit her lip.

'Have you just got here?'

'To the bench, yes, but once we'd arranged to meet, I got the train down last night. Stayed in a guesthouse just off The Lanes. I needed to be on my own with my thoughts.' Vic's eyes filled with tears. 'Let me save you the trauma of coming out with it yourself. You've got HIV, haven't you?'

The handsome blond took a long, hard drag of his cigarette and remained silent for a second. 'Oh Vic, no, please tell me no, you're not positive too, are you? You can't be.' He saw the pain etched on her face. 'It would be so unlucky. No! It can't be possible.'

'I wish I *had* slept around more now; at least the law of averages would have made more sense.'

'I can't believe how upbeat you're being.'

'It's that or slit my wrists, so I guess I have to stick with the first option.'

'Vic. I'm so, so bloody sorry. I never thought for one minute you would have it. I just knew I had to talk to you about getting tested, just in case, but shit, I never ever thought that...' He shook his head. 'Oh, Jesus!'

'We used a condom – I half remember the conversation.' Vic sighed. 'So I don't understand.'

'We did. I was adamant – it's just the respectful and sensible thing to do. But, Vic, we had all sorts of wild sex, in many positions, and when I went to wrap the condom to throw it in the bin, I noticed that it had split.'

'For fuck's sake. And you didn't think to mention it at the time?' Vic grabbed the cigarette from Danny and took a drag. 'Please tell me you've got more than one of these?'

'I thought you only smoked when you were drunk.'

'Spare me the lecture today, perlease.'

A large wave crashed on the shore ahead of them as a light drizzle began to fall. Vic rolled her hood up over her hair.

Danny took a packet of Marlboro Lights out of his jacket

pocket. 'My consultant said that I have to try and live a healthy lifestyle from now on.'

'Danny, just give me a cigarette. If you tell me you knew you had it already, I will have to murder you, though, so get ready to run.'

Danny snapped. 'What do you take me for, Vic? Of course I didn't know. Jamie only told me three weeks ago. His open-relationship house had been entertaining visitors for a lot longer than he had made out.'

'His?'

'Yes, Vic, and sorry I omitted to tell you that. I just didn't think it was relevant, as I figured we wouldn't be running off into the sunset together. I liked you and I meant what I said about the gallery, but I think we both realised that that night was just what it was.'

'It's fine, I understand.' She held her cigarette up to Danny's offered light. 'I accused Nate of giving it to me, too. Fuck! If only I'd listened to your message before I spoke to him. Nate, that's my fella – ex fella, maybe. God knows what I call him now.'

Danny lit a cigarette for himself. 'I didn't contact you straight away as I was waiting for the results of my second test, which seemed to take forever. I didn't want to believe it was true. Stuck my head up my arse, to be honest. And like I said, I honestly thought it would be impossible for you to have it. Nate will have to test now, anyway, so you had to tell him.'

'Yes, I know that, thank you,' she sighed, then shut her eyes and, taking a large drag of her cigarette, let the nicotine work its toxic magic. 'But I've just scared the shit out of him, maybe for no reason. I blamed the poor bastard for giving it to me, and it wasn't him.'

'Let's walk.' Danny stood and took Vic's hand to help her up.

They found themselves drawn to the sea's edge. The

melodic noise of the waves rushing up onto the shingle beach did nothing to calm their melancholy. The grey of the sea and the dull December morning just served to amplify their sadness.

'I must call Nate.'

'Does he know about me, and that you're here?'

'I told him I slept with someone, yes. He walked out of the flat and has gone completely AWOL, so he has no detail. What about Jamie?'

'It's over. I can't even tell you how much I despise that man. I mean, there's parting gifts, and then there's parting gifts.'

Vic frowned. 'I'm so sorry.'

'I'm not. He's a tosser.' Danny's voice lilted and he let out a little sarcastic laugh. He camply half-spoke, half-sang, 'So, it's just little ol' me and the HIV.' He sighed. 'I can't believe *I'm* being so upbeat now.'

'What's the alternative? Lie on the floor and pummel it with our fists, shouting "why me?" Saying that, I actually did that for a few days after I found out.' Vic took a drag of her cigarette.

'Oh, Vic.' Danny reached for her hand and squeezed it. 'I just got horrendously drunk, then ran down here and swam in the freezing-cold sea. Went a bit mad, if I'm honest.'

'It's a lot to take in.' Vic sighed. 'I have to call Nate again. Give me a sec.' She walked ahead but turned back within seconds. 'Voicemail.'

'Did you leave a message?'

'Yes. Another one trying to alleviate his fear, but I know him so well. He will be in such a state.' Vic started to cry. 'I've hurt him so much, Danny. We have hurt each other so much. What a mess! What a complete and utter mess.'

'Yes. It really is. Please don't cry, Vic.' Danny coughed to clear his throat of emotion. 'I don't know how I'm ever going to get over what I've done to you.'

'Well, you need to be brave, because what else can you do? We can't change it. How are you feeling, anyway? Have you started any treatment or...' The rain had stopped, so Vic pulled her hood back down.

'No.' Danny sighed. 'It's early days and it's all about the CD4 and viral load, isn't it? I've already forgotten which one has to be up and which one has to be down. I start treatment when one of them drops, I think.'

'Yes, same for me.' Vic yawned, throwing her cigarette butt into the sea. 'If the viral load is high and the CD4 count drops then we're in trouble.' She took on a dramatic tone. 'Then the ART begins!' Her voice softened. 'We're never going to be free of this, even in our minds, are we?'

'We will be. I hope. Like everything. In time,' Danny replied sagely, in a staccato fashion.

Victoria stopped and looked up and down the beach. Granted, the weather wasn't good, but it seemed eerily quiet considering it was that never-ending holiday period between Christmas and New Year. The pair walked along the water's edge in silence for a while, until Danny spoke up. 'Why are you not angrier with me, Vic? Being honest, I know I could never be as calm.'

'Because we were having consensual sex, and you didn't know. It's just bad luck on my part. And what good would throwing anger in the mix do, when we are already feeling like shit and so full of fear?'

'You are the coolest, strongest woman I think I have ever met, Victoria Sharpe.' Danny threw his finished smoke into the water.

'Maybe. But inside, there's a whole disco of disaster going on with my immune system.' They both laughed. 'We are going to need each other, Danny Miller. To ride the stormy waters of this shit virus. Because I, for one, don't think – even with all the best treatments in the world – this is going to be plain sailing.'

Danny stopped and clasped Victoria's hand. He then clumsily pulled her towards him and brushed her lips with his.

Vic pulled away. 'No... What are you doing?'

'Maybe we should make a go of it.' Danny became animated. 'I've been thinking about it a lot.'

'What, as in you and me together... as a couple?'

'Why not? I mean, what's the worst that can happen? And it means that we'll never ever have the awful scenario of having to tell prospective partners. Because we will be partners.'

Vic shook her head. 'Danny, stop it, you're just knee-jerking...'

'You can come and live with me down here. Sell your work in my gallery and...' His voice tailed off. 'We'll never be alone, then, Vic. In sickness or in health.'

'That all sounds like a very fucked-up happy ever after to me. When realistically you've never seen any of my work, and not forgetting I do still need to fathom what's happening between me and Nate.' Vic blew out a huge breath.

'Come on, Vic, do you really think once Nate has thought this through, he will want to be with you?'

Vic opened her eyes wide with shock. 'I can't believe you just said that.' Her voice turned into a wail. 'Because if he doesn't, that means that nobody probably will.'

'But Vic, this is huge. Huge for anyone to take on. You could get ill; we don't know what's going to happen.'

Vic felt her stomach drop to her knees. 'Stop! Danny Miller, just stop that right now.'

'It's the facts, Vic. We have to face them. We're stuck with them.'

'And each other? The ridiculous suggestion you just made about us being together... do we have to settle for that, too?'

'Like you may be settling for Nate, you mean.'

'I didn't say that,' Vic screamed. 'And maybe I don't want the facts right now, or ever, eh!'

The rain started tipping down again. Victoria strode forward towards the sea. 'I could just walk into this ocean and keep going, and it would be done. My life's fucking over anyway.' She started to sob. Danny ran to the frothing sea's edge after her and grabbed her shoulders.

'Vic, listen to me. Don't you ever think like that again, you hear me? Whatever happens, we always have each other, OK? I promise to do right by you forever. And I really mean that.'

Vic's cheeks were strewn with tears that mingled with the rain. 'I'm scared, Danny.' She wiped her coat sleeve across her face.

'So am I, but we've got this. We've got this together. The treatments are getting better. We are young and fit and, who knows, they might find a cure soon and all of this will just have been an awful nightmare.'

Leading her back to the shore, without a word, they turned to face each other. The rain plastered Vic's hair to her face and soaked through their clothes, but in that moment, none of it mattered. All the fear and hurt that had built up suddenly dissipated. For in the vastness of a wild ocean, they sensed their own smallness, their shared humanity. They wrapped their arms around each other, gripping on as if just being together would make them strong enough to withstand any storm.

'I'm so sorry,' Danny whispered, his voice muffled against Vic's neck.

'Me too,' Vic replied.

The rain fell harder, drenching them further, but they barely noticed. The world as they now knew it had narrowed down to the warmth of their embrace, the steady beat of each other's hearts and the quiet acceptance that their chance meeting had led to a whole lot more than either of them had ever bargained for.

SIXTEEN
WINDSOR

New Year's Eve

Vic was in Orla's place making a cup of coffee when she heard the front door fly open and a loud commotion in the hallway. She poked her head around the door to see her spirited house-mate throwing her bags and coat onto the floor, then stumbling to the lounge with an anguished groan. On following her through, and finding her friend face down on the sofa, Vic couldn't help but laugh.

'I am never fecking drinking again,' Orla stated dramatically, running her free hand through her unruly black curls. Vic was not in the mood for going anywhere, let alone wishing anyone a happy new year, and she breathed a huge sigh of instant relief.

'Ma O'Malley decided that a leaving party for her firstborn in the local pub was a clever idea. I mean, Ireland is only an hour's flight away and I'm already booked to go over on my birthday. You would think she's never seeing me again. Anyways, I'm ruined. I had a whisky on the flight home to try and ease my head, but I don't think I've ever felt this shit before in my whole life.'

'If I had a pound for every time I've heard you say that... Coffee?'

Orla looked up at her friend. 'Bejasus, you look pretty banjaxed yourself.'

Vic took a deep breath. This was her chance to tell all. But once she did, their friendship would be different and she didn't want it to be different. Maybe just one more day. Tears rushed to the back of her eyes. 'I haven't slept much. Nate has gone AWOL and...'

'He'll be back. You know what he's like. Shit, I take it you told him about Blondie, then?'

Vic nodded. Telling him she had been unfaithful would have been like telling him she had won the lottery now she knew what she knew. One thing her dad had taught her was that in life there was always a solution to everything – except for death. He should have added death and HIV because, at the moment, it felt nothing was going to be easy now that she knew she had a virus with such fear and misunderstanding connected to it.

Orla groaned. 'I think I just need to get into bed for a bit; a nana nap will sort me right out and I'll feel grand later.'

Vic bit her lip. 'Orla. I'm sorry to let you down but I don't think I'm up for a big one later. What with me and Nate and...'

'Don't be stupid, the craic is what you need. It'll do you good to let your hair down.'

'Says the woman who's never drinking again,' Vic replied flatly, then shouted back as she walked through to the kitchen, 'I'm really sorry, Orla, but I'm going to go to Mum's for the night. All I feel like doing is watching Jools and his Hootenanny and snuggling up with Chandler.'

Taking Orla's silence as a sulk, Vic walked back through to the lounge, shook her head, and managed a smile. For, lying flat out on the sofa, was her beautiful friend, absolutely sparko, a thin line of dribble running from her mouth.

Vic turned into her mum's road to see an RSPCA van parked on the driveway.

'For fuck's sake,' she said aloud, standing still for a second to gather her thoughts ready for the fight to keep Chandler where he really did belong.

Tentatively entering the house, Vic saw no sign of Chandler, or any occupants from the van, for that matter – just her mother at the kitchen table, a large vodka and tonic in hand.

'You said they'd come and take him.' Kath emitted a huge ugly sob. 'I always feed him, and I know I don't walk him as much as I should, but he loves running around the garden and he's healthy, Vic, and happy. I know he is. What am I going to do without my boy?' She began to wail.

'Slow down, it's OK.' Vic continued talking to her mum as if she were a child. 'Where is Chandler? Did they take him? Where is he, Mum? The van is still out there. I don't get it.'

'I don't know. I was upstairs, came down and he was gone.'

'So you didn't let anyone in?'

'No.' Kath made a noise of complete despair.

'Was the back door open?'

'Yes, but they can't get round there. Albie told me to keep the back gate locked at all times, and I always do.'

Vic went to the front room to see the van pulling off the drive. As soon as it was out of sight she marched around to Joti and banged on her front door. So much for all the love thy neighbour, happy Christmas bollocks, the pretty new neighbour was showing her true colours now, wasn't she? Joti opened her door wearing a nurse's uniform, with a splodge of mud on her face and what looked like a twig sticking out of her hair.

'I knew you were trouble. All this pretence of—'

Joti put her hand up to stop Victoria's tirade of abuse and said calmly, 'Get in here, Vicki. Don't give those bastards opposite the satisfaction of another show.'

Victoria frowned in confusion but did as she was told. Walking through the house and through the double doors into Joti's garden, her face broke into a huge grin, for there was Chandler contentedly chewing on one of his favourite bone snacks, with not a care in the world.

'I don't understand.' Vic was now full of both joy and bewilderment. 'I thought that—'

'Vicki, you need to trust me. I'm the last person who'd want to see your mum even sadder than she already is.'

'So what happened, then?'

'Well, someone clearly wanted to make trouble and report your mum. Luckily, I'd just come off shift and saw the van pull up. I launched myself under the back hedge, snuck in your mum's back door, grabbed Chandler and his food and water bowl, then ran to stop them in front of your mum's front door before she had a chance to open it.' Joti took an exaggerated breath. 'I explained that Kath had had some health problems and that I had now taken charge of Chandler's care until she got back on her feet.'

'Oh, Joti.' Vic burst into tears. 'I'm sorry I'm such a bitch. Look at you. You really are a real-life angel.'

'And a tired one at that. I work in A&E and this time of year is always madness.'

'Bless you. I wondered where you were heading off at all hours. I paint things; it's hardly lifesaving – or life-changing for that matter.'

'I disagree. Creativity takes courage. So few people stick at doing what they love.'

There was a loud bark from the garden. 'Chandler?' Kath Sharpe screamed and ran out into her back garden. 'Chandler? Is that you, my precious boy?'

Vic gasped. 'Shit. Poor Mum. We forgot about her.'

As soon as he saw Vic, Chandler's tail started wagging furiously, and he jumped up and barked even more loudly.

'Chandler? Chandler!' Kath shouted.

'We're coming, Mum.' Vic grinned at Joti.

'Here. Quick.' The nurse handed Vic a carrier bag containing the dog bowls. 'Take this little fella to where he rightly belongs.'

'I'd love to talk some more,' Vic said, without thought.

'Me too.' Joti put an arm on Victoria's. 'And I need to start getting my life back on track in the new year, which includes exercise, so I'll make sure I get some walks in with this little fella, if that's OK.'

Vic suddenly felt an unexplained closeness around this clearly kind-hearted woman, and began to well up again. 'Of course. That's amazing. Thank you so much. Oh, and thanks for getting a bed downstairs for Mum, and the Christmas food. I take it that was your intervention, too?'

'I'd love to take the credit, but no, not me. Although I did hear an almighty crash through the wall the other afternoon.'

'Oh, Jesus.' Vic put her hand to her head.

'I couldn't get an answer round the front, so I shimmied through the hedge and luckily the back door was open, as it usually is, so I let myself in.'

Vic tutted. 'Thank you, thank you so much.'

'Your mum was anaesthetised with vodka by the look of her. I checked her over; she was lucky. Just bruised, nothing broken. I had to get off to work so I was relieved to see your brother arrive a while later.'

'I'm sorry for you having to get involved. How about we share numbers and then you can just call me if you need me? If that's OK, of course.'

With numbers shared, Joti's voice softened. 'It is such a good thing that your mum has a bed downstairs now, though

– less of a worry. She's not of a mind to stop drinking, I take it?'

'Sadly not. It would take something pretty big to get her even to start thinking about it, I tell you.'

'Right. I'd better get my hair washed.' Joti pulled the stray twig out of it. 'I'm filthy.'

'Have you got plans tonight, then?' Vic picked her phone up off the side.

'Yes, a hot chocolate, a comfy sofa and trash TV. I'm exhausted.'

'Same! Happy New Year, Joti.'

'Happy New Year, Vicki.'

Vic grimaced, took a breath to say something, but decided to let the 'ki' go. More important was the mystery: if it wasn't Joti or Albie who had helped move the bed and get the Christmas supplies, then who was it?

Leaving her mum with a mug of strong coffee and a large slice of Christmas cake, in the hope that she might sober up for the evening, Vic made her way to the river path with a tail-wagging terrier. As she headed towards the town, it sounded like the New Year's revelry had already begun.

On reaching her favourite bench, Vic lengthened Chandler's lead so he could have a good sniff around, then retrieved her mobile from her bag. Still no word from Nate, which was giving her a pain in her stomach now, since she had called him every day, followed by a goodnight message, but got nothing back. She had even phoned his dad to wish him an early happy New Year in the hope he might let slip that Nate was with him, but he was just heading to the airport for a week in the Canaries with his partner, so no clues there.

Nate wasn't at work, either. She had rung – imitating a call from a potential frozen dessert supplier – to be told that he wouldn't be back in until the ninth of January. She was sure he would have told her that he had booked a week off, so that worried her even more. On the other hand, after she had left him the message telling him it was Danny who had given her HIV, maybe Nate had got tested, and he was positive and didn't know how to react – because she sure as hell still didn't. He probably hated her, in fact. His previous declaration of three little words, null and voided by the three little letters that had caused such a maelstrom of suffering already. Suddenly big, silent tears began to fall slowly down her face. As if sensing her distress, Chandler came to her feet and whimpered. Then, out of nowhere, somebody was standing right in front of her.

'Come on, sweet Victoria, let's get in the warm and get us both a nice hot drink, shall we?' Norman the Jack Russell barked his approval as Jake led the way to the festively lit *Lazy Daze*, the boat which he called home. Once inside, Vic sat down in one of his comfortable armchairs and felt an instant sense of both familiarity and relief. The dogs tumbled around the floor playfighting until Jake threw them a chew each and they lay down in front of the wood burner, paws outstretched, munching away. Jake sat down opposite Vic and handed over a steaming, milky drink. 'Funny to say, but it's a dry boat in here, as you know. Not even a sherry trifle at Christmas. I hope you like Ovaltine?'

'This is just perfect, thank you.' Vic cradled the steaming mug in both hands. 'Alcohol isn't helping to numb anything at the moment, anyway.' The kindness of the man she had known since childhood caused her to cry again. 'I'm sorry,' she blubbered.

Jake went to the toilet, grabbed her a wad of toilet paper and set a Simon & Garfunkel disc to play in his dated CD player.

'Never apologise for showing emotion,' he said gently. 'It is our greatest strength. Because, when it boils down to it, in this crazy world, all we have is ourselves to give.'

Vic blew her nose. 'I never did find out why you ended up here. Mum has always been very protective over you, and I assume there must be a story?'

'Has she indeed.' Jake smiled enigmatically. 'I thought you seemed sad last time I saw you, too. What's up, love?'

Vic sighed. 'That was nothing compared to now.'

'Let me guess, Mum or men?'

'Neither. Well, both but... Mum is a constant worry. It's...' Vic rubbed her eyes and prepared herself. 'I don't think I can... not just yet. I haven't even told Mum and I don't know how to.' She began to cry again.

Jake looked visibly upset. 'What do you mean? Tell me what's wrong, love. You're safe here. I don't see anyone to tell.' Despite his smile, Vic was sure that his usually weathered face had paled slightly. 'Bridge Over Troubled Water' started to play.

'My mum used to love this track.'

'I know,' Jake replied quietly.

Vic wiped her eyes and took a sip of her drink. To her surprise she found herself reassuring him: 'It'll be OK.'

'And if it's not OK, it's not the end.' Jake held out his hand to Vic and squeezed it. 'You can tell me, little lady, in your own time – or you can tell me to bugger off. I'm not going anywhere soon.'

They sat in silence for a while, enjoying the warmth of the wood burner and the peacefulness of the river, until Jake began to talk.

'You are right; there is a story. I lived down in Wiltshire. I bought a huge pile of an old detached house. I'd made my money on the stock markets. I had everything anyone could want. I could holiday wherever I wanted. Dress like a right dandy if I wanted to.' He laughed. 'My parents lived nearby. I loved the fact that I could treat them, too. Paid off their mortgage and made sure they never wanted for anything. Sadly, no siblings. Mum had wanted more kids, but it didn't happen. I was in my early thirties and living like a king.'

Vic leant down to stroke the now-sleeping dogs. She wasn't sure if she was ready for what was to come, because her gut and Jake's tone were telling her that there was not going to be a happy ending to this story.

'I decided to travel whilst I was still young. And that was when I met the most beautiful soul. Her name was Malini. She had the eyes of a doe, and the longest black mane of straight, shiny hair that I'd ever seen. Like some mesmerising sea creature, she was. I fell immediately in love. In fact, we fell in love so hard that I realised at last I had found a reason for my life. Love just took over.' His face suddenly fell. He reached forward to turn the music off.

'You don't have to tell me, Jake – it's fine.'

'I want you to know, Victoria.'

'OK.' Vic put her empty mug down on the small hand-crafted table in front of them.

'Mum and Dad were minding the house when I went travelling because I had a couple of dogs then, and they really did love it at my place. The grounds were impressive, and they both enjoyed pottering about together in the pretty walled garden. It had an indoor swimming pool, too, so for them, it was like being on holiday themselves.'

'Sounds idyllic.' Vic slipped her boots off.

Tears filled Jake's eyes. 'There was a fire.' His voice wobbled. 'The night before me and Malini were due to travel home. A spark from the huge inglenook fireplace took hold whilst they were sleeping. I lost them all: Mum, Dad and the dogs. Probably a good job they all went, really, because if any of them had survived, those who were left would have been bereft – and that includes the dogs.'

'Oh, Jake. I am so sorry.'

'Yes. So am I.' Jake looked for his tobacco to roll a cigarette.

'How do you ever get over something like that?' Vic's face was full of compassion.

'You don't, Vic.'

'And you and Malini?'

'She was amazing, a complete rock. Flew back to England with me, helped me with the funerals and sorting out the insurances, et cetera. We lived in a rented place for a while, but it appears that sometimes love doesn't always win. Because in this instance, grief did.' Jake's face contorted in anguish. 'I became hopelessly lost, and I began to drink heavily. Malini tried – she tried so hard – but I wasn't a nice person to be around, and I don't blame her for leaving.'

'So, how come you are here? What brought you to Windsor?'

'I studied at Eton many moons ago and I remembered the boats along here, and how I loved living near to this river. I wanted to be a nomad. In my drunken haze I thought that was a good thing to be. No houses to lose, no people to lose. Just me and the boat.'

'And Malini – did you ever see her again?'

'I knew the drink or not seeing her again would kill me, so I got myself sober and I tried to find her for years. But there was no internet then and she loved to travel. In the end I paid a private investigator to go to her hometown and see what he could discover.' His voice tailed off. 'And he found her.'

Vic put her hand to her heart. 'That's amazing.'

'Not that amazing, because she wasn't actually there. He found out that she was married, with a little girl, living in Australia. Timings added up that she had waited less than a year to get hitched and have a kid after being with me. He was a doctor.' Jake shook his head. 'So at least she married well.'

'And you didn't want to speak to her again?'

'Of course I did. I wrote her a letter, in such a way that if her husband did see it, he wouldn't have known that we had been lovers – just friends – but included enough information to let her know that I was sober and that I still loved her and would wait for her as long as she was on this planet.'

'Oh, Jake, that is so romantic. Please tell me she replied.'

'Nothing. For two years, I checked that PO box every single morning. I was so torn but also so hurt. I figured if she had really loved me, she would have waited for me, or at least replied to the letter. It was a raw love, Vic. One that, if you haven't already experienced it, I really hope that you do, at least once in life. We said we had found a "diamond love" because it sparkled. Our chemistry was effervescent. We even noticed that our eyes shone brighter in each other's company. Which is why I was so surprised that she moved on so quickly and didn't reply.'

'Aww, Jake, that is so sad.'

'Yes, really sad. But I had to get on, and there's not been one minute that I have regretted living here. Money is of no interest to me. I like the simple life. I love waking up to birds singing, the water sloshing and all this nature. And Norman's a great little companion. Nineteen sixty-nine, I arrived. Sober and ready to sail off down the Thames.' He laughed. 'And then I met your mother.' His voice tailed off again and he jumped up. 'Good gosh, it's eight o'clock already. Won't she be wondering where you are?'

Vic leapt up too. 'Shit, yes. We need to eat, and I need to feed this little man, too.' She looked down at the sleeping pair by her feet. 'They've been such good boys.'

She put the lead on the snoozing little terrier, who shot up and started running around her feet, barking. Norman joined in, the two of them causing a right old commotion.

'Send her my good wishes, won't you?' Jake squeezed Vic's shoulder. 'Your mum, that is, and hope I didn't bore you too much. I don't tell many people my pitiful life story, you know.'

'I'm glad you did.' Vic squeezed his arm and slipped her boots back on. What a kind and caring man Jake Turner was.

Clever, too. She had only known him at a surface level before. Maybe he had been hoping that with his outpouring of truth she would share what was troubling her, as she had quite often used that tactic in the past with friends. Sadly, she felt her truth was so huge that even learning about the trauma of dead parents and dogs and lost loves couldn't release it. Not yet.

Jake opened up the tiny front door and helped Vic and Chandler onto the deck. 'It's been so good to see you, Victoria, and how about instead of worrying about what you can't control, shift your energy to what you can create, eh? Short of that, just breathe.'

Suddenly feeling a stronger sense of self through Jake's own resilience over adversity, Vic carried Chandler off the boat and placed him down gently on the river path. Waiting a minute for a pleasure boat blaring out its party music to pass, she looked up at the wise and distinguished white-haired gentleman in front of her and smiled.

He smiled right back. 'Happy New Year, Victoria.'

'Happy New Year, Jake.'

SEVENTEEN

LONDON

The Confrontation

9 January 2006

Victoria's first week back at work after the Christmas break went by in a complete blur. It seemed like months since she had received her diagnosis, not just a couple of weeks. Ray was having his usual extended new year break and Penny was more interested in arranging after-school clubs and wine soirées with friends than in chatting to Vic. So it was an ideal time for Vic to get her head down and catch up on the smaller jobs that she had missed before her unplanned time off.

She had emailed Jerico to thank him for his wonderful gift and had got the reply of an out-of-office message stating, *Writer at work, I will reply when I reach a suitable climax*, which had made her laugh but also feel a little sad. If she were to tell him about her positive status it would change everything. She would miss the easy flow of conversation that she had got used to with him. But this was the thing: how would people react? And should she tell them at all? If she wasn't having sex with them, then surely she didn't need to. It was so awkward and weird, because if she had any other illness then she would probably tell everyone and there would be an element of pity or sadness. But from what she knew from constantly reading up on the subject and how people dealt with it, it would be a rollercoaster of a conversation. Would they or wouldn't they accept her for having the virus? Because that's all it was: a virus. A virus that could be treated. The flu was a virus, and the flu could kill too. But nobody gave a damn about that. The bigoted hangover from the eighties had a lot to answer for. Maybe it would just be a case of knowing when the time was right to tell someone, and it would just happen naturally.

Danny had checked in with her every other day either by text or a quick phone call, which was comforting to know – that someone was there and supporting her. But this comfort was marred by the fact that despite her leaving several messages on Nate's mobile, she had still not heard from him, and she was beginning to get really worried now. She was not only worried, but also angry that he knew what she must be going through, and he hadn't even bothered to check in with her. It was eating her up inside that she may have given him the virus and again, selfishly, as much as part of her would have preferred it to be him rather than Danny with whom she had to share this HIV journey, she wouldn't wish it on anyone.

The weekend came and she had even gone to their flat on the Saturday to see if she could speak to him, but it was clear that Nate hadn't been staying there, as nothing had moved since he had stormed out the day she had told him the awful news. His work had told her that he would be back on the ninth. Which was why now, at ten fifteen on a Monday evening, she was sitting in the kitchen of the Wandsworth flat she had once shared with her boyfriend, with a cup of coffee in hand, waiting for him to come home.

At eleven o'clock, she was just about to give up and go back to Orla's when her friend called her, sounding full of anguish. 'Vic, you gotta come back. Nate is here. He's drunk and talking complete gibberish.'

Vic pushed open the kitchen door of Orla's place to find Nate slumped on the breakfast bar. Orla was drying up some mugs and putting them away.

'He's all yours,' the feisty Irishwoman snapped. 'I've got to be up at fecking five a.m., as I'm flying to Düsseldorf for my big event, and there was no way I could leave him like this. He's been crying and saying all sorts of weird shit about worrying about you dying. I couldn't get an ounce of sense from him.'

'I'm so sorry, mate.' Vic hurriedly took off her coat as Orla stropped off to her room.

'Vic. Is that you?' Nate remained head down on the counter.

'You know it is, Nate. Are you all right?'

He slowly lifted his head and looked at her. 'Of course I'm not.'

Vic was too frightened to ask if he'd been for a test, but she had no need to worry, as alcohol was working its lip-loosening magic. 'I'm not all right, because you're not all right. I've had a couple of tests. The second came back negative today. I wanted to be sure before I saw you.'

Vic felt a complete sense of solace at the news. 'That's such a relief.' She went to kiss his cheek.

Nate put his hand up and recoiled. 'Sorry, I can't.'

Feeling physically sick at his reaction, Vic turned to put the kettle on. 'I'm making you a black coffee to sober you up, and then we can talk. Where have you been, anyway?'

'I've been downing shots of vodka during my shift.'

'I mean, where have you been for the past two weeks? I've been worried sick.'

Nate sat up properly on the high stool and brushed his hands through his unkempt mop.

For fear of him spilling the scalding coffee given the state he was in, Vic put some cold water in the mug before she handed it over. 'You need a haircut.'

He drank the tepid drink down in one.

'Not been on the top of my list, surprisingly.' Nate burped loudly.

'Oh, and you look brown?' She moved closer. 'You've got a suntan?'

'I joined Dad and Melissa in Gran Canaria. I just had to get away. I got a test before I went. And despite your message letting me know Brighton boy had given it to you, just waiting for that result has been crucifying me. I can't even tell you how stressed I've felt since you told me. I don't understand, though, Vic. You said you'd used protection. Are you sure you're positive – like, really sure?'

Vic nodded slowly. 'I'm afraid so.'

Nate burst into tears. She rushed to comfort him but again he pushed her away.

'Please let me in, Nate.'

'I just can't, Vic, I just can't. I'm so angry with you. I know I cheated, but fuck me. I can't cope with this. HIV – it's huge and I... I've been thinking so much about everything, about us, about what all this means and... and I'm sorry, so, so sorry, Vic, but I don't think I can be with you.'

'What do you mean, you can't be with me?' Vic had a level of panic in her voice she didn't even recognise. Tears began to roll down both of their faces.

'Vic, be honest. I know you so well that I'm not even sure you want to be with me anymore anyway.'

Vic squirmed.

'And how can we possibly ever lead a normal life now? If

you did decide you wanted kids, then there would be so much to think about.'

'I don't care about that now,' Vic cried. 'In fact, that's the least of my bloody worries.'

'And I can't bear to see you suffer either.' Nate's face was pained.

'Nate, the treatments are so much better than they were. You are being short-sighted. Who knows what's going to happen to anyone? You could get run over by a bus tomorrow. I need you.' As she said it, she realised it was true.

'You could have fucking killed me!' he suddenly shouted.

'Ssh, you'll wake Orla.' Vic reached for some kitchen roll and blew her nose loudly. 'You're being fucking ridiculous now. And of course I didn't know I had it when we had sex. Who do you think I am, Nate? And we could make this work. I don't even have to start taking the drugs for ages. I may have got this virus inside me, but I'm not any different. I'm still me. I'm still the same old Vic. Nothing changes. We just have to have sex using a condom. That's all.'

Nate's voice dropped to a whisper. 'I'd be too frightened.' He reached for his coat. 'I'm so sorry, Vic.'

'Nate, don't do this, please. We can learn about it together.' Vic felt like she could hardly breathe.

'I'm going to go back to the flat.' Nate patted his jeans pocket to check for his keys.

'I'll come with you.' There was desperation in Victoria's voice.

'No. This is hard enough as it is.' Nate went to use the toilet and came back. 'And be honest, Vic. You haven't been happy for ages, have you? And whilst the honesty box is out, I never felt good enough for you, ever!' He shouted the last word.

Vic felt a pain of sadness shear through her.

'Oh, Nate. I had no clue.'

Nate carried on his drunken tirade. 'And I want to be somebody's choice because they see the value I bring to their life, not a default option because of some stupid fucking virus.'

Vic dropped her head. 'OK, yes. Maybe I felt like I wasn't living life the way I wanted to with you. But I still cared. I still loved you.'

'Loved? You still loved me? And there I rest my case.' Nate shook his head. His voice softened. 'Because, rightly or wrongly, you clearly don't love me anymore, Vic. And that's OK. It is what it is.'

Vic welled up again, then said softly, 'But I need you, Nate. Please don't leave me. I need you more now than I ever have. I can't do this on my own.'

Nate started to cry again. 'I can't.' Tears rolled slowly down his face. 'Call me a coward, call me what you will, but I'm not staying with someone who is just with me out of fear of being alone. I want someone who stays because they can't imagine life without me.' He faltered. 'And call me weak, but the only reason I cheated on you was because your signals were so mixed and I needed to feel wanted, Vic. I have needs, too, you know.'

Vic let out a massive sob and blubbered, 'I know you do. I can't imagine life without you. Especially now.'

The graveness of the situation and the black coffee had brought Nate to his sober senses. 'You can't imagine life without me now, Vic. Now that you think nobody else will want you, you mean.' He reached for his phone and rang a taxi. 'Five minutes. I'm gonna wait outside.' He walked towards the door and turned around. 'But you mustn't think like that. You have a beautiful soul, Vic.' He managed to gulp back his emotion as he turned the catch. 'And scared or not scared of catching this wretched virus, I can't just stay with someone who doesn't love me because I feel sorry for them, either.'

'I need to move back to our flat this weekend,' Vic blurted, then added, 'Aletta is coming back here. We can talk more then. Please, Nate. I can't do this without you.'

Nate took a deep breath and shook his head. 'Let me know how much I owe you, because I'll be gone on Sunday.'

'What do you mean, gone?' Vic screwed her face up in anguish.

'I'm going back up to the Lake District. Someone Dad knows is looking for a live-in chef/handyman. It's beautiful grounds and I get a cottage to live in included with the job. I grew up in the area. I love it up there, Vic, and it will make this easier for both of us.'

'You never said anything about still loving it up there.'

'You never asked me.'

'For fuck's sake.' Vic shook her head.

The cab tooted outside.

'I'm doing it, Vic. Give me a bit of time and maybe we can be friends – just not right now, OK?' His voice went to a whisper. 'I'm so sorry.' His voice rasped into a sob.

Vic quietly shut the door behind him and slid down it to the floor. Drawing her knees up to her chest and wrapping her arms around them, she sank deep in thought. Nate was right: he did know her so well. She *was* clinging on to what she knew, because she was so scared of the unknown. Before her HIV diagnosis, time away from him had made her realise that she needed to step up and out of the relationship. To find her way with her art and realise what exactly it was that would make her happy. And as much as she did still have feelings for him, they had been drifting for a while – *she* had been drifting for a while – and as much as Nate said he felt like a coward for walking away, she appreciated that it had also taken a hell of a lot of guts to make that decision. Of course, he had every right to be angry, every right to be afraid. And, HIV or no HIV, he had every right to leave her.

EIGHTEEN

LONDON

The Reactions

Three days later was Ray's first day back from his holidays, and he called Vic into his office. She sat opposite him with a coffee and a sad face. Thankfully Penny wasn't in, so Vic didn't have her inquistive eyes burying into the back of her through the glass wall. Her long-standing boss shut the file that he had been fingering on his desk and leant forward with his hands clasped in front of him.

'I was going to say happy New Year, but with your face looking like a smacked arse and those sad red eyes, I don't think I dare. Do you want to talk about it?'

Vic sighed heavily. 'I've had a terrible few weeks.' Her bottom lip wobbled.

Ray took a sip of coffee. 'I guessed that,' he replied gently. 'It's not like you to have any time off work, so when you said you had an emergency to deal with before Christmas, I knew it was serious.'

'Mum's not good. She's drinking far too much and she had a

fall.' Vic closed her eyes and took another breath to centre herself.

'Oh no, I'm sorry to hear that. Is she OK now?'

'She clearly bounced.' Vic managed a smile. 'Bit of a bruised face and that was it.' Ray remained silent. Vic took a big drink from her Glovers-branded mug. 'Nate and I have split up.'

'As in split, "we're on a break" like Ross and Rachel?' He used his fingers to make fake inverted commas. 'Or as in, split "it's big shit and we are really over this time"?'

'It's big shit, Ray.' Vic sighed heavily. 'He's moving up to the Lake District at the weekend.'

'Wow. That does sound pretty final. How are you feeling?'

'How do you think I'm feeling?' Vic spat.

'Stupid question alert. Sorry.' Ray leant over and squeezed one of her hands.

'No, I'm sorry for snapping. We both cheated, Ray, so we weren't happy. I know that.'

'Whoa, OK. Newsflash!'

'Yes, yes, I kept it all in. I wasn't being the best of partners, but I still cared.' Her voice had gone to a whisper. 'I just didn't know where the relationship was going. We didn't communicate. I got stressed and then didn't fancy sex and that's why it happened.' She shook her shoulders as if to pull herself together and made a funny whining noise.

'I think you should stop beating yourself up, Vic. He made the choice to cheat. And you have no God-given duty to have sex with anyone, even your partner, if you don't want to.'

'I guess not,' Vic whimpered.

'I know not,' Ray confirmed.

Vic's face screwed up into an ugly ball of hurt and pain. 'Everything is such a mess, a fucking mess.' Suddenly, it was like a dam had burst, and rivers of anguish began to flood out in a gush of uncontrollable sobbing.

Ray went off to the loo, came back with a toilet roll and

handed it to her. He awkwardly went to hug her from behind and then danced back again before he reached her, but when he decided to go for it again, she pushed him away, mortified. Through her sobs, she said, 'This is so unprofessional. I'm sorry.' She blew her nose loudly, calmed down a bit and her breathing began to hitch.

'If I'd employed you for your professionalism, you'd have been lucky to have made a year, not ten.' Ray sat back in front of her and peered at her, evidently keen to see what reaction this attempt at humour would get.

'I can see why you want to just employ men.' Vic sniffed loudly and managed a weak smile through her now ebbing tears. 'I'm an emotional wreck.'

'You know I'm joking with you. You're such an asset to this company, Victoria, but I also class you as a friend. And I'm glad you can be this open with me.'

This was it: the time felt suddenly right. She didn't know how, or why. It just was.

'Ray.' She blew out a noisy exaggerated breath and began to babble. 'I have something else to tell you, and I totally understand that it may change the way you view me, but I feel it's only fair that I tell you, as we work so closely together, and I may need to take a bit more time out for appointments, et cetera.'

Ray looked at her flat tummy. 'Vic, if you're pregnant, I'm not that much of an ogre, really. I mean, Penny's got two and she's still here.' Then his brow furrowed. 'No wonder you're upset with Nate going off.'

Vic shook her head. 'Not pregnant, sadly.'

'Oh my God, you're ill, aren't you?' His voice wobbled slightly.

Vic inhaled deeply. It was now or never. 'I'm HIV-positive, Ray.' She looked up at the ceiling and sighed. 'I've got HIV.'

Ray looked her right in the eye. 'OK. That's OK. How long have you known?' His voice remained level.

'The week before Christmas. I just couldn't face coming in.'

'Of course you couldn't. And Nate?'

'He's tested negative.'

'OK.' Ray nodded slowly. 'So, what happened with you?'

'I had a one-night stand in Brighton. We used a condom, but it split. What are the chances, eh? That'll teach me for me being unfaithful.'

'You poor girl. And Nate can't deal with it, I guess?'

'No. He's scared and angry. And rightly not wanting to be with me because if I were to be with him, it would be fear-based on my side and I think he knows that now.'

'So tough, Vic. So tough. I'm sorry.' Ray lifted his bin for Vic to put her pile of tear-sodden tissues in and sat back at his desk.

'You can't catch it from mucus or saliva,' Vic said weakly.

'I know that,' Ray replied wisely. 'I have a friend; he's positive too. He's been on the drug therapy for a year now and is living a normal life. It's never such a shock for us gay boys. We've lived with it around us for a long time.' He reached to squeeze her hand.

Vic felt her sadness lift, just a little. 'I guess not. I'm just learning about it all. Your friend feels OK on the drugs, then?'

'There were side-effects when he started, I believe, but he has a great doctor who seems to be on top of everything for him. It really isn't the death sentence it used to be, Victoria.'

'The clinic told me that 2005 had seen a large increase in the diagnosis of heterosexual men and women, so at least I'll make it to the Office of National Statistics, if nothing else.'

'Yes. Trust you to have made the grade.' Ray smiled sadly. 'Have you told anybody other than Nate?'

'Danny – he's the guy I slept with in Brighton – knows, of course, but none of my family or friends yet.'

'I take it this Danny didn't know he had it?'

'God, no. He's a decent bloke. He's absolutely mortified. In fact, he suggested we be together to make our lives easier, but that wouldn't work, either. He will be a great mate. I know that for sure.'

'And you're going need a few of those.' Ray put his hand on top of hers and squeezed it.

'That's what the guy at Terrence Higgins said to me.' Vic felt tears stinging her eyes. 'It's a whole different world I know nothing about.'

'And a world where research and improvements in medicine are happening all the time, and seemingly very fast,' Ray said gently.

'Thank you, Ray, for being so realistic about it all.'

'I feel very privileged you've told me,' Ray said quietly, standing up and leaning against his filing cabinet. 'You're an incredible artist and designer, Vic, you really are, and I will do anything I can to support you.'

'I just thought that...' Vic stuttered.

'You thought what? It's the lack of education around it that causes the stigma. You're no different to me, Vic, from last week to this. It's really all right. OK?'

Vic felt tears brimming in her eyes once more. 'Does Penny have to know?'

'*Nobody* has to know, Vic, and please, no more tears. You'd've thought you'd used up your ration for the month with that last outburst.'

Vic gave a watery smile, then Ray became serious.

'I wanted to talk to you about something, and it actually seems like the right time.'

'Oh, God, that sounds ominous.' Vic grimaced.

'No, far from it. I know I'm lucky to have you. I see your talent, but also know you well enough to see that you get frustrated sometimes.' He laughed. 'That face when another cereal

packet brief comes in! I'm thankful I haven't been knocked out
by a flying box of Krispy Wheats.'

Vic managed to laugh too. 'I do love it here, Ray, you know
that, and I love you. I just hoped maybe I'd do more with my art
outside of this, I guess. And being very honest, I could have
done, but life got in the way, and I've been fundamentally lazy,
too.'

Ray nodded. 'We do what we do, but with all this going on I
just want to make sure you are doing whatever makes you
happy, and I would never stop you following whatever that path
may be. You could set up an exhibition, or offer your work for
sale online, even.'

'Nate said that, too. About never stopping me.' Vic bit her
lip. 'So, I guess that only points to one person who does stop me,
then.' She reached for a tissue in her bag and blew her nose.

'Look, Vic. You've had a terrible shock. And I guess with
Nate going... well, you may have stuff to sort at home. Why
don't you take some time out, call it a little holiday... get yourself
back on track?'

'Yes, I do have decisions to make. I can just about afford the
flat without Nate's contribution, or maybe I'll just move out and
get a smaller place. The least of my worries at the moment, to be
honest. You're such a diamond, Ray. If you're sure, that would
help me out so much.' Vic stood up and smoothed down her
dress. 'I'll probably just need a couple of weeks, is that all right?'

'Take as long as you need. Have a think about what you
want to do, and let me know what you decide.' He smiled. 'But I
know what I want to do before you trot off.'

'Go on,' Vic urged.

'How about we go for a nice long lunch at Ricardo's and put
the world to rights over a glass of something cheeky.'

. . .

Vic could see Ray typing frantically at his computer as she sat back at her desk. He didn't look up once. Then she saw an email arrive in her inbox.

Dear Victoria,

I meant for you to receive this before Christmas, but I forgot to press send. On top of your Christmas bonus of one thousand pounds, I'd like to offer you a pay rise of five thousand pounds a year, backdated from December. Your work last year was exemplary, and Jerico Flint assures me he is going to write a series based on your amazing illustrations, so that will cover it!

Cover it! Ha, ha. Get it?

Best regards
Ray Glover
Managing Director

Feeling warm and fuzzy inside, Vic looked directly at Ray through the glass of his office. He sensed her gaze and looked up. Blowing him a kiss, she mouthed 'thank you' and in return received her boss's beaming smile and a shrug.

Whether or not Ray Glover had intended her getting this pay rise before Christmas – or at all – didn't matter. Because what did matter was that her boss was an angel in human form, and telling him about her situation had suddenly made her feel a whole lot lighter again.

Full of the most delicious lasagne, tiramisu, and a couple of glasses of wine, Vic returned to Orla's garden flat, feeling incredibly sad about the loss of her six-year relationship with Nate but, amazingly, with the thoughts of HIV banished to the back of her mind. Then she noticed that the dustbin out the front was packed so full that the lid wasn't able to shut. She went towards it and was confused to recognise the pattern of her duvet cover, which was still on the duvet that had been clumsily stuffed in there. To the side, in a black bag, were two pillows, again from her bed.

On entering the flat, she could hear loud music coming from her bedroom. Wondering what was going on, she walked in to find Orla wearing a mask and rubber gloves, scrubbing the mattress of her double bed. A bowl of water cloudy with a strong-smelling disinfectant was on the floor. On catching Vic out of the corner of her eye, Orla screamed loudly and dropped the scrubbing brush to the floor. Vic bent down and handed it back to her. Then turning off the bedside radio, said calmly, 'I didn't think you were home from your event until tomorrow.'

Orla continued to look startled. 'I got an earlier flight. I'm er... just cleaning your room before Aletta comes back. You know. Umm. And she's coming back earlier, too, so I'm... er... just getting her room ready and I umm... was going to talk to you when you got in tonight, as I need you to go back to your old flat tonight – and you're early, too.'

'Looks like we're all early, doesn't it?' Vic took a deep breath to slow the anger that was rising up within her. She stormed down the corridor to the bathroom, used the loo and was just washing her hands when she noticed that her toothbrush had been taken out of the pot that she and her friend had shared for the past few weeks and placed on the side of the sink.

Orla was in the kitchen, kettle on, two mugs out, when Vic walked in. 'You had that flu and you said yourself you'd soaked through everything so would probably buy new sheets, so I'm saving you a job,' Orla gabbled.

'I think chucking out the duvet and pillows is a bit extreme, though, isn't it?'

Vic noticed her friend now had tears running down her face. 'I'm so sorry, Vic.'

Vic felt her heart drop. 'You know, don't you?' Orla's face twitched. 'Did Nate tell you?'

'No. I overheard you the night before I flew to Düsseldorf.' Orla continued to gabble. 'I didn't know what to say or do. I've felt sick since I've been gone. Oh Vic, you poor thing.'

'I don't want your sympathy, Orla, just your fucking support. I haven't got leprosy. I've got a virus, that is inside of me and unless you want to start sharing bodily fluids or shoot up some heroin together, then you're going to be fine. OK?'

'Vic, I'm so sorry. I just didn't know what to do... or... say.'

'So, you thought, *I'll leave my mate to deal with this whilst I'm away. I'm sure she'll be all right. I mean, she's only got HIV.*'

'That's unkind, Vic. It wasn't like that. I had to work. I... er... Please just try and understand from my point of view. I didn't know how to react. You hadn't even told me properly.'

Vic's anger took over. 'And how do you think I felt when I saw you'd chucked out the duvet and the pillows without a word?! And I hope you don't expect me to replace it all.'

'No, no. I have bought new. And I'll get you another cover.' Orla put the two identical mugs of steaming tea down on the breakfast bar. 'I don't want you to buy anything.'

Vic took a sip of tea as Orla returned with the sugar bowl, and hesitated. The mugs were sitting parallel in front of them. 'Which one did you just drink out of?'

'That's enough; that really is enough!' Vic growled. 'Any fool knows you can't catch it from saliva. If you don't want to be alongside me on this journey – 'cos it's gonna be a long, hard one – then I'm no longer calling you my friend.' She grabbed her handbag.

'Vic, you're being sensitive and overreacting. Talk to me, help me understand.'

'I don't want to. I just want to be on my own.' Vic headed for the door, then turned back. 'I guess you've told Mandy?'

'Umm... yes, but she won't say anything. I needed someone to support me.'

Vic was almost speechless. 'You needed support? *You* did? For fuck's sake, Orla. And now she'll tell Steve, and soon everyone we know will know.'

Vic's anger was compounded by a surge of sadness on realising that Mandy, her oldest friend, had known all this time and hadn't reached out to her either.

Orla looked perplexed. 'Vic, what's going on? Of course she won't. We're your friends. Stop this.'

'Friends? Friends support each other, Orla.' Vic's voice tailed off.

Short of words, Orla turned to practicality. 'What about your clothes and stuff? Do you need them now?'

'Just chuck them in the landfill too. That's fine. I hear a lot of people catch it off buttons. Oh, and you better burn my toothbrush, whilst you're at it, and God forbid if I've used your hairbrush by mistake, too!'

'Vic! *Stop!* I can be there for you. We will help you.' Orla put her arm on her friend's. 'We love you.'

'I don't need your help. Here! Educate *yourself.*' Vic reached inside her bag and threw a stray leaflet at her mate. 'And yes, call me bitter, because with the amount of men you sleep with, you're damned lucky this is happening to me and not you. Keep shagging strangers, Orla O'Malley – because it's clearly *not* making you happy. Or short of that, grow up and get into the real world.'

Dragging her case up the Wandsworth flat steps, Vic let herself in and turned on the kitchen light. With a heavy heart, she immediately noticed that the multi-coloured rug Nate had insisted on buying at Athens airport when they last went away was no longer on the floor. She ran to the bedroom and flung open the wardrobe. All Nate's clothes were gone too. He'd said he wasn't leaving until the weekend, hadn't he? She ran back to the kitchen to see if he had placed any kind of note on the cork board where they had always left messages for one another. And there it was, on a yellow Post-it, scribbled in black marker pen.

> Sharpie, you know I'm rubbish at goodbyes, so let's just say, see you when we're older. I'm so sorry.
>
> Your Nate X

With a high-pitched scream, Vic ripped the cork board off the wall, threw it to the floor and began to sob.

NINETEEN

LONDON

The Three Musketeers

'TFI Friday.' Ray Glover flew into the kitchen and poured himself a coffee from the jug. 'Marcus and I are off to a reassuringly expensive spa hotel in Hampshire. I cannot wait.'

Penny was at the water cooler, filling her water bottle. 'All right for some. I have a weekend of rugby practice.'

'I don't think you've quite got the thighs for that, dear,' Ray laughed.

Penny rolled her eyes. 'Funny, funny. I am the official terrible twins' chauffeur, as darling husband is off on a golf weekend. You men have it so easy,' she harrumphed and marched back to her desk as Victoria, coming in to get herself a coffee, crossed with Ray on his way out.

'How's things?'

'Fine,' Victoria replied, her voice hollow.

'When a woman says fine... even I know what that means. Have you got time for a chat?'

Vic sat opposite Ray at his desk.

'What's the matter, *chica*?'

'I haven't spoken to Orla since my outburst.'

'Oh, OK. Has she tried to contact you?'

'No.'

'And you her?'

'No. Because she was the one who acted like a complete arsehole. Cleaning like a madwoman as if she thought I was contagious.'

'Friends are the family you choose, Vic, so if she can't take a few Fs being thrown at her then she never was your friend. But from what I've seen and heard about her, she'll be back.'

'You do make me laugh.'

'Good.' Ray looked at his inbox as an email pinged in.

'I just don't know what to say to her.' Vic stuck out her bottom lip. 'Funnily enough, though, it was Orla who said if you don't know what to do, do nothing, say nothing and the answer will come to you. Maybe I should just be the bigger person here and hold out the olive branch and meet her for a drink?' Vic paused. 'Because as much as she's an annoying bitch sometimes, I do miss her. And as for Mandy not picking up the phone to me, well, I'm not surprised. Orla O'Malley has always played the Pied Piper in our friendship group.'

'There you go. Nobody likes a stubborn old mule. If you miss her, just do it.' Ray slammed his hand on the desk, making Vic jump. 'Right. Midday already. I'm leaving early for my weekend in the shires.' He looked down at his mail again. 'Jerico Flint. Poor bastard. His dog has died. He wanted to explain his delay in paying his invoice. Said he would be in contact in due course.'

'Oh, no, poor Jerico.' Vic put her hand to her chest. 'I sent an email and received an amusing out of office from him. Just his way, I guess.'

'Yes, we're all guilty of hiding the tracks of our tears. Well, maybe not you.' Ray laughed and then grimaced slightly, worried of Vic's reaction.

'You're such a sod. But you're right. I could fill the Thames at the touch of a button at the moment.' Vic smiled, got up, opened Ray's office door then turned around in the doorway.

'Talking of Jerico, what does he do for a day job, do you know?'

'No. I know as much, if not less, about him than you. Why?'

'Just interested.' Vic was casual in her reply.

'Because she fancies the arse off him, that's why.' Penny strutted past on her way to the toilet.

Vic shook her head at her blonde colleague. 'You know that's not true.' However, if she were honest with herself, Vic did find the eccentric author intriguing, as well as attractive, sexy and funny – very funny. But with Nate now gone, she had already resigned herself to the fact that no man would want her, and that hurt. It hurt a lot.

'What did he get you for Christmas, then?' Penny wasn't going to be letting up any time soon, it seemed.

'A Jack Vettriano book. I bloody love his work. Some of it is so tastefully raunchy it literally sizzles off the canvas.'

'Nice,' Ray chipped in. 'That sounds like a gift that some-body who is pleased with two great illustrations would give. How were your clients' gifts this year, Penny?'

The woman said nothing, just harrumphed.

'Now, back to work, the pair of you. I'm off to get pampered with my beau.' Ray started to clear his desk.

Once Penny was out of earshot, Vic gave her boss a grin. 'Have an amazing weekend, and thanks for being such a stal-wart in my life, Ray Glover.'

As she headed back to her computer, the door buzzer sounded. She walked over and pressed the intercom.

'Vic, Vic, is that you?' Vic's soul soared at the sound of the familiar Irish tones. 'It's Orla... and Mand. We've come to take you for lunch, you moody eejit.'

Vic poked her head around Ray's door. By the smug look on his face, he'd clearly heard already.

'It so annoys me when you're right.' But Vic couldn't hide her elation.

Ray cocked his head to the side. 'My dad brought me up to never to say I told you so.' Then he winked.

'I love you, Ray Glover.' Vic blew him a kiss.

'Steady on.' Ray grinned. 'Now get your arse downstairs. And remember: those who mind don't matter and those who matter don't mind.'

Once Mandy had managed to stop crying and they had at last been able to put in their lunch order to one of the suave Italian waiters in Ricardo's, Orla spoke up. 'I am so sorry, Vic, that I reacted so badly.'

'I won't lie, I was surprised, and very hurt. But I get it too. I've had to educate myself.' Vic took a drink of her cola.

Mandy took a slug of water. 'I promise I haven't told anyone, not even Steve, and I won't unless you say I can. I realise you might not want people to know.' She started crying again. 'And I feel so bad about not calling you, but I didn't actually know what to say.'

'"Hello" would have been a start.' Vic's face remained stony. 'And what's with the bloody waterworks? I am not dying – well, not yet, anyway.'

'Oh my God, don't say, that,' Mandy wailed again, making Orla and Vic laugh.

'I'll start on the treatment when required, and that's it.' Not quite believing herself how relaxed she was being – and, in this moment, feeling – about the whole situation, Vic picked up a bread stick and took a bite.

Mandy blew her nose. 'I'm not sure this is the right time or place, but I have to tell you both something too...' She put her hand to her stomach. 'I'm pregnant.' Orla and Vic instinctively looked to her already-large tummy.

'Jesus. No wonder you're a bag of water,' Orla blurted.

'Tell me about it. I'm even crying at reruns of *The Office*. I'm not sure what's happening to me because I also lied to the school and said I was ill today so that I could come here. I'm turning into a charlatan.' She burst into tears again.

'Oh, Mandy, that's the best news ever! Congratulations!' Orla enthused. 'And as for being a charlatan, don't be daft. I clearly hold that title, not you.'

'When are you due?' Vic asked quietly.

'July the first.' Mandy blew her nose again. 'I was pregnant at the hen weekend and didn't even realise!'

'Shit, if it's a girl you'll have to call her Tequila.' Orla smiled.

'Wow. That seems quick.' Vic felt a tinge of sadness, which quickly passed. 'I don't think having a baby is an option for me now. It would be too much of a risk that the baby might contract it too.'

'I knew I shouldn't have told you.' Mandy started wailing again.

'You should have told me. I am still the same old Vic. Please don't wrap me in cotton wool. I've thought about it and I'm genuinely OK about not having kids. I was never sure, anyway – you know that. And the decision has been made for me now. And that sits well with me. Another tick to my future, in a weird way. And I could always get a dog.' Vic grinned.

'You're so brave.' Mandy sniffed.

'No, just realistic, and trying now to deal with the cards I've been dealt.' Vic picked up the menu.

'No, you are fecking brave,' Orla insisted, taking another big slurp of her wine.

Three huge wood-fired pizzas and a fresh and appetising-looking side salad to share were put down in front of them, along with a beaming smile from the same handsome waiter, whom Orla, surprisingly, hadn't once attempted to flirt with.

They ate in silence until Orla spoke up. 'I went and got tested myself.'

'OK.' Vic nodded, her pulse picking up. 'Because you were worried you'd caught it from me, in the flat?'

Orla looked scandalised. 'Of course not! As you yourself said, I enjoy a one-night stand from time to time. I guessed if it could happen to you, then... I do use condoms but sometimes I get very drunk, as you know, and, well... it's reckless of me.'

'I mean, the law of averages does say it should be you and not me, but I was in the wrong time at the wrong place.' Vic's voice wobbled. 'I'm sorry, I was such a bitch to you, Orla.'

'Shut up, mate. My behaviour towards you was nothing short of diabolical. How dare I treat you like that? It came from a complete place of ignorance and fear. I didn't actually know how to deal with it. How to deal with you. And for that I am truly sorry.'

'I appreciate you saying that.' Vic sighed. 'I was so hurt.'

Orla rarely cried but Vic was sure she caught a glisten in her eyes. 'And what you said to me was right, Vic. I do need to sort myself out. I float along saying I don't want a man, or kids or commitment of any kind, but if I'm honest with myself I think I'm frightened that nobody will want me. I equate sex with love. I know I do that. But this isn't about me today, so tell me to shut the feck up. And anyways, my woes are completely irrelevant compared to what you're going through.'

'No, they're not.' Vic sighed. 'Everything is relative, and like I just said, I don't want you to treat me like I'm ill, or like you have to tread on eggshells, worrying about what to say around me, as we've all got to just muddle on the best way we can. So, do you want to talk about how *you're* feeling, Orla?'

'Jesus, no. We'll be here till next fecking Christmas, but I am thinking of getting some counselling, maybe.'

'I'm going to, as well,' Vic added in solidarity.

Mandy welled up again. 'I'm scared to ask this, but does Nate have it too?'

Vic shook her head. 'I got it from Blondie. The condom split.'

'Fuck.' Orla took another glug of her wine.

'Yes, fuck, indeed.' Vic sighed. 'And despite us sleeping together just the once after, it looks like Nate dodged the bullet, thankfully. What I am finding hard to get my head around, though, is that he's got a job up north, and left already.'

'Oh, mate,' Mandy said through a mouth full of pizza. 'What a fucker, though.'

'He couldn't cope with it,' Vic stated plainly.

'But come on, Vic, you've been with him six years.' Orla shook her head.

'I cheated on him. And he cheated on me. There was a lot going on there, and people are going to react differently. And, without knowing what I know now, I think I would initially be dubious about sleeping with someone who told me they had it, to be honest.'

'I think he's being weak,' Orla said stoutly.

'No. I think we'd run our course, to be honest. It wasn't just him being scared of contracting it; he didn't want to stay with me knowing I wasn't all in. I actually think that's quite brave.' Victoria's voice remained level. 'I want to concentrate on me and my art now. I need to get my head around what having this virus means, and maybe spending some time on my own isn't such a bad thing.'

'I can't believe how calm you're being.' Orla spooned some salad onto her plate.

'I'm not, really. When I think about how impossible it's going to be to find love again now I've got *this*, I feel anything but calm. I mean, who in their right mind will want me?' She puffed out her cheeks and looked up to stop tears from falling.

'Oh, darling.' Mandy put her hand on hers. 'We're here for you. And you are beautiful inside and out, Victoria Sharpe, and don't you ever forget that.'

'The gorgeous Ray gave me a Christmas bonus and a pay rise so I can afford to stay at the flat, but I don't know what I want to do anymore.' Vic blew her nose.

'Sit with it, Vic.' Orla was now welling up, too. 'No rash decisions. Your job is safe, and the flat is fine. Just stick with the familiar, for now.'

'I think you're right. Ray didn't even break his stride when I told him. But we've agreed for me to take a couple of weeks off to work out what I really want to do.'

'He's so cool, that man.' Mandy picked up another piece of pizza, and Orla looked sheepish.

'Yes, he really is and I'm glad for that. You need that support at work too.' Orla took a sip of her wine. 'So what happens now, with your hospital appointments et cetera? What's the next step?'

'Regular check-ups with my specialist. Dr Anna, I call her. On first impressions, she's really nice. She'll let me know when I need to go on medication – and it could be years. It just depends how the virus takes hold.'

'I read that's the process,' Orla added. 'You'd think they'd put you on the medication right away.'

'It does feel odd, but I have to be advised by the experts.' Vic shrugged. 'And if my body is doing what it should be at the moment, then I guess there's no reason to. The medication isn't side-effect free, either.'

'You also have to allow us to support you,' Orla added. 'You're not on your own, mate. And however small the problem may seem, pick up the phone to one of us, OK?'

'Thank you,' Vic said quietly, then her voice lifted slightly. 'What was our mantra, when we went on that crazy weekend at Butlin's in Bognor?'

'Oh my God, the one when Orla ended up screwing that clown and got his red nose stuck in her foo-foo, and we all had to go to A&E so someone could pull it out.' Mandy's tummy shook as she giggled.

'And how handsome was the doctor who had the unenviable task of doing that?' Orla put her hand to her mouth. They all started laughing hysterically.

Vic lifted her glass. 'I remember what it was. *One for all and all for one.*'

The others raised theirs too and repeated, '*One for all and all for one.*'

'I always did fancy D'Artagnan,' Orla added.

'That's an improvement on Coco the Clown, I guess,' Mandy said, which set them all off again.

TWENTY
WINDSOR

The Lasagne

11 February 2006

'Mum? What are you doing?'

'Oh, hello, love.' Kath Sharpe, wearing rubber gloves and an apron tied tightly around her waist, continued to furiously mop the kitchen floor. Chandler was whining outside the back door, wanting to be let back into the warm.

Vic stood in the kitchen doorway and peered around, dumbfounded. All the kitchen sides were clear of clutter, and even the stainless-steel draining board had a gleam to it – and it brought her right back to days of old. Her mother's bark of, 'Shoes off first, madam,' made her jump.

She smiled in bemusement as Kath Sharpe blurted, 'I mean, I clean for all these posh, fancy women and this place is a complete and utter shambles. I should be ashamed of myself.' Kath then let out a big sigh, took the mop out of the bucket and tipped the dirty water down the sink. Grabbing a tea towel, she opened the back door, greeted her beloved pooch with a stroke, then lifted his paws to wipe them of any mud he may have picked up whilst charging around outside.

'This is 28, Simpson Crescent, isn't it?' Vic grinned. 'Am I in the right house?'

Kath whipped off her apron. 'You cheeky mare. I wasn't expecting you this weekend, was I?'

'No, Mum.' Vic took a deep breath. 'I just needed to get out of London.'

'How are you feeling, darling?' Kath threw the dirty tea towel into the washing machine.

Tail wagging furiously, Chandler leapt up at Vic's legs until she picked him up and cradled him like a baby. 'Aww, my precious boy.' The little dog scrabbled until she put him back down.

'So, you're feeling OK, Vic?' Kath repeated.

'Umm. Yes, I'm all right.' Despite it being wonderful that her mother was for once showing interest in her only daughter, Vic cringed inside. The drama that would ensue if she told her just wasn't worth it. She'd rather simply be here, in the familiar family home, with her secret safe inside. Sleeping in her old single bed with a dip in it, pretending that nothing had changed. It had been a relief to see Dr Anna earlier in the week, and to be told that nothing had changed with her viral load or CD4 count since the last check, and to just continue as normal until their next appointment in three months' time.

'And how's that Nate? I haven't seen him for ages. Last summer, wasn't it? You two went off Monday night horse racing?'

'Umm. He's the same as usual.' Just hearing his name made Vic want to burst into tears. For, even though they had long been like ships passing in the night, she had been missing him greatly. It was sad and a little strange that when they had been together, knowing someone had been coming home to her, at whatever time, had been enough for her not to feel alone. But now that void was huge, and her nights quite often devoid of sleep. And as much as she probably should share her feelings of woe, Vic wasn't ready to open up that whole assortment of problems either – not yet, anyway.

Just thinking of her ex-love gave her the sudden urge to message him and tell him that her mum could actually be sober. He was one of the only people who would really get the significance of that for her. But to what end? And why would he care now, anyway?

Kath filled the kettle. 'Let me make us a nice pot of tea. I got some chocolate digestives when I went shopping this morning, too. Note to self: don't shop on a Saturday, especially not the weekend before Valentine's Day. It was packed everywhere.'

Romance being the last thing on her mind at the moment, Vic hadn't even registered what date it was. 'Tea and biscuits sounds lovely, thanks, Mum.' She opened the back door under the pretence of wanting to run up and down the lawn with Chandler and took a quick look in the recycle bin – no bottles. Then opened the dustbin and lifted the bin bag in there and shook it – no glass clanking in there, either.

After she had checked the little fella's paws for mud, they went back inside.

'The garden looks tidy, Mum.'

'Yes. I can't take the credit for that. It's a bit wet for mowing, so your brother just gave it a bit of a strim on the edges and sorted out the old pots that were out there. He's popped some rhubarb in the top corner, too, and I'm looking forward to getting some sweet peas out there this year.'

'It's great that you're getting organised again, Mum. You used to love your garden.'

'Yes, yes, well... with Albie helping, it makes it a bit easier. He's paying off his national debt, as he calls it. He came over with Lisa and her boys and they helped me put the bed back upstairs, too. I can start using the dining room table again for my jigsaws. Looked like an old people's home in there before – it's much better now.'

Vic was feeling quite shocked at the huge transformation of her mother in such a brief time.

'Have you met her, Vic? Lisa, I mean. She's a lovely girl, that one.'

Vic didn't want to spoil the moment and convey that of course she'd met Lisa – once here, even, when they'd all had a Sunday lunch together – so just replied with a quick, 'Yes, yes, I have.'

She opened the packet of biscuits as her mum filled the teapot with boiling water. 'I know what I meant to ask you: who helped you get the bed downstairs before, Mum?'

Kath Sharpe took off her apron and threw it in the washing machine too. 'It was Albie, wasn't it? I think but...' Kath sighed. 'OK. Hands up. I'm ashamed to say I have no recollection of it happening.'

They moved through to the living room, which, Vic noticed, with a dart of pride, was also clutter-free, with not a spot of dust in sight. Chandler jumped up on the sofa next to Kath and snuggled into her ample thighs.

'So, how's work, love?'

'It's all right, thanks.' Vic laid her head back on the armchair. It had been lovely to have a couple of weeks off in January, and she had gone back to Glovers with renewed vigour – and a plan. She had also put her thousand-pound bonus in a high-interest account and was saving as much money as she could afford so that, when the time was right, she would at least have some behind her when she started to make a plan with her art. She found that when her mind was cluttered and worried, she couldn't release her full creativity, and she was in that kind of mental state at the moment.

'You look tired, darling. Are you sure you're OK?'

'I'm fine, Mum. I promise.'

'So are you here for the weekend, or is it just a flying visit?'

'Until tomorrow night, if you'll both have me?' Vic looked at Chandler, who was now lightly snoring.

'We'll do better than that. How about a nice home-made lasagne for our dinner? And I've got some rhubarb in the freezer – I could do a crumble, too. Your favourites.'

Vic felt herself welling up. 'That'll be really lovely, Mum.'

'Good. Good.' Kath Sharpe took a big slurp of her tea, then released her hair from the bobble that had been tying it back and gave her head a shake.

'Wow. You've had your hair cut.' Vic took in her mum's new shoulder-length bob, which had been coloured deep brown to cover the greys. 'I can't believe I didn't notice it straight away. It's lovely, and that colour really suits you.'

Kath Sharpe patted her head. 'Thanks, love. I did an extra few hours for the Overton-Hattons, so Sally Jenkins – you know, who used to come here and do it – well, I called her up. I found a pair of your old straighteners in the back cupboard, so used those on it the other day, too. Hark at me with my "new hair, don't care" attitude.' Kath Sharpe grinned.

'Hark at you.' Vic smiled, delighting in Kath's happiness, but also feeling distinctly perplexed at her mother's new-found positive attitude, which had seemingly come out of nowhere.

She thought back to a conversation with Joti, about it taking something big to even get her mother to think about stopping drinking. But whatever she was thinking, Victoria Sharpe certainly wasn't going to either question or comment on the matter. Instead, as she had done on many other occasions, she would just quietly take in and enjoy this long-awaited moment of sobriety. And pray that, this time, it would last.

'Hello, Vicki. How are you?' Joti was on her knees refilling an outdoor pot with soil as Vic came out of the door to take Chandler for a walk along the river.

'I'm all right, thanks. It's a bit early for bedding plants, isn't it?'

'Just repotting a rose. Your brother kindly strimmed the grass out here last week, so I wanted to get it looking nice, ready for spring. He's quite the charmer, isn't he? I meant to ask you, what age is he? Mid-twenties, I guessed?'

'Charming when he wants something, usually.' Vic smiled. 'And don't let that babyface fool you, he was thirty last birthday. I hope he didn't ask you for money.'

'No – said he worked for beer, so I will get him some cans for next time I see him.' Joti rubbed her hands together to clean them of earth and stood up.

'He must like you, then.' Vic shook her head at the cheek of her brother asking for anything. Joti blushed. But cheek aside, if he'd asked for beer over money, maybe he had tried to put the brakes on the gambling, and for this Vic was incredibly happy.

'Let me just change my coat and wash my hands and I'll come with you for a walk – I assume that's where you're going.' Joti was slightly hesitant. 'If you don't mind, of course.'

At the word 'walk' Chandler barked his disapproval at being kept waiting for his. 'No, no, that'll be lovely,' Vic replied, and meant it.

'Give me a minute, mister.' Joti ruffled the impatient terrier's ears and went inside. She appeared, fresh-faced, wearing a smart beige mac and black, knee-high boots. Her long, black, poker-straight hair was brushed flat, accentuating just how shiny it was.

'I didn't recognise you with your proper clothes on,' Vic commented. 'You look gorgeous.'

Joti laughed. 'Yes, I still brush up OK when I can be bothered.'

As they headed out of their close and on to the road towards the river path, they passed a tall blond man carrying a huge bouquet of red roses.

'Someone's a lucky girl,' Vic exclaimed when he was out of earshot.

'Or not,' Joti replied darkly. 'If I never have a man again, it will be too soon.'

'Oh dear. You got divorced, didn't you? I remember you saying when we first met, and I was in the middle of abusing you.' Vic felt a surge of guilt at being rude to the clearly kind and soft-hearted woman walking by her side.

Joti sighed. 'Yes, my dear darling *Mister* Johnson had an affair.' She accentuated the word 'mister'. 'And woe betide anyone who dare call the bastard *Doctor*, for he is a *Mister*! A surgeon, same as my dad was. Rob was a brusque Glaswegian – and the reason why I ended up in Edinburgh, following my cheating husband's career dreams of being the best heart surgeon in Scotland.'

'Were you together long?'

'Ten years.'

'Wow! So, yes, then.' Vic tightened Chandler's lead as another dog owner approached them.

'It was great at the start, as it always is. In fact, the honeymoon period was a long one. But I've always wanted kids, Vic, and although we discussed it and he said that when the time was right, he would be open to it, when the conversation arose, he wasn't sure. And I wasn't going to have kids with someone who didn't really want them – and at the grand old childbearing age of thirty-eight, I didn't have the luxury of time to wait. So, the arguments began, as did his affair. She was the clichéd model – ten years younger than me, and despite him saying he had always preferred dark-eyed Eastern beauties, she had long blonde hair and made no demands, I heard, other than being the recipient of regular gifts and her promise to him of no-strings-attached, regular sex.'

'Oh, shit,' was all Vic could muster.

'As you can hear from my voice, I'm clearly not bitter.'

Both women laughed.

'Are they still together?'

Joti's voice assumed a sarcastic tone. 'Yes – and guess what? She's only gone and got herself pregnant.'

'Oh, Joti, that's terrible.'

'Yes, heartbreaking. And one of the other reasons that I moved to the other end of the country – so I never ever have to see them playing happy families.'

'I'm so sorry. So Adams is your birth name, I take it?'

'Yes. A good old common English name – my mum was Sri Lankan. And please don't be sorry. Shit happens and I've got to get on with it now. I guess the only good thing that has come out of it is the divorce settlement, which has enabled me to buy a house in a lovely part of the world, and I have no mortgage on it. I could also take some time out of work, too, but I don't want to. Nursing is a vocation and I love my job.'

'So why Windsor?'

Joti's voice wobbled slightly. 'It's a long story.'

'It's a long path.' Vic smiled as they reached the river entrance opposite Browns. Swans were streaming onto the concrete riverbank area as excitable kids threw them bread and grains bought from the café on the front. Vic loved these magnificent birds when they were swimming gracefully on the water, but if they dared to stretch their wings and come towards her, it reminded her of when she nearly toppled into the river when she was just five, and which caused her to scream every time they came close, even now.

With Chandler barking like crazy at the majestic birds, the two women quickly made their way through them and, reaching a quieter spot on the path, were able to hear each other again.

Jake was having a smoke on the deck when Vic and Chandler reached his boat. Joti had held back to take a quick call from someone at work about her shift pattern. On recognising Chandler, Jake whistled, then on seeing Victoria, looked slightly surprised. 'Oh hello, young'un. I expected to see your mum at the end of that lead.'

'So that means she's been out walking, then?'

'Yes, yes. She has.'

She couldn't be sure, but Vic thought maybe Jake's cheeks had gone a light shade of pink.

'She's been trotting along here every day this past week, with this little fella. Have arranged to go on a longer walk with them both tomorrow.'

'Ah, she didn't mention it.'

'Umm... Well, I did only suggest it in passing. She's probably forgotten. And she'll want to spend time with you, no doubt.'

For once, Vic didn't air the inquisitive thoughts that were spinning around her head. 'She's great, though, Jake. I don't know what's happened. She's like a different woman. It's a breath of fresh air to see her so happy and sober.'

'I'm so pleased.' Jake paused. 'For both of your sakes. How are you doing anyway, Victoria? You weren't in a good place when I saw you last.'

'I'm fine.' She looked down and straightened a kink in Chandler's lead as he tried to jump up on the boat. Jake was emotionally aware enough not to question the 'fine' on this occasion. 'Not now, matey.' Vic pulled the errant hound to her side. She looked back to see Joti now walking towards them down the river path and waved to her. 'That's Mum's neighbour. We're just having a walk together. She's lovely.'

Without looking down the path, Jake checked his watch. 'That's nice. I'm always here with an ear. You know that. But for now, as you have company anyway, I'm going to love you and leave you, as there's a programme on Radio 4 I've been waiting to listen to. See you soon, love.'

He disappeared inside.

TWENTY-ONE

SLOUGH

The Drop-in Centre

April 2006

Taking a deep breath, Vic took hold of the bee-shaped knocker and banged the door to the jaded Victorian end-of-terrace house. It was opened by a woman of around fifty, Vic guessed, with dyed blonde hair tied back loosely in a clip. She was wearing jeans, a navy sweatshirt with the words 'Positive Hope' in white on it, and a friendly smile.

'Sorry for taking so long,' she said in a strong Liverpudlian accent. 'I had the blender going in the kitchen.' She wiped her hands on the sides of her jeans.

'Hello...' Vic felt suddenly nervous. 'I'm Victoria.'

'Well, it's lovely to meet you, Victoria – or would you prefer Vicki?'

Victoria stopped herself from visibly cringing. 'Just Vic or Victoria is fine.'

'OK, Vic. Well, I'm Chrissie. I'm one of the support workers here. It's your first time, isn't it?'

Victoria felt her breath catch as she nodded, and Chrissie clearly noticed.

'We are a friendly bunch here. We have a chef who comes in and does a lunch for one-ish; I was just making a cake for later, as I'm working in the office upstairs till late.'

They arrived at the kitchen door. Chrissie addressed the well-built, tattooed bald man who was stirring something on the hob. 'All right, Doug. We have a new diner, so you best make an effort with today's scran.'

'You cheeky...' The guy grinned and looked at Vic. 'Hi. Don't listen to this one. She boils eggs in the microwave. But welcome to Hope Cottage.'

'Oi.' Chrissie mock-swiped him.

'Actually, whilst we're in here...' Chrissie walked further into the kitchen and pointed to the labelled canisters on the side. 'Help yourself to tea and coffee, and there's always biscuits or cakes in the green tin there. Actually, come on, let's make a brew.'

With hot drinks in hand, Chrissie was then off again down the hallway, Vic following close behind. 'Living room to your right – people just come and chat or watch television, or just sit and have some peace.'

Vic noticed a long leather sofa and armchair and a television that was showing a news channel with the sound down.

'Between ten and three every Tuesday, fifty-two weeks a year, rain or shine, this whole place is yours to use as you wish.' They carried on to the end of the corridor. 'Toilet and shower room to the left, should you need it, and this – without really needing any introduction – is the dining room.' They entered a large, airy room housing a long wooden table with mis-matching chairs. Double doors led out onto a garden, where there was a small brown shed and two bench-seated tables.

'You're the first in today.'

'How many people usually come?'

'Depends, really. Six, sometimes up to twelve. Some of the same faces have been coming for years; some just pop in immediately after diagnosis to see what it's all about, then drift off. Others, well, it's part of their weekly routine.'

'Ah, OK. So informal, then?'

'Yes. We do have a circle session around the dining table on the last Wednesday of the month, where people come in and share whatever is on their mind. Sometimes we have a guest speaker to talk about health or wealth or whatever the boss thinks may be of use to our service-users. That's what we call you, by the way: a service-user. You don't have to book, and one of the volunteers usually hosts it.'

'Ah, OK.' Vic nodded. 'Handy to know.'

'You found us all right, then?' Chrissie's voice lifted.

'Yes, yes. I got a taxi. Easy to find the road, though not the house – I expected a sign of some sort, I guess.'

'Yes, we keep it low-key here now. Used to have one, but some stupid cock decided to spray paint the fence with abuse.'

Vic bit her lip. 'I hate this side of it.'

'Let's sit.' The women sat down opposite each other in the dining room. Vic noticed that the walls were blank, apart from a poster saying 'Help yourself' and an arrow pointing down to a huge basket of condoms and what Vic assumed must be femidoms.

'Here at Positive Hope, we're doing our best to stop the stigma, but it's a tough job, unfortunately, and as we are a charity, we have to work hard to keep the funds coming in. We are always putting the message out to try and combat it, but it ain't easy.'

'Good for you, but hearing that makes me so angry.' Vic sighed. 'I keep repeating this, but if I was sat here with any other illness, people would be feeling sorry for me, not making me feel like a total outcast.'

Chrissie sighed. 'Yes, but I do think the cause of that fear and ignorance is clear. Granted, back in the eighties, the treatments weren't there, and a lot of people were dying, so we did need the public to be as informed and aware as possible. But although successful in its messaging, the lingering shock from those tombstone ads around the virus didn't help. Along with the association with the gay community, the ignorance and bigotry carries on and, sadly, the path from that to the continuing stigma is well trodden, I'm afraid to say.'

'I guess I need to just be as informed as I can,' Vic added.

'Or just keep away from the idiots who aren't.' Chrissie put her hand over her mouth as she coughed. 'How did you hear of us, by the way?'

'A leaflet.' Vic thought back to how a leaflet for this place had randomly come through the door at her mother's with a bunch of other junk mail. 'I spoke to another lady – I can't remember her name now – about coming today. I took a day off work. I'm staying at my mum's tonight.'

'You don't live around here, then?'

'Does that matter?' Vic replied, more defensively than she meant to.

'Not at all. Hope Cottage is an open house.'

'I live in London. At the moment, anyway. I did think about going to the Lighthouse but I liked the idea of this being small and personal, and it's not far from Mum's, so...'

'Well, it's a big well done for coming. I can't imagine it's easy. Do you want to tell me your story?' Chrissie looked Vic right in the eye.

'I was diagnosed just before Christmas.' Tears hit the back of Victoria's eyes. 'Condom split. The guy I slept with didn't know he was positive.'

Chrissie tutted. 'Oh, Victoria. That really is a tough one to swallow.'

'Yeah.' Vic let out a huge sigh. 'I always try and see the good in a situation. Like there's a reason for everything, you know? But I'm struggling with this one.'

'Trust in the timing of your life, Victoria. One day, you'll see, and I'd bet good money on that.'

'I like that.' Vic smiled and repeated, 'Trust in the timing of your life.'

'Are you in a relationship now, Vic?'

'No. *He* left me when I told him.'

Chrissie's face dropped. She put her arm on Vic's. 'Oh, love. You really have been through it, haven't you.' Her voice then lilted. 'All I can say is, don't rush to find love, because I can imagine that's a lot of what's on your mind right now.'

'Yes and no. Nobody will want me. I have to face that.'

'If you think like that, then of course they won't. Be patient. Love is blind. He'll walk through the door when you're least expecting it. I bet you.'

Vic raised her eyebrows. 'I didn't put you down as a romantic, Chrissie.'

'Romantic, nah, just a realist. This game of happiness is formulaic. Stop rushing around and looking for it, then – what is it they say? It'll have a chance to sit on your still shoulder like a butterfly.'

'Aww. You're sweet,' Vic crooned.

Chrissie let out a loud, dirty laugh. 'I've been called many things before, but that ain't one of them.'

Vic smiled. 'So did anyone come and sit on your shoulder, then?'

'I'm not supposed to say, but yeah, that bald-headed auld fella in the kitchen. Moved down here, minding my own business and he'd been in that kitchen waiting for me all along.' A grin formed on the blonde woman's face.

'Aw, that's lovely to hear.' Vic took another slurp of coffee. 'There could be a chance for me yet.'

'Keep the bigger picture in mind, girl. You're going to be just fine. Right, I better go and help my Doug, before he starts kicking off.'

Vic sat and looked down the garden. Maybe the only reason she had come here today was for Chrissie's wise words. Because right now, she had a sudden urge to flee this building, which reminded her of everything she didn't really want to be talking about to complete strangers – not today, anyway.

She checked for messages on her phone and, finding none, closed her handbag and stood up.

Chrissie noticed her walking past the kitchen and followed her to the door. 'You're off already?' she asked gently. 'Was it something I said?' She smiled, seemingly keen to show she wasn't offended.

'It was everything you said, actually.' Vic paused. 'In a positive way, I mean.'

'Good job I'm not in charge of service-user retention.' Chrissie grinned, but on noticing Vic's downturned lips, put her hand on her shoulder. 'We are here, every Tuesday. No judgement. It's not as hard as you think to open up to strangers. I mean we did all right, didn't we?'

'Thanks, Chrissie. And yes, we did just fine. And just knowing that is enough – for now, anyway.'

As Vic arrived back home in Windsor, Kath came to the front door with Chandler at her feet.

'I didn't even hear you leave. Are you OK, love?' Kath looked concerned. 'Been somewhere nice?'

'Just into Slough, I... er... needed to take a top back that I bought last week.' Wishing that was what she had been doing, Vic leant down and ruffled Chandler's ears. Despite – and indeed because of – her mum going through a sober patch, she just wasn't ready to worry her and cause an explosion of drama by telling her. Not yet.

They walked through to the kitchen.

'It's been lovely having you home more lately. And I'm so glad you told me about Nate, love.'

Despite it being months since Nate had left, the time had only recently felt right for Vic to tell her mother.

'You can't be going through that on your own. So I've made a vegetable soup this morning, for your lunch. Full of goodness, it is, and I'm just off into town to get some fresh bread. There's a sliced loaf in the bread bin if you can't wait.' Kath put her hand to her daughter's chin and moved her face from side to side.

'Mum! Stop it!'

'You look much better than when you arrived. Good, good. See you later on.' Kath fixed Chandler's lead to his collar. 'Our Albie is coming round for his tea tonight. In fact, I've seen a lot of him lately. He's been helping Joti out with odd jobs as well as me.'

'I'd heard.' Vic was finding the obvious change in both her mother and sibling quite unnerving.

'I told you, he's a good lad, really. Oh, that reminds me: I need to get some mince. I'll do a lasagne, shall I?'

'I'll be looking like a lasagne soon,' said Vic fondly, over-taken by the warmth of love from her mother.

'Well, if your old mum can't feed you up with your favourite food, then who can? See you later, darling.'

Vic was sure her mother had tears in her eyes. She found it so heartening to see the change in her, and if Kath carried on like this, Vic would have no hesitation in confiding in her about her HIV. Because a sober Kath Sharpe was a tour de force and a mother like no other – two things that she could really do with right now.

'Bye, Mum.'

Vic was just about to shut the door behind her when Joti pulled onto the drive. As she lifted her hand to wave at her, Vic noticed that she was crying. Not wanting to pry, she turned to go inside again.

'Vicki? Have you got a minute?'

Joti handed Vic a steaming mug of tea and sniffed loudly. 'I'm being stupid. I'm all right now. It's just, it would have been my dad's birthday today.'

The magical sound of birdsong coming from the apple tree at the bottom of Joti's garden gave relief to the mood for a second.

'It's so lovely to be sat outside, at last. But no wonder you're upset. Gosh, with you being the age you are, I'm assuming your dad must have died fairly young?'

'No, he was eighty-eight when he died a year ago – my mum was much younger than him.' She let out a little laugh. 'Ironic that a heart surgeon should drop down dead from a heart attack, but a good way to go, I reckon. Instant; no suffering. At a ripe old age.' Joti's voice tailed off. 'Sadly, unlike my mum.'

'Oh no. So your mum has passed, too?'

'Yes, she died in a car accident in Sydney, just two years after I was born. I was in the car and survived without a scratch. The headline was: "Miracle Baby Survives Horror Crash". My one claim to fame.'

'Oh, Joti, I'm so sorry. I don't know what else to say. You've lost your dad, your marriage has ended and you've moved to the other end of the country in the space of a year.'

'I know. Some days I don't know how I put one foot in front of the other, and now, well... What is happening today is just, well, on a different level.'

Vic was beginning to think that maybe being HIV-positive

wasn't the worst thing in the world, when put into the context of other people's lives. 'Oh shit. What is it?'

'Can I show you something, Vic? It's personal, but I feel I can trust you.'

'Of course.' Vic took a sip of her tea.

Joti ran inside, then came out holding a letter. 'My dad's solicitor in Australia gave me this when he read his will. And I'd like you to look at it, as it is the reason I chose to live in Windsor.'

The beautiful writing on crisp white paper caused Vic's thoughts to turn to Jerico Flint for a fleeting second. 'It is so him, another Mister, just like my ex-husband. *Mister* Jonathan Selfish Adams this time, and the brusque bedside manner he was so famous for.' Joti huffed.

Vic began to read.

Dear Joti, my beautiful daughter,

If you are reading this, then your stepmother and I must be dead. I felt the time was right to tell you that I am not your biological dad. Never doubt that I have loved you as if I was, as did Katy.

'Katy was your stepmother, I take it?' Vic asked. Joti nodded. Vic carried on.

But maybe if your real father is still around, he will want to meet you and you won't be all alone in this world.

I loved your mother dearly. Who wouldn't? She was kind, gracious, undeniably beautiful and so much fun, but she could never love me like she loved your real father. Never. I knew that.

He sent a letter, you see, to our house in Australia. Your mum never knew I read it, of course, even though I had discreetly torn through the PO box number, so she couldn't reply. So all she had to go on was that he was sober and missed her, and that he probably lived in Windsor and had signed off as JT. And despite him professing to be a friend, she had mentioned a Jake, and when she had said his name her whole being lit up. I could feel the love through the pages. I also worked back the dates of when you were born and I knew you couldn't possibly be mine. When she told me that she was taking you to see a great-aunt in England, I knew where she was going. She was going to him. She'd packed for weeks, not days. I'm not stupid. You were a mile from the airport when the accident happened. Like I've told you so many times, your mum wouldn't have suffered and I still can't get over the absolute miracle that you survived. Even more reason that you must know where you came from. As must he. You are a special girl, Joti. You really are.

You have reminded me so much of her all my life. And even though you moved away, you gave me such joy when you came over to see me and Katy. You really did.

I am so sorry for only sharing this with you now, though, my darling. I didn't want to confuse you. But if I'm honest, more selfishly, I didn't want to lose you.

Please forgive me, my cherub, but most importantly, be happy.

Please be happy XX

An open-mouthed Vic put the letter down on the garden table.

'Mad, isn't it?' Joti smiled.

'Wow. Just wow.' Vic's voice was now shaking. 'So you are taking the chance, that this... this Jake is still in Windsor, I guess?'

'It's a long shot but a good start to make enquiries, and quite frankly it's all I have. And it was easier than putting a pin in the map when I knew I wanted to get out of Edinburgh.'

Vic then had to ask the question. 'What was your mum's name, Joti?'

With tears in her eyes, Joti replied, 'Malini. Her name was Malini.'

TWENTY-TWO

The Boss

Two weeks later, Victoria decided that she should embark on a keep-fit campaign, which consisted of just walking more for now, but it was a start, and hence the reason she decided to stomp the thirty minutes into work rather than take the train that morning.

Her chat with Joti about Malini had made her realise just how short life was, and rather than using the excuse of saving money to hold her back from the freedom of creating art for herself, she realised it was time to take life by the balls. Which was why, on a beautiful sunny morning in April, she had arranged to meet Ray in their favourite café next to the office, away from the prying ears and eyes of Penny Clayton.

Thinking of Joti made her feel a sudden surge of guilt that she had not yet revealed that it was highly likely she knew who Joti's real father was. Not because she didn't want Joti to know, but because the whole thing was so huge, and she felt she had to speak to Jake first. She had known Jake for years, and she also knew just how much he had loved Malini. And as much as it would delight him that he may have a daughter, it would also break his heart when he realised that Malini had actually been on her way to him when she had died, and he had been unaware of this all these years. The whole thing would have to be treated with sensitivity.

But Vic had to put her own lifejacket on before she sorted everyone else out. She'd been thinking long and hard about her future, and today she was actioning what she should have done a long time ago. Jake had waited so many years that another few days wouldn't hurt. So she would go and talk to him at the weekend, and then it would be up to him to decide if he wanted to meet Joti or not. And in the unlikely event that he decided not to, it would be a secret that Victoria would have to bear.

'Two cappuccinos and a lemon Danish, please.' Ray looked at the waitress and then back at Victoria. 'Are you sure you don't want anything to eat?'

'Go on, then, I'll have a croissant, thanks.'

The waitress headed off.

'Good weekend? You're looking well.' Ray smiled.

'I decided to walk here this morning, hence the rosy glow.'

'And you're feeling OK in yourself, are you? I haven't had a chance to ask lately, and I never will if Penny is hovering, of course.'

'Yes. I've recently had another check-up, and everything is where it was before.'

'That's brilliant. I am slightly intrigued by the impromptu breakfast meeting request, though.'

'I wanted to be out of Penny's earshot, too.' Vic paused as the waitress delivered their pastries.

'You're leaving me, aren't you?' Ray pulled off a tiny piece of lemon icing and popped it in his mouth, then put his big hand on top of Vic's tiny one. She remained silent. 'And that really is OK.' His kind brown eyes met hers as the waitress put their coffees down in front of them.

Vic began to gabble. 'I'm so appreciative that you gave me a pay rise, but I think the time is right for me to get creative for myself. I know you've never stopped me, and never would, but finding out about – well, you know what... It's made me reassess... well, made me reassess everything, really.'

'It's OK, Vic, calm down.' Ray grinned his wide smile. 'Business is business. Life moves on. I've been so lucky to have you for ten years. What I will say is that the door will always be open for you at Glovers. And, like I've said many times before, you are the most talented illustrator I've ever met.'

'So that is why I have a proposition for you.' Vic broke her warm croissant in half.

'Oh, here we go. I like the sound of this.' Ray grinned again.

'Would you consider me doing some freelance projects for you? No pressure, but I think it could work in both of our favours.'

Ray put his cup back down on the saucer. 'Yes, definitely. I'm glad you've suggested that. What a great idea.'

Vic smiled. 'Really? Well, that was easier than I thought. I'm going to buy myself a new Mac, so I'll be able to work from anywhere.'

'Vic, no justification required. It's fine. Honestly, I think it's an amazing compromise. I don't lose you completely, and you still have your freedom and will have some income to launch your own plans.'

'That's what I thought.' Vic was beaming.

'I will see what work comes in. You can price job by job, and invoice me, if that suits?'

'Sounds good to me.' Victoria took a sip of coffee.

'When do you want to start working this way?' Ray reached in his jacket pocket for his Filofax.

'I was thinking I would stay until the end of this month so I can get all my pipeline jobs finished, and May Day heralds a new start.'

'Perfect. I'm so proud of you, Victoria.' Ray's voice cracked slightly.

'I'm actually a little proud of myself.' Vic looked up to contain her tears. Her voice lifted. 'Anyway, I thought you were only interviewing men from now on.' They both laughed.

'Yes, what am I thinking? I could have said no to your proposition, then I would be one pesky girl down already,' Ray quipped, setting them both off again. He took a mouthful of coffee. 'But hang on, Jerico would be distraught if you were to leave me completely.'

Vic squirmed in her seat.

'You like him, don't you?'

Vic purposely shoved a big bit of croissant in her mouth and made the universal 'I can't talk, I'm eating' sign with her finger.

'That's a yes, then.' Ray raised his hands dramatically and began to recite: '*Love is a smoke made with the fume of sighs.*'

'Don't you be going all *Romeo and Juliet* on me now.'

'Well, love *is* elusive, and I think Jerico is a great person. You could do a whole lot worse. Smoking hot, too.'

'Great, maybe, but he's also slightly mad. And who said anything about love!' But despite her declared reservations, even thinking about Jerico Flint made Vic smile and she couldn't keep the one that had formed off her face.

'All the best people are slightly loco.' Ray grinned. 'Does he make you laugh, though, Vic?'

'He makes me unattractively snort.'

'Well, to be honest, once the initial lust has passed, the nose hairs start growing and our hips start giving way, what do we all really want? For me, it will be enjoyable conversation, a sense of humour and my dick sucked now and then. I don't know about you.'

Vic laughed. 'I think you'd best leave the romantic notions

to the great bard. And being honest, I want to concentrate on my work at the moment. It's taken me a long time to get to this point.'

'If advice from a middle-aged homosexual who has never himself been great at love counts, I agree that's the right decision. You've had some life-changing news, so just be still for a bit. See what happens. Do what makes you happy and surround yourself with people who care about you. And when you are ready for romance, don't settle with anyone, just because you're afraid, Vic.' He put his hand on hers.

'Thank you. Thank you so much.' Vic smiled. 'And I class you as one of those – people who care, I mean. You've helped me so much.'

'You always were completely deluded.' Maintaining a straight face, Ray popped another chunk of pastry into his mouth.

TWENTY-THREE
BRIGHTON

The Gallery

It was May the second and Victoria's first day of freedom from Glovers. Boarding the train at Clapham Junction, she balanced her large art porfolio case in front of her legs, put her bag on the seat next to her and cosied herself in a window seat.

The previous week had been one of big changes, what with leaving Glovers as a permanent employee and giving notice on her Wandsworth flat. To her mum's delight, she had decided she would spend more time in Windsor while still living in London until the lease expired.

Getting ready that morning, she had felt like she was going for a real interview, not just to show Danny her artwork. Her ultimate goal was for him to exhibit and sell some of her creations, but he had been really straight with her, saying that he had a business to run, so it wasn't guaranteed he could take her work. As the train made its merry way down to the south coast, she began to feel rather nervous.

She had chosen to take a post-rush-hour train so there was

room for her portfolio case, and also because, with her new-found freelance freedom, she could now enjoy that luxury. Feeling thankful that nobody had sat next to her yet, she stuck her earphones into her iPod and laid her head back on the seat.

She was in the habit of playing 'Nobody Knows' by Pink over and over, not just because she loved it, but also because it was about feelings that one can have but not show to the outside world. Pink had described it as the most vulnerable track on the album. And vulnerable was how Vic felt these days. In fact, she loved the whole *I'm Not Dead* album because, at that moment in time, even its name was almost amusingly relevant, and many of its tracks were powerful, too. And that was what she needed in her life just now. A bit of Pink power to get her through the uncertain times ahead.

Putting her phone on the tray in front of her, she was just about to relax and listen to her album when she saw a message come in. Seeing that it was from Nate, she took a sharp intake of breath. Then, on taking in the postcard-like verbiage, she shook her head in disbelief.

> Really hope you're OK. Ace here. Job great.
> Nate x

She was just ruing the fact that this was the best her ex of six years could muster, after the limited contact they had had since March, when another text popped in, from Ray.

> Hope you're good. I've told Jerico you're a free agent now – professionally, I mean – & have given him your number. He has another book on the bubble – do you mind? Rx

Vic shook her head at Ray's comment and replied imme-diately.

> I'm all good, and that's great, thanks! Vx

She was just walking from Brighton train station in the direction of Danny's gallery, when her mobile rang. She answered, and hearing the posh tones of Jerico Flint brought an instant smile to her lips.

'Queen Victoria? It's Jerico Flint. How dare you run away and not tell me? Mr Pigeons is really quite furious. And is that the squawk of seagulls I hear?'

Vic laughed. 'I totally understand that the consequences for Mr Pigeons would be far too great to bear if I did that.'

'Yes, yes, indeed.'

She knew he was smiling. He then took an exaggerated breath. 'Well, I won't bother you now, as I'm assuming you're away.'

'I'm just in Brighton for the day. I understand Mr Pigeons needs another jacket? I'm happy to help you with that. In fact, I'd love to,' Vic laughed. 'Dare I ask where he's off to now?'

'Sidmouth, actually.'

'Oh.' Vic giggled. 'Not far then.'

'*Mr Pigeons and the Devon Donkey Sanctuary.*' Jerico slipped into a fine Devonian twang. 'Subtitle: *The Perils of Perissodactyla.*'

'Of what?' Vic shook her head. 'And not St Lucia this time? I kind of thought *Mr Pigeons and the Perilous Pitons* had a certain ring to it.'

'Very good, very good. Maybe that *should* be the next one. No. I think I need to keep his detective work on our hallowed turf for consistency, for now at least. The Waterloo clock murder went down a storm. Reached five thousand in the *Detective Tales* chart this time.'

'That's great. Hmm, so, I understand him detecting in cities like Glasgow and London, but do any major crimes actually happen in Devon?'

'Oh, dear girl, Agatha Christie will be turning in her grave at that preposterous comment.'

'Oh shit, yes. Silly me.' With her portfolio case gripped tightly to her, Vic shimmied her way through a group of people who were milling around outside the twenty-four-hour café where she had confessed all to her girls. It made her think back to that fateful night with Danny, seven months ago now. How time had flown. And how things had changed since then. And how ironic that what had happened then – the worst thing that had ever happened to her – was now leading her to potentially fulfilling one of her dreams of exhibiting her work in a real-life gallery. Granted it wasn't her own place, but... one step at a time...

'Are you there? Sounds awfully noisy.' Jerico jolted her out of her thoughts.

'Yes, yes. Just thinking it would probably be easier to meet you in person for the brief, rather than you doing it over the phone, but I'm staying in Windsor with my mum for the rest of this week.'

'Really? That's perfect. I'd rather not travel into town either, to be honest.' The author was back in his posh southern accent now.

'Oh, I assumed you were London-based.' Vic stopped on the corner of the road that led down to Danny's gallery. She tilted her face to the sky and took in the sun's warming spring rays. Just seeing the ocean spread out in front of her lifted her soul. A relaxed smile crossed her lips.

'One must never assume, for it makes an ass out of you and me.' Jerico continued without taking a breath, 'Anyway, how about this Friday coming? Say, midday? And I know exactly the place to meet you, Queen Victoria.'

'Go on.' Vic checked her watch and grimaced. She had five minutes until she'd said she'd be at Danny's and she hated being late. But she also loved the banter of this crazy man. whom she had found so attractive since their first meeting, and who now stirred up a maelstrom of feelings within her every time they spoke.

'At your namesake's statue, near the castle.'

'Sounds good to me. I've got to run, Jerico. See you at the bottom of Queen Victoria.'

Jerico laughed.

'And I'll bring my sketch pad,' Vic sang.

'Fabulous. Toodlepip!' And he was gone.

Vic realised that she was laughing again – something she hadn't done in a long while.

Danny Miller Arts was a smart and trendy outfit, set back from the seafront in the busy Brighton Lanes. As Vic approached, she noticed that the gallery had a large, curved front window, where one large, dramatic watercolour was currently displayed in pride of place. Abstract statues sat either side, on plinths of differing heights. A piece of interestingly shaped driftwood was displayed below, to frame the look. She had been so drunk the night they had staggered up to the flat above the gallery that it was as if she was seeing it all for the very first time.

Danny greeted her with a kiss and immediately offered a whirlwind tour of the premises. The walls of the gallery were painted a stark white, hung with original framed watercolours, acrylics and prints of varying sizes and prices – some still-life pencil drawings, a variety of coastal views and portraits depicting the Brighton of old and today. He informed her that local artists regularly supplied the gallery, mostly with colourful seascapes. A stylish touch was provided in the body of the shop by smart black easels, each holding a white-framed, limited-edition print. To the rear of the shop was a curved white counter, behind which a hallway led off to a discreet kitchenette, a toilet, a compact storeroom and another back room that had been converted into an art studio. On top of the counter was a small display stand of hand-painted greetings cards.

'Victoria Sharpe, I am literally blown away.' Danny Miller stood back and admired her paintings, which he had set up on easels in his back studio.

Vic could feel her whole body tingle with pride and excitement.

'Really?'

'Your seascapes are something else. The way you capture the light on the water and your use of colour on the riverboats in this one.' He pointed to one that included Jake's boat on the Thames at Windsor. 'You're a great artist, Vic.' He had excitement in his voice. 'Show me the smaller ones in there, too, please.'

Vic went to her case and reached for the book cover sketches she had worked on for Jerico and handed him a couple.

'Wow, the girl does people, too. And look at those hands. I find hands so hard to paint well, and you've really nailed it here.'

Vic thought she would burst with pride. 'Looking at the quality of the artists you have out front in the gallery, I don't know what to say.'

'You don't have to say anything, Vic, but please know your worth. Don't be giving any of this work away, now, will you?' He looked at one more painting in her case. 'Why's this one still in here?'

'Umm. I'm not sure about it. You like the others – let's just leave it at that.' Vic went to shut the case.

'I'm intrigued now. Show me. There's no right or wrong with art – you know that.'

Vic reluctantly lifted out the large picture. Danny immediately took it and placed it in front of one of her seascapes on an easel. They both then stared at the colourful, dynamic piece in front of them. Danny was in awe. Vic thought it looked more vibrant somehow in this setting than when it was sitting on the easel in her kitchen in Wandsworth.

It was certainly very different from all the other work she had shown Danny. A completely abstract piece. At the centre, a burst of fiery orange and deep red radiated out in what looked like swirling waves. Surrounding the intense core were softer hues of lavender and sky-blue strokes suggesting a reflective calm body of water.

Vic broke the silence. 'I painted it last week.'

Danny suddenly kissed her on the cheek. He had tears in his eyes. He moved away to stare at it again. 'It's dynamic and emotive. It's chaos and tranquillity, all rolled into one. It invites multiple interpretations. I absolutely love it!'

Vic promptly burst into tears.

'Darling girl, what's the matter?'

'They are happy tears. Honestly. I got back from my recent hospital appointment and suddenly I was taken over by an urge to drop everything else and just paint. I know you get that.'

'I really do.' Danny's eyes were shining.

'I feel that this painting is me now,' Vic enthused. 'And you could say the fire within is the virus, but also I think it's my core. It's my energy to make something of myself and use my creativity. The blue I feel is the love emanating from the people around me who really do care.' Vic laughed. 'And maybe even an element of peace, which sounds so fucked up, considering.'

'I get that too. I'm so happy for you.' Vic could tell Danny really meant it. 'Do you think this could be a new style you work with moving forward?'

'I don't know. I enjoyed being so free with it.'

'See what comes out of you, eh? But for now, I would like to make you an offer that you hopefully can't refuse.'

. . .

The bright orange orb of the sun was slowly slipping down on the horizon as the pair of them sat cross-legged on the shingle beach.

'Our bodies are supposed to be temples, Danny Miller.' Vic finished up her plastic glass of wine and hiccupped. 'Dr Anna will be furious.'

Danny smiled. 'Dr Anna need never know, and we're celebrating you being a celebrated artist in Brighton from July, aren't we?'

'I am so excited. To be exhibiting in an actual gallery. It is like a dream come true for me.'

'And me, now I've seen what you can do. And I'm so glad the timing fits with you.'

'Summer is perfect. I will have other work to do for Ray before that, but it will still give me time to create some new masterpieces. Are you sure it's OK to leave my portfolio at yours until then?'

'Of course. It makes sense. Shall we go and get another bottle, or not?' Danny lit a cigarette and offered her his packet.

Vic shook her head. 'That's something I really must say no to from now on.' She let out a contented sigh. 'I was intending to get home tonight. Shit. Actually, I forgot, I'm going back to Windsor tonight, so I'd better check the train times.' She burped. 'Oh my God, excuse me.'

'Intention requires action, Victoria Sharpe.'

'Then, no, I don't want more wine, thank you very much, but how about we walk along the beach towards the train station, to try and get me nearer home at least?'

They linked arms as they walked and talked. 'It's certainly warmer than the last time we did this,' Vic offered.

'Yes, that wild weather literally signified how we were both feeling that day.'

'I know it hasn't been that long, but you were right about time lessening the blow.'

'Yes,' Danny confirmed. 'And it sounds like you're coping much better now.'

'Yeah, now the actual shock is over, I am. And because I'm not taking medication yet, I guess the only life change at the moment is that I go for my regular checks at the hospital. I feel fine in myself.'

'Yes, me too. I totally get that. So you and Nate are definitely over, then?'

'Yes. It looks that way. He does text every so often to see how I am, but that's it. He's up in the Lakes now, and sounds like he's living his best life.'

'Silly question maybe, but do you miss him?'

'I don't know if I miss him, or the company of someone, to be honest. What I do miss is being held. I think bear hugs are very underrated. Just that human touch we all need, especially when we're feeling a bit fragile.' Vic felt herself unexpectedly well up, and she cast around for a change of subject. 'I forgot to say, I went to an HIV drop-in centre.'

'Oh really? How was it?'

'A woman there implied that everything happens for a reason, but...' Vic blew out her lips. 'We can all grab at straws to make us feel better, can't we?'

Danny took her hand and squeezed it, the approaching darkness and rhythmic noise of the sea washing its way up the beach giving them both space for thought. 'I'm not into going to those places, to be honest. I don't really want to talk about it with strangers. That's why I'm so happy to have you in my life.'

'Aww, yes, I do hear you. It was nerve-wracking knocking on the door, and then I just met a support worker, who was lovely. No one else had arrived, so I had a chat with her, then left. I wasn't sure if I was ready to open up to a group of strangers but it felt like a comfortable and safe environment.

And I would go again, if I felt the need to. Enough free condoms to make a life raft, too.'

'So remind me, Vic, who have you told now?'

'Nate, of course, and my two best friends, Orla and Mandy – although they found out by accident, really – and my boss. And they've all been great. But they don't understand everything – not like you do.'

'So, not your family?'

'No.' Vic sighed. 'I don't want to worry them.'

'And dare I ask if there are any new men on the horizon?' Danny asked quietly.

'God, no. I'm not ready for that yet. Maybe not ever, the way I feel at the moment. You?'

'Well...'

Vic let out a little gasp. 'Wow, go on.'

'I have met someone, yes. Philip. He's great. A session musician, which is pretty cool. So he's around enough to keep me interested but not so much that he gets under my feet. I felt comfortable enough with him to be honest from the start and he seems to really like me for me. He is fully aware of the situation, so we are getting to know each other and having fun.'

'Aww, that's amazing – and no wonder you've been busy!'

'I will *always* have time for you, though, Vic, and it is early days but I feel good and, to be honest, I can't believe how easy it was to tell him.'

'I do think telling a hetero man will be so different to telling a gay or bi man. It's kind of... just different, I think. HIV has been around in your world for so much longer – or maybe it's just me and my own lack of exposure and awareness to it, I guess.'

'I think you're overthinking it, Vic. Of course it's going to be hard and frightening to tell anyone but if that someone is decent and emotionally aware, they will be straight with you. My advice would be, a couple of dates in, if you like them, then throw it out there. It's their loss if they can't see what kind of amazing person is in front of them.'

'You make it all sound so damn easy, Danny Miller.' Vic sighed deeply. 'I feel *dirty*. And I know I shouldn't, but that is how I feel. And what if they're really horrible to me? I don't know how I'd cope.'

'You, my lovely girl, are not dirty. In fact, you are possibly one of the most fragrant women I've ever slept with. Saying that, I've only slept with you and one other.'

They both laughed. Then Danny stopped walking. Small waves crashed against the shoreline, the moon now highlighing its twinkly path across the infinite ocean. 'Come here, you.' The handsome blond pulled Vic towards him and, wrapping his toned arms around her, held her closely to his chest. 'Is that tight enough, madam?'

'No. Tighter.' Vic exaggerated her grip around Danny's back, then nuzzled her face into his neck and breathed slowly and deeply. After what seemed like an age, and only when she felt fully hugged, did she pull away.

'I so, so needed that. Thank you, so much.'

'There's lots more where that came from, my little painter girl. And you'll be here for the summer, so you can claim as many of them as you want.'

It was gone midnight when Victoria arrived back in Windsor. She'd really enjoyed seeing Danny, and even without his amazing hugs, she had felt held by him. He had been and continued to be her constant support through everything, and for that she was truly grateful.

The brisk walk from the train station had woken her up slightly but she certainly felt ready for her bed as she turned the corner into Simpson Crescent.

She was just reaching in her handbag for her door key when

she noticed Joti's outside light come on, then a figure strolling down the path, then on towards a van parked on the opposite side of the road to where Vic was walking.

Nosily wondering what her mum's neighbour was up to at this time of night on a Tuesday, she hurriedly walked as near to the back of the van as she could, then wished she hadn't. For there, sitting in the driver's seat with a contented look on his face, and rolling a cigarette, was her Albie. She tapped on the passenger window, causing him to nearly jump out of his skin.

She lowered her head to talk. 'You all right, bro?'

As the window went down, she clocked his 'guilty face' immediately. 'Jesus, sis, you scared the shit out of me. What are you doing?'

'I think it's me who should be asking you that question, don't you?'

Albie bit his lip, then lit the cigarette, forcing his sister to go first.

'Well, I've been to Brighton to see a mate.'

'Nice. I'm heading home now myself, so let's catch up soon, all right?'

'Is Mum OK?' Inspector Sharpe wasn't letting this go.

'Yeah, yeah. I've er... just been helping Joti. Umm... she had a problem with her stop cock.' He couldn't stop himself from laughing, which set Vic off too. 'Look, it's not what it looks like.'

'Is it ever?' Vic smirked.

'She seemed upset. I comforted her.'

'I bet you did. And where does Lisa fit into all this?'

'Not now, sis, I've got to get home. She thinks I was having dinner with Mum, and it's really late. You won't say anything, will you? Like... to anyone, I mean.'

'If you can't trust your blood, then who can you trust, really?' Vic blew him a kiss through the open window.

Albie looked her directly in the eyes. 'Ditto, Vic, ditto. And, I really mean that, OK? I love you, Vic.'

'Blimey, you must be feeling guilty.'

After waving her errant brother off, Vic tiptoed through the hall so as not to wake Chandler, who was on his bed in the lounge, then headed to the kitchen to get herself a glass of water. She laughed to herself at the scenario. Despite Joti stating that she wanted to be forever single, she clearly needed comfort. Albie was without doubt a chip off the old block, but despite all her misgivings, he was still her brother and she loved him with all her heart.

TWENTY-FOUR

WINDSOR

The 'Date'

Three days later, Victoria popped her sketchpad, a couple of pencils and an eraser into her bag, then shouted goodbye to her mum, who was digging a small vegetable patch in the back garden, to Chandler's delight. She made her way down the path and towards the town centre.

The Windsor streets were teeming with tourists, who were not only making the most of the spring weather, but also checking out the various market stall-holders, who were exuberantly selling their wares along the centre of Peascod Street.

Victoria carried on walking past the delicious-smelling sausage stall, and smiled at the confectionery stall, with happy memories of going with her mum and Albie to Ferry Lane Market when they used to holiday in Cornwall with her gran and grandad, and where they would get their penny chews. She had always been a Fruit Salad girl, whereas Albie loved the Black Jacks that left a dark, liquoricey stain on his tongue.

Checking her watch, Vic was happy to see that she still had half an hour before she was to meet Jerico. She needed to buy

Mandy a birthday gift, and on entering Marks and Spencer, she noticed that they had moved the underwear section to the front. She loved good underwear, and Nate had loved her wearing it. A memory of her prancing around the bedroom drunk as a skunk one Valentine's night in a sexy red lace ensemble, suspenders included, then tripping over the hairdryer and stubbing her toe on the bed leg and ruining the moment, caused her to smile to herself.

She walked towards a mannequin dressed in a beautiful, white-silk balcony bra and matching panties. As she felt the material between her fingers, a huge wave of sadness engulfed her. How could she ever feel sexy again, now? The constant fear of telling someone, if she hadn't already, would be there, plus the fear of passing on the virus, or the doubts about what the other person might be thinking about her, even if they had taken it all on board.

In fact, would anyone ever find her sexy or attractive again?

Overcome with emotion, she aborted her present-buying mission. Keen to compose herself before meeting Jerico, she walked back down the street, engineering a loop through the King Edward Court shopping centre so she could get some sun on her face and try to clear her mind of this negativity.

Arriving early at the castle, she was amazed that she managed to get a space to sit on a bench near the impressive statue where they were to meet. She was just scrabbling around in her bag in panic because she thought she had forgotten her shiny new Nokia 8800, which was still a novelty to her, as it had so many different features, when a familiar voice greeted her.

'So, my real life Queen Victoria – what kind of adventure shall we have today, then?'

Startled, Vic grinned, then stood up to an enthusiastic kiss on both cheeks from the handsome author, which caused her to flush slightly.

She noticed that Jerico Flint was a man who wore his long

beige shorts with the effortless style of a European. His predominantly green, patterned shirt brought out the emerald of his eyes, and his khaki-coloured fedora made him look like some kind of unassuming movie star. In fact, she saw a couple of Japanese tourists giving him a second look, as if they were wondering about him. Maybe they could sense the Vince Vaughn vibes, too, or had caught the same delicious whiff of expensive-smelling sandalwood aftershave that had just reached her on the breeze.

'I've always wanted to meet someone here,' Jerico enthused. 'A bit like meeting someone under the Waterloo clock – it holds an element of mystery and romance, doesn't it?'

Vic laughed and took on a dramatic tone. 'Maybe pass on the Pitons then, for I have a new title for you. Once your donkeys are done with, of course.' She raised her voice slightly. 'I can see it now, *Mr Pigeons and the Queen Victoria Statue.*'

'Love it already.' Jerico threw his arms out wide. 'An eccentric author meets a mysterious artist and they find themselves solving a murder that takes place in the chapel within Windsor Castle.'

'As long as you're not murdering me, then fine.'

'*Au contraire*, dear girl, *au contraire*. Also, this is quite the statue. I had a little read-up about it last night. Did you know that it's made of bronze and was erected in 1887 to mark the great monarch's Golden Jubilee? The cost of it was covered by subcriptions from the people of Windsor and surrounding districts.'

'A generous lot, us Windsorians, clearly. I didn't know that, and I guess I really should, considering I was born here. And isn't that always the way? I've only ever been around the castle twice, too.'

'Are you hungry?' Jerico suddenly enquired, above the babble of a group of Chinese tourists who had appeared out of nowhere and started taking photos of the statue and the castle walls.

'I can be.' Vic smiled. 'There are loads of places to eat around here.'

'No, dear girl. I have taken the liberty of bringing us a picnic. We have a river and sunshine – why on earth would we want to sit inside with the stinking masses when we can be outside with nature?'

'That backpack is like Doctor Who's TARDIS,' Vic laughed as Jerico pulled out a blanket, a bottle of wine in a clear chiller pack, plastic glasses and various Tupperware containers. They had managed to find a quietish area of riverbank down near her favourite bench. With swans for company and boats quietly meandering their way up and down the river, it really was quite idyllic. They sat down with their legs out straight towards the river bank.

'I can't take credit for anything, I'm afraid. The sausage rolls, mini quiches, mini pizzas and egg custard tarts are all from the posh deli near where I live.' Jerico started to lay out all the goodies between them.

'Which is where, exactly?' Vic quizzed.

'Bray, and that's not a command for your best donkey impression.'

Vic laughed. 'Very posh.' She raised an eyebrow. 'Other than you living in a fancy village not far from here, all I know is that you write books about murders and dress like somebody out of a Dickension novel.' She cocked her head. 'No spectacles today, I see. Or maybe you are going to bring out a monacle in a minute?' She smirked.

Jerico remained deadpan. 'They are purely for show, but isn't everything we wear on the outside, including ourselves? For show, I mean.'

'Perhaps,' Vic said, eyeing up the delicious-looking food as Jerico snapped the lids off the plastic tubs. 'Oh, and also I heard that your dog died. I'm so sorry to hear that.'

Jerico suddenly looked intently at Vic with his deep emerald eyes, which she realised were watering with sadness. His dark lashes were longer than hers, and she noted, with a dart of alarm, that his shoulder-length raven hair made him a ringer for Nate – just an older, wiser version. And boy, did she fancy him.

'Grief is the price we pay for loving, Queen V.' His voice became animated. 'Fat Frank was a joy. Better than any human I've ever known. I never knew to this day which mixture of breeds he was, or even how old. I found him wrapped in a blanket in a bus shelter one Christmas Eve. A label around his neck said, "Please love me like I deserve to be loved".'

'Aww.' Thinking maybe she should try that for herself, Victoria put her hand to her heart.

'Yes, my little boy. He had a bark as deep as Frank Bruno's voice, hated exercise and I overfed him. But despite him being overweight, he lived a long and happy life, so put that in your healthy-living pipes, everyone. Maybe that's the answer, Queen V: that happiness and dog treats are the key to longevity.'

'I'll stick with sausage rolls, for now.' She wiped her mouth free of flaky pastry. 'These are delicious.'

'I really appreciate you meeting me today. I feel I'm on a writing roll. In fact, I think grief has turned me into a literary demon. I knocked this one out in three months. It's with the editor – hence me having this delectable breathing space.'

'Yes, I umm... I needed some breathing space earlier in the year too.' The ever-wise Jerico gave her silence to expand if she wanted to. There was something about his expression and his manner that made it easy to open up to him; he felt safe. 'Had a bit going on myself. I split from my fella of six years. It's been tough.' She sighed and suddenly spiralled into her thoughts.

Should she tell him the real reason? Was Jerico Flint someone she could just could divulge her diagnosis to? She hardly knew him. And was this what her life was going to be like from now on? Was she supposed to live a lie, and in fear of how people would react if she did want to be honest? But why did he need to know, anyway? Their relationship wouldn't change if he didn't know. And maybe it wouldn't if he did. But she liked him and didn't want his thoughts of her to be any different to what they were now.

Maybe, when the shock of it all had passed and she had got used to living with the virus, then these thoughts wouldn't even cross her mind. So what? She had HIV. But it *did* matter. What if she were to cut herself badly, like she had done during the Albie debacle on Christmas Eve? Then, out of respect, he would need to know.

Jerico put his hand on hers. 'I'm sorry you're going through a difficult time. And who is this fool to let such a beautiful creature go? I've a good mind to set Mr Pigeons on him.'

Despite Vic's breath hitching at his touch, she was brusque in her delivery. 'I don't want to talk about it anymore.' Then more softly, 'If you don't mind.'

'Of course not.' Jerico refilled her plastic glass. 'Cheers.' He held his glass to hers.

Vic's mind darted elsewhere. 'I love the Vettriano book you gave me – thanks again. I haven't read the text yet – just flicked through the paintings – amazing. And... how thoughtful of you to remember that I liked him.'

'Rarely happens – that level of thoughfulness on my part, that is – so make the most of it.'

When Jerico laughed and the skin around his eyes crinkled, he looked even more attractive, Vic thought. He had lips that would give Mick Jagger a run for his money, too. Full and kissable. She suddenly had an image of them pushed against her own well-defined ones, today coated with a slick of peach lip gloss. They both shared the same thick, dark wavy hair, too. They would have made beautiful babies, she thought sadly.

Vic took a sip of wine.

'So tell me about Victoria Sharpe then. Are you from around here? Are your parents still about?'

Vic took another drink. 'Yes, born in Windsor and I guess I have to thank them for my path to creativity.'

'You don't sound very enthused by that.' Jerico wiped his mouth on a napkin.

'Oh, just, it wasn't always easy – a drunk mother, an absent father...' Her voice tailed off. 'It was by drawing in my room that I got through some of the darker days of my childhood.'

Jerico's voice softened. 'And out of the darkness came a beautiful light.'

Vic was sure she actually felt her heart flutter.

The ebullient man drained his glass. 'It's really quite divine here today, isn't it? We needed this sunshine.'

'I've just realised you said you wrote a book in three months, but last time we met you mentioned that you wanted to write full-time, so how on earth do you find time to work?'

'If you have the will, you will find a way, my dear.'

'Wow, you must never sleep. What do you do for work, anyway?'

'Oh, a bit of this and a bit of that, mainly for charities. Anyway, enough about me – we need to talk about Mr Pigeons.'

Once they had agreed on a sketch for the new cover, hours passed in what seemed like a matter of minutes, with fun, easy chat and banter. Until Jerico suddenly checked his watch and started furiously packing his rucksack with the empty plastic containers. 'Shit, I'm late. Shit. I'm really late. I have to go. I need to be somewhere. Shit, shit, shit!' He shoved a piece of chewing gum into his mouth. 'I can get to Slough on the train from here, can't I?'

'Yes, yes, it's just six minutes from the central station.'

In his haste to jump up, they bumped heads. And then Vic found Jerico awkwardly pulling her up towards him, and then he was cupping her chin in his hand and then looking right at her. Then without inhibition, they were kissing. Clumsy at first, and then curious, passionate, meaningful. Lost in the moment, not caring, or knowing who or what was around them, until, 'Shit, I'm sorry, Vic, so sorry. I really do have to go.'

With his rucksack on his back, Jerico Flint careered off to the station, leaving Vic standing looking out over the river, feeling like she had literally just had her socks blown off. A lone swan appeared on the bank next to her and she burst into tears.

Jake was smoking a cigarette, Norman sunbathing quietly at his feet, when Vic appeared on deck, sobbing her heart out. Ignoring the annoyed bark from Norman for the interruption, Jake butted his cigarette and stretched his arms out wide to her.

'Victoria, sweetheart.' He ushered her inside and onto an armchair. A cool breeze rushed through the boat. 'You sit down there. I'll make you a nice cup of tea.'

Vic, slightly drunk from the half bottle of wine she had just consumed on the riverbank, began to gabble. 'I kissed him, and I liked it, but I can never be with him. It's not fair.'

'Slow down – what's not fair? Who have you been kissing?' Jake put a mug down on a side table. 'And have you been drinking?'

'You judge me, too; that's right. You're all the same. I'm going.' She went to get up, but Jake put a firm but gentle hand on her shoulder.

'Victoria, stop. I judge no one – you should know that by now. All I care about is if you are OK. And you don't have to tell me anything, but I'm not letting you leave this boat until you've calmed down. All right?'

'OK,' Victoria said, her voice small. Jake handed her a piece of kitchen towel and she blew her nose noisily. 'It's fine. You wouldn't understand, anyway.'

'What, an old man like me, you mean?' He cocked his head to the side. 'You know damn well from our chat the other day, I've loved and lost along with the best of them. Age is a number, Vic, and never forget that. And with age, comes sage – well, sometimes.' Jake smiled.

'I think I may have found my "diamond love",' Vic whispered.

'Really?' Jake took an intake of breath and sat down on the other armchair.

'Exactly.' Vic sniffed. 'I've known him literally five minutes, but he makes me feel alive and attractive and cared for all at the same time. But there's no way I can be with him.'

'Why?' Norman came running in and plonked himself down at their feet.

'If I tell you something – and I know this is a big ask – will you promise not to tell my mum?' Victoria realised she sounded like she was eight years old again and had just run inside the galley kitchen to sneak a glass of cold orange squash.

Jake nodded and put his hand on top of hers. 'I promise.'

'I've just been diagnosed as HIV-positive.'

Saying nothing, he squeezed her hand. After a moment he said, 'I'm grateful you feel you know you can trust me enough to tell me.'

'You don't seem shocked.' Vic screwed up her face. 'It's like you knew already.'

Jake got up and went to the kitchen, so she couldn't read his face. 'Nothing shocks me, Victoria. Not anymore. How are you feeling?'

'I'm fine physically, just struggling with it mentally.'

Jake came back to face her. 'Do you want to talk about it?'

His face was open and kind. Vic felt a warmth emanate from him that gave her the urge to hug him. Instead: 'No, no,

I'm all talked out. I'm more bothered as to why would Jerico... that's his name, by the way.'

'And a mighty fine name, at that!' Jake enthused. 'And the phantom weekday kisser, I take it?'

'Yeah.' Vic smiled. 'Why would he want me once he knows I've got this?'

'Because, like everybody else who knows you, he may just see the amazing person that you are. Kind, capable, loving, creative, fun... Need I go on? Or, on the other hand, he might not.'

'Oh. Thanks for that.' Vic shook her head.

'See what you did there? You homed directly in on the negative. We don't know what other people are thinking, Victoria. We can make up all sorts of things in our head about what they might be, but until we communicate with someone, it's all our own fabrication. You will do what you will do, whatever anyone else says. But all I can say is, if it is a "diamond love", then maybe, just maybe, it is worth taking that chance on.'

At that moment, Vic's phone rang. 'Who's that?' she groaned. Then, on seeing it was Nate, groaned again. 'Oh, God, I'm so not in the mood for a Nate chat.' She took a drink of tea. 'Whilst we are on difficult subjects, I need to talk to you about something else. Something really serious.'

Jake sat down again. 'That sounds ominous, but before that, do you want to talk more about what's going on with you?'

'No. No, I don't.' Vic ran her hands through her hair. 'This is so hard to tell you. And I'm not sure if it is even the right thing to be doing.'

'Harder than telling me what you just did? Surely not. Come on, Vic. Like I say, nothing shocks me.'

'Malini received your letter.'

Jake's hand began to shake. He sat down and put his hand to his head. 'How on earth do you know this?'

'She was driving to the airport to fly to England to find you, with her two-year-old little girl in the car, and was killed instantly in a car crash.' A look of complete horror swept over his face. 'She never stopped loving you, Jake.' Vic had tears pouring down her face now.

'And her daughter?' Jake whispered.

'She survived... And this is the hardest bit to tell you,' Vic stuttered. 'The woman I was walking along here with the other day – I think she's the little girl who was in the car. I think she could be your daughter, Jake.'

Jake took a huge intake of breath. 'How do you know her?'

'Her name is Joti. She's Mum's neighbour. She showed me a letter from the man she had always thought was her real dad. After his death he wanted her to find you so she was not alone in this world. He selfishly didn't tell her before he passed, as he lived in Australia and was scared he would lose her, because she used to go home and visit him and his new wife every year, without fail.

'This is all so meant to be, because if you hadn't told me your story the other day, I never would have known.'

'Did you say you knew me?'

'No. No, I wanted to talk to you first.'

Jake gripped Vic's hand again. 'You don't know what this means to me. I could die right now and be the happiest man alive. I can't believe Malini has been dead all these years, though.' He let out a wracking sob. 'And it's all my fault.'

'No, Jake. No. It's not. She chose to leave you and marry someone else.'

'Yes, but only because nobody could have lived with me at that time. She did what was right for her child... our child.'

'But clearly not what was right for her – as when the time was right she felt that she had to come to you. It's so romantic and so sad, all at the same time. And don't you ever be blaming yourself again, Jake Turner. She experienced a great love with you – like no other – and Joti has grown into the most amazing woman. She's a nurse and is the kindest, wisest person. Your Malini shines through her.'

'To think I could have bumped into her when I went to your mum's.'

'You went to Mum's?'

'Yeah. I, er... I knew you were struggling around her drinking. I think the world of both of you kids and her... and... I umm... wanted to make sure you had a decent Christmas. Your mother told me what you both liked, so I got the food shopping.'

'And the bed?'

'Yes, that was me too. Your mum was out of it. I took it apart and sorted it for her. She thanked me, but I could have been the milkman for all she knew.'

'Oh, Jake, you've gone beyond the realms of friendship. Thank you, thank you so much.'

'And, Victoria, there's something else that you should...' Jake stopped himself short. His brow furrowed as if deep in thought.

'Yes, what is it, Jake? Say it.' From his face she could tell he had said too much already.

'Umm, nothing. It's fine, it can wait...' Jake shuffled in his chair. 'But how do I work this, Vic? I have to see Joti. We must talk.'

'I've said enough, and it's over to you on this one, I think. Rather than me playing matchmaker, you know where she lives.'

'Yes, you're right. I have to deal with this in my own way.'

The Proposal

Victoria arrived back at Simpson Crescent to raised voices and a barking Chandler.

She walked in to find Albie and Kath eye to eye across the kitchen table.

'What's going on?'

'Albie wants to move back in because Lisa has chucked him out.' She gestured angrily towards Albie. 'I knew your flipping gambling would cause this. I'm just getting myself together, then you and your sister want to move back in – and I refuse to pick up the pieces this time.'

'Don't bloody start on me, thanks very much.' Vic shook her head in disbelief.

'It's not my gambling, Mum, I promise you.' Albie's voice stayed on a level.

Kath Sharpe sighed. 'So tell me, you couldn't keep your dick in your trousers – was that it?'

Vic winced at her mother's choice of words. 'Mother, really, do you have to?'

'Yes I do – you'd be the first to slag your father off about his philandering.'

'But we are talking about Albie now and none of this has got anything to do with me.' Vic's voice was raised.

'So what *is* going on then, lad?' Kath spat.

'Who says that we haven't just fallen out of love?' Albie shifted from foot to foot.

'Because you're Barry Sharpe's son, that's why. God, I need a drink!' Kath suddenly exclaimed.

'No, you don't!' Albie and Victoria shouted in unison, as there was a light knock at the door, followed by a 'Hello'.

'Who the hell is that now?' Kath Sharpe grabbed the kettle off the side and started to fill it.

Joti appeared in the kitchen. 'The door was open, so I hope you don't mind.'

'Sorry about all the shouting, love,' Kath said, visibly attempting to calm down as she put teabags into mugs with a shaking hand. 'Fancy a cuppa?'

'What shouting?' Joti convincingly lied. 'And thanks, but no thanks. I'm on nights. I need to get a nap in this afternoon, or I'll be a walking zombie. I did want to talk to you, though. I'm er... thinking of getting a lodger. Where do you think would be a good place to advertise?'

Luckily only Vic, and not her mother, saw Joti's sneaky wink to a now-smirking Albie.

'Maybe I can save you the trouble, Miss Adams,' Albie flirted. 'As it happens, I'm looking for a place myself.'

'Oh. OK. Really? Erm... brilliant. Message me later. I'll be up again around six. Bye for now.' A pink-faced Joti let herself out.

'Oh, so you *don't* want to live here now, then?' Kath Sharpe snapped, once Joti was out of earshot.

'Women!' Albie exclaimed, heading out of the back door for a cigarette.

Kath shut the door behind him and breathed a sigh of relief. She had just sat down opposite Vic when the doorbell rang.

'Jesus, it's like bleeding Clapham Junction around here,' Kath huffed.

Vic went to the door and, on seeing who it was, her mouth fell to the floor.

'Nate! What are you doing here?'

Though comforted by his presence, Victoria thought it odd that Nate would reach for her hand as they entered the Long Walk, near the castle gates. They began to walk down the famous straight road, flanked on either side by grassy areas where families and tourists alike were chatting, playing games, sunbathing, or picnicking on the Queen's famous carriageway.

'Please pick up when I call you, or reply to my messages. You scare the life out of me, Vic. When I don't hear back from you, I think – well, I think... maybe...'

Nate pushed back his messy fringe and looked at Vic through puppy-dog eyes. His uniform of distressed jeans and Oasis T-shirt were achingly familiar.

'Nate, I've just been busy. Sorry. And I'm not just going to drop down dead. It's fine. I'm being looked after, well and close-ly.' Vic pulled her hand away. 'I wish you'd bloody educate yourself.'

'I didn't mean that. I'm just worried about you in general. Are you feeling all right?'

'Apart from being a complete mental wreck, then yes. I am starting to get my head around it, as I have to. Because whatever is going on inside this body of mine, I am still Victoria Sharpe.'

'The one and only.' Nate smiled. 'I'm so sorry I left you like I did.' He sounded sincere.

'Yes, well... You did what you felt was right for you and I'm sorry, too, that I put you in a position where you could have been in the same situation as me.'

'You didn't know, Vic.'

'But I still slept with someone else, Nate, and that wasn't my finest hour.'

'We both obviously had shit to sort out, which we didn't face.' Nate pulled a can of lager out of his rucksack. 'Do you want one?'

'No, thanks.' Vic sighed. 'Why are you down here anyway? Don't tell me you've left the job already. You said it was good in one of your texts.'

'One of the texts you ignored, you mean.'

'No need to keep on.' Vic wasn't quite sure she could take much more today. It was only a few hours ago that she had been lip to lip with Jerico, and so much had happened since.

'I wanted to talk to you face to face. I was a coward. Six years is a long time, Vic. We've shared a lot and I miss you.'

'I miss you too,' Vic replied quietly.

'I think you'd love it where I am in the Lakes. I'm staying in this beautiful little cottage, surrounded by the most stunning countryside. All paid for by the mansion house owners. And my day consists of making a lunch and dinner for whoever is in the house, just five days a week. Plus, looking after the grounds, and you know how much I enjoy being outside.' Nate was on a roll now. 'There's a decent town just fifteen minutes away – and all the food produce and the air just seems fresher somehow. I love it up there.'

'It's good to hear you sounding so happy.' And Vic meant it.

'But it's not the same without you.' Nate took her hand again. 'Come back with me, Vic. I can set the spare room up as a studio. There are so many gorgeous places where you could paint. I will do anything to help you find your way. You won't have to pay rent and I get my food, too. We will manage until you are on your feet.'

Tears sprang into Vic's eyes. 'And what about my hospital visits? I'm all set up in London now, and I want to stay that way whilst it's all so new.'

'You can travel down for those. You'll want to see your family and friends, too, I guess, so you can combine it.'

'You've thought of everything.' Vic blew out loudly.

'I have. There's not a day goes by that I don't think of you. Sometimes I think I even see you in the street or hear your laugh, and my heart leaps a little bit. And as the old adage says, your absence really has made my heart grow fonder.'

'Well, this is taking a turn,' Vic said aloud. It had been shock enough Nate just turning up unannounced, let alone turning into Saint bloody Valentine. And his previous messages had given no clue that he was feeling this way – but that was Nate all over. A bag of free and reckless wonder.

'I want to be with you, Vic. I've never been so sure of anything in my whole life.' He led her off the path and onto the grass. 'Let's sit.'

They sat next to each other in silence. Legs stretched out, their thighs touching.

Nate's closeness made her immediately think of Jerico. The sexy author sparked her mentally. He had a huge presence. He was a joy to be around. He had made her heart beat extremely fast when he had kissed her earlier. She thought he might be her 'diamond love'. But Nate was her Nate. They had shared the reality of life, had lived together, slept together, left the bathroom door open in front of each other and he'd even held her hair back on the few occasions she'd been sick. It may have been messy a lot of the time, but whatever it was, it had been real.

A 'diamond love' was all anyone could aspire to. What Jake and Malini had did sound magical. But even so, it had still crumbled in the face of his addiction. Maybe that level of desire was just too intense ever to last?

Vic looked directly into Nathaniel Carlisle's brooding

brown eyes. He was offering her his heart and soul. It would be so easy to walk back into his life now. Being able to make love to him and not have to worry about telling him what was wrong. She automatically picked up his hand and kissed it.

'Please say yes, Vic. Sort out what you need to here and I'll be waiting for you. I know it will take work, but we can do this.'

Tears of past hurt and regret began to fall slowly down Vic's cheeks, and instead of a flat no, the words, 'I'm not sure,' flew right out of her mouth and into the sunshine.

'I'll take an unsure over a no, any day.' Nate wiped Vic's tears away with his thumb.

She managed a smile. 'I'm just starting to get back on my feet again.'

'I get that it's a big decision. But I promise you, I will make it so worth it. No rush. I'll be waiting.'

'Don't put your life on hold for me, Nate. I'm going to be working in Brighton for the summer.'

'Oh, are you now?'

'Yes. I can't wait. Danny, well, Danny and I, we're friends, and it's nice to be around someone who totally understands what I'm going through. He's also going to exhibit my work in his gallery, so it's such a big chance for me.'

'Danny, eh,' Nate said softly under his breath, took a second to compose himself then reached for her hand. 'Do what you need to. No pressure. OK?'

'Thank you,' Vic replied. 'When are you heading back up north?'

'Shortly. I've got to work this weekend.'

'So you've done the Lake District and back in a day just to see me.' Despite herself, Vic was impressed.

Nate nodded. 'Yes, that's how serious I am, Vic. I miss you so much.' He checked his watch. 'But shit, I mustn't miss this train.'

He jumped up, threw a soft kiss on her lips, then, after

shouting back the words, 'Call me,' he was gone, leaving her standing halfway down the Long Walk.

Vic retrieved a screwed-up tissue from the bottom of her handbag and blew her nose. Why had the words 'not sure' come flying out of her mouth? She had made up her mind that it was over with Nate, but him standing there in front of her, offering his heart and soul and really seeming like he meant it, had messed with her head – and her heart. It would be so easy to revert to the factory settings of life.

But it was fine, she convinced herself. Brighton would be a new start and Nate was now an option on the backburner. And if thinking of using him as that made her a bad person, so be it, because life had thrown her one hell of a lemon and she felt justified in making lemonade wherever she could.

TWENTY-SIX

The Boss

The following week found Vic back in London, sitting opposite Ray in his glass office. Penny had already left for the school run.

'How's it all going?' Ray enquired. 'I have to say it's far too quiet in here without you.'

'To remedy that, if it's OK with you, I may still come in and work when I need to –once the flat lease is up, that is. The signal at Mum's place is so shite.'

'Of course, that's a given. You know that. Did you manage to sort out Jerico?'

'Er, yes. I'm hoping he'll be happy with this design without any alterations.' Vic reached in her bag for a brown envelope and handed it across the table.

He opened it up. 'Donkeys, eh?' Ray laughed. 'But I love that. Well done. And you've expertly drawn it in a way that makes it fit with the series.'

Vic's smile was abruptly washed off her face with Ray's next enquiry. 'So, I take it you won't be giving this to him your-self, then.' She squirmed under his knowing gaze, but didn't say anything. 'That's fine. I'll sort it' – he smiled – 'but now you have to tell me the reason why. You haven't been upsetting my clients already, have you?'

Vic felt her face twist, and Ray peered at her sternly. 'Victoria Sharpe, I know you so well. Has something happened between you two?'

Vic grimaced. 'Just a tipsy kiss.'

'How delightful.' Ray smiled.

'It kind of was, but in the cold light of day, I've realised I'm not ready even for tipsy kisses.'

Ray looked right at her. 'Is that your head or your heart telling you that?'

Vic groaned. 'I... I... er... I just can't. It's work as well, and I don't want it ever to be awkward.'

'OK.' Ray nodded wisely. 'But you don't have to worry about me in that equation. If you're happy, I'm happy – you know that. And, well, what's a few lost cover designs between friends, if it does go tits-up?'

'That's very sweet, but not forgetting, I have to tell anyone I decide to have sex with that I have HIV.'

'Lady, are you telling me you want to have sex with Jerico Flint? I mean, I don't blame you at all if you are. I'd leave Marcus for him if he was of my persuasion.'

Vic wiped some coffee froth from her mouth and chose not to answer directly. 'It will take him at least another three months to write his next book, so he won't need another cover until at least then. Oh, and just another small thing: Nate wants me back.'

'Shit.' Ray reached for the glass of water on his desk and took a swig. 'But you're surely not contemplating it?'

'Maybe better the devil you know isn't such a bad option for me. At least he knows about the diagnosis.' Vic grimaced and checked her watch. 'Sorry for the flying visit – I have to go. I'm having dinner with the girls later and I need to pop into the estate agent's first, about the inventory on the flat.'

'No worries.' Ray thought for a moment. 'And the only chink of wisdom I can offer on what you've just told me is what my old mum used to say to me, bless her dear heart. I can hear her as if it were only yesterday, and I did all right with my Marcus, so maybe you should heed it.' He began to relay in a deep Ghanaian accent: '"Raymond, don't settle for the one you can live with, wait for the one you can't live without. You hear me?"'

The Three Musketeers

May 2006

'I mean, who gets pregnancy cravings for pickled onions and lime milkshake? I bet there's not a single real lime in it, either,' Mandy ranted as the three musketeers sat in her bright and airy kitchen.

'Onions are good for you, though,' Orla said loyally.

'Poor Steve,' Vic added, looking at Orla. 'She trumps like an elephant at the best of times.'

Orla and Vic fell about laughing. Mandy shook her head. 'Children, I'm doing pizza and garlic bread for tea, if that's all right. I couldn't be bothered to mess about.'

'Perfect,' Orla declared.

'Where is Steve, anyway?' Vic popped open a bottle of wine.

'Working away tonight. Hence me actually making some kind of effort for my friends.'

Vic filled her and Orla's glass then cleared her throat. 'I've got something to tell you all.'

'That sounds ominous.' Orla took a large slug of wine. 'Are you OK?'

'Yes, yes I'm fine.' Vic smiled weakly. 'It's just, Nate has asked me to go and live with him in the Lakes. Wants us to try again, says he loves me and can't be without me.'

'Wow. OK.' Mandy took a sip of her fizzy water.

Orla jumped in. 'The same Nate who said he didn't want to be with you just a few months ago. Who turned his back on you when you really needed him?'

'I'm not going,' Vic said softly. 'I need time to think. Because also...' She sighed deeply. 'I kissed Jerico Flint.'

'Jerico Flint?' Mandy screwed her face up. 'He sounds like an actor, with a name like that.'

'He's a client of Ray's. I do illustrations for his book covers, but he actually does look like he could be on the set of a film.' Vic smiled as she thought about him. 'He's handsome and clever – so quick-witted and fun, really fun. He doesn't seem to realise just how hot he is, and I love that about him too.'

'Listen to you. I've never heard you talk about Nate like that once.' Orla topped up her own wine glass. 'And just kissed, you say?'

'Yes, just kissed. I can't be with him either, though, girls. Actually, I could, but I can't tell him. Because I really like him. And if he can't cope with the HIV then I'm scared I might lose him, and I don't want him to look at me as this tainted woman. I want him to see me as me – just Victoria; just me – without this fucking-awful time bomb of a virus.' Tears pricked Vic's eyes.

'Oh, darling.' Orla squeezed her hand. 'But what if he's totally cool about it?'

'I don't think I can bear to take that chance.'

'Well, you can just see him and not have sex with him – be friends?' Mandy suggested innocently.

'She can't,' Orla replied wisely. 'You really like him; I can tell.'

Vic nodded. 'But then there's Nate.'

'You're not in love with him, are you?' Orla sighed.

'But does that really matter?' Vic breathed out noisily. 'We could have a good life. It would be OK, and maybe OK is as good as it gets now.'

'No!' Orla banged her hand down on the table. 'Be careful not to compromise what you want long term, in favour of what you want or feel you need right now.'

'Wow, that's very profound, Orla.' Mandy got up to turn the oven on.

'My therapist actually said it to me the other day.'

'Ray said that to me as well, in so many words,' Vic added.

Orla looked smug. 'See.'

'I'm so glad you've decided to have therapy.' Vic smiled.

'Me too.' Orla bit her lip. 'Thanks to you.'

Mandy's brow furrowed. 'But, Vic, what are you going to do about Nate – or this Jerico, for that matter?'

'I know exactly what I am going to do. I'm actually taking your advice, Orla O'Malley, and I'm going to do nothing and see what comes to me, because I've also got some other big news, which is going to take up a lot of my time.'

'I feel like I need to sit down for this.' Mandy sat at the kitchen table and put her hand to her pregnancy bump.

'Well, you know how I'm working freelance for Ray now?'

'Yes,' Orla and Mandy answered in unison. Mandy suddenly looked worried. 'This will pay your rent and allow you to live, will it?'

'I will be fine. I saved a bit of my Christmas bonus and Ray gave me a decent pay rise so I've saved a bit of that, too. Plus, I will have the deposit from the flat. And, well, the other news is that I'm moving to Brighton for the summer to exhibit and sell my work at Danny's gallery. As well as still doing any bits for Ray if he needs me, of course.'

Orla was wide-eyed. 'Oh my God, mate. That's what you've always dreamt of doing.'

'Well, my own gallery would be my ultimate,' Vic replied modestly.

Mandy rushed over and threw her arms around Vic. 'Proud, so bloody proud of how far you've come with everything you've had to deal with.'

'He says in July I can have the front display window, which is saved for the big shots, usually.'

'He clearly thinks you are a big shot,' Mandy enthused.

'Maybe he feels obliged to,' replied Vic, who, despite Danny's reaction to her work, still felt she needed reassurance.

'No, of course not, Vic.' Orla was stern. 'He has a business to run; he's not going to do anyone any favours.' She went to the fridge to retrieve more wine. 'I bloody love Brighton. Are you going to be staying at his?'

'Yes, in the two-bed apartment above the gallery where it all happened that fateful night.'

'Maybe you can just have wild unattached sex with him – then you're sorted. New job, new knob, all in one go.' Orla refilled her glass then topped up Vic's.

Mandy shook her head. 'Is that even an option?'

Vic smiled. 'Me and Danny work far better as friends, and he's seeing someone now anyway.'

'See, he's done it,' Orla said knowingly. 'Found somebody pretty quickly too.'

Mandy stood up. 'Let's get these pizzas in. I'm starving, but before that, a toast to our gorgeous girl, Victoria Sharpe.' Mandy put a thimble of wine into a glass and lifted it into the air. 'Here's to Victoria having the best time and selling all her paintings in Brighton.'

'To Victoria,' Mandy and Orla said in unison.

'*One for all and all for one,*' added a now-tipsy Orla.

'*One for all and all for one,*' they all repeated.

TWENTY-EIGHT
BRIGHTON

The Gallery

July 2006

'Vic? Vic! Are you awake?'

Vic turned over in bed and groaned at the voice coming through her bedroom door. 'What time is it?' she answered sleepily.

'Just after eight thirty. I'm going out to meet a potential new artist shortly, so if you could open up the gallery today, that would be really helpful.'

Vic sat up and rubbed her eyes. 'Bloody hell. Sorry, Danny. I've had the most amazing sleep for once.'

Danny knocked lightly and poked his head around the door. 'See, I told you that the old "sea, air, sleep" mantra has something to it.'

Vic smiled and pushed her hands through her messy hair. 'Excuse the bed head. I dreamt that Robbie Williams commissioned me to illustrate an album cover for him, and he would only accept payment of a sexual nature.'

Danny laughed. 'Lucky you. Anyway, I've got to run. See you later, mate.'

Vic yawned, got out of bed, threw open her bedroom window and delighted not only at the early sunshine streaming in and hitting her face, but also the indefatigable cries of seagulls soaring on the summer breeze. Quickly throwing on some clothes and tying her hair back in a high ponytail, she made herself a large mug of coffee and, with a spring in her step, headed downstairs.

Today was an exciting day for her, as it was the day that she was to set up the shop window purely with her work. She had wasted no time in getting her chosen pieces professionally framed. Danny had also kindly ordered in some smaller-sized new easels on which she could display them on the plinths.

Wedging the gallery door open to let in the warm summer breeze, she wished a 'Happy Monday' to a young guy walking past, and for the first time in a long time felt a sense of joy.

Danny was one of life's good people, and despite the somewhat unconventional and unfortunate way they had met, she was truly glad that he was now in her life. After he had offered her the window display, he had also suggested that she get away from life as she knew it for as long as she needed and, after a couple of long, thinking walks along the river, and with encouragement from Jake, her decision to spend the summer in Brighton had been cemented.

She had received her deposit for the London flat back a lot quicker than she expected. The little furniture that she and Nate had accrued was second-hand and nothing special. Nate had already taken what was rightfully his, and she had agreed to leave the rest for the new tenant. So, after storing stuff back in her old bedroom in Windsor, with just a large suitcase, her portfolio of artwork and an invigorated sense of self, she had headed to the south coast. It had been sad to say goodbye to her still thankfully sober and much happier mother, but she had assured

Kath that she was only just over an hour down the road, so she could go home and visit anytime.

She had insisted she pay Danny rent for the spare room in his apartment, which he had declined, saying that if she could cover him in the gallery for two days a week in the summer peak, he would be so grateful, and would consider it payment for her accommodation. And other than that, she could help him out as much or as little as she wished. Which still gave her the freedom to paint and to do whatever else she wanted. It was a perfect scenario. So, here she was now, in the centre of Brighton, in an established gallery, about to exhibit her work for the very first time in her life. She was just unpacking her box of newly framed artwork when a text beeped in.

> Hey. Hope you're good. Any chance I could come down and see you this Sunday? I really need to talk. Joti x

Vic sighed. Maybe Jake had at last spoken with her. Before she left, his procrastinating had not only become tedious, but had also got quite awkward. As it wasn't her place to tell Joti the huge news, every time she spoke to her new-found friend, she had felt like she was harbouring a guilty secret. Which, in effect, she was. Without a second thought, she typed a speedy reply.

> Of course! Nowhere to park. Easier to get train. Let me know which one you're on & I'll meet you at the station. Vx

Vic finished unwrapping her newly framed originals and began to set up the easels ready for her display. As previously instructed by Danny, she also gently dusted around every other item in the gallery, then walked out to the front to gauge how she would position her work. She was just heading through to the kitchen to make herself another coffee before placing her masterpieces when her mobile rang.

'Sharpie, it's me.' Vic was sure Nate's northern accent had got stronger since he had moved back to Cumbria.

'Hey.'

'Just wanted to say thanks so much for the deposit cheque from the flat. What a welcome surprise.'

'No worries.'

'So, how's Brighton?'

'Great, thanks. Just about to display my exhibit in the front window now.'

'I'm so chuffed for you. It's what you've always wanted. But it's just a window, and if you come here, then – well, I've already spoken to a couple of people I know, and there are a few empty units to rent nearby that would make a great gallery just for you and your work.'

Vic sighed. 'Like I said before, Nate, I want to get myself established here first and I'm not making you any promises. OK?'

'I just miss you, that's all. How about you come and stay here for a long weekend soon, just to see what it's like?' He paused. 'No pressure, but I just know you'll fall in love with the place. I mean, what's not to like? It has beautiful scenery, lots of scrummy food – and me!' He laughed.

Vic couldn't match his enthusiasm. 'Nate, I don't know what I want at the moment – and I know that's not what you want to hear but it's where I'm at, I'm afraid.'

'It just gets a bit lonely up here, that's all.'

'You're not listening to me, Nate.' Vic tried to shift the conversation. 'But it sounds like you've fallen on your feet with your job, and that's important.'

'Is it... is it really?' His voice softened. 'Because you mean so much more to me than anything else.'

Vic put her hand to her heart. It seemed like the more she put Nate off, the more he wanted her there. Why was it that absence made the heart grow fonder? Why was human nature such that if you couldn't have something, you began to want it more? Maybe living with someone was a bit like eating your favourite food over and over: you eventually got sick of it. That when something isn't new, novel, or different, it commands less of your attention. No wonder people had affairs, then never left their partners. Perhaps they were thinking the grass would be greener, but in reality, on the other side of the fence the lawn was actually a bit patchy and in need of a good old sprinkling of fresh seed, too.

And maybe *this* was what real love felt like. Not an all-consuming 'diamond love' like that of Jake and Malini. But more like a chip-of-zirconium kind of love, which offered half the excitement but was not only far easier to insure but also wouldn't hurt as much to lose.

But Vic was surging forward with her own life now, and despite selfishly hanging on to Nate for fear of being alone, upping sticks to the other end of the country just didn't seem the right thing to be doing – not at this moment in time, anyway.

She heard a customer enter the gallery. 'I'm sorry, Nate, I've got to go, but I'll give you a call soon. I promise.'

With a reluctant 'OK' and a huge sigh, Nathaniel Carlisle hung up.

With the happy customer leaving with a moody-looking Constable print of Brighton Chain Pier, and Danny texting to say he wouldn't be back until after lunch, Vic set about arranging her window.

There was space for a large painting in the centre and three around the edge of that. She'd had nine smaller illustrations framed and had decided that she would rotate these throughout the month. Thinking which would make the best display, she came to the decision that the prints of the book covers she had created for Jerico would look really cool together and show her range, plus would be a bit of advertising for his books. She could imagine him saying, 'It'll get me to at least two thousand in the *Donkey Tales* chart, once they see those.'

Then, to the big one in the middle. As she walked through to the back studio, a feeling of excitement surged through her belly as she started to remove the bubble wrap. She hadn't seen it framed yet, and knew that the shade she had chosen for the frame would enhance the colours even further. She gasped as she saw it in its full glory. Even seeing her swirly trademark signature of *Victoria S* made her feel proud of what she was actually about to do. She propped it up on the easel in the middle of the room and grinned broadly. Who'd have thought the abstract she had created post-diagnosis would be the one that was going to be her first exhibit piece? She put her hand close to the glass and started to swirl it around in various huge virtual paint strokes. She had named it *Fire & Blues*.

Giving the glass of the framed book-cover prints a dust-off, she read aloud: '*Mr Pigeons and the Glasgow Kiss*,' took a deep breath and suddenly felt sad. If Jerico hadn't kissed her, then everything would be OK, wouldn't it? But he had, and even when she was telling Ray that she had brushed it off as a tipsy kiss, she had realised it had been more than that. She had felt her toes curl. She had felt an electric current go through her. She had felt like a teenager again. Not dissimilar to what she had felt with Danny. But that *had* been lust and longing, and if she was honest with herself, in that moment of life-changing madness, she had also subconsciously sabotaged her relationship, in order to push herself to make a decision regarding Nate.

Jerico had messaged her the night of the kiss. Not apologising for it in any way, but saying sorry for rushing off. She had ignored his text. He had tried to call her a couple of days later, but not knowing how to deal with her emotions, she had stared at the phone as if it were some kind of alien, then had let out a little groan as it rang off. His last attempt at contacting her had been via text, after Ray had shared his latest book cover with him, as she had instructed. Unlike with Nate's, she'd been pleased that this message didn't include a question mark. And trust Jerico to make sure that his reply didn't pressurise her in any way either.

> Dear Queen Victoria. Mr Pigeons and the donkeys are simply delighted with their new cover. Now, find what brings you joy and take yourself there.

Victoria was suddenly awash with a sense of sadness and regret. What a beautiful thing for Jerico to say. If she didn't have HIV, maybe – just maybe – there would be a chance for them to make it work. Because she liked him, and he clearly liked her. But her shame was too great, and telling him was a risk that she was too frightened to take. For, despite only knowing this charming man such a short time, a life without Jerico Flint in it – in whatever capacity, and however difficult it may be – was something she was not prepared to take a chance on.

A while later, Danny came rushing through the front door. 'Wow, wow, wow, Vic, the window looks fucking magnificent. I'm so happy you decided on your new one. I didn't want to push you but it really is so, so special. Amazing! I hope you don't mind, but when I change the window I get the local paper to do a little piece on the artist showing. I actually met my journalist mate for lunch so he can get it in this week's. It just helps to bring in the business, and all of these certainly will. They're all fab, Vic! He's going to call for a quick chat in around an hour if that's OK. Do you have any prints of them, as well as the originals?'

'The books covers are just prints. The author kept the originals.' Vic felt slightly overwhelmed. 'I got fifty of each of them. But I wanted the main one to be a one-off.'

'I agree. Someone will hang that in their home and people

will be asking who painted it. I'm excited for you. And what price are you putting on them?'

'I've no idea, Danny. This is all so alien to me.'

'Well, I say put a thousand on the original abstract and two hundred and fifty each on the cover prints.'

'That much?' Vic's eyes widened.

'Vic, you're good. Really good. I've seen a lot of artists come and go here. You are going to be a name. I just know it. Your work is incredible.'

Vic felt herself tingle from head to foot.

Danny smiled. 'It really is. Now, sorry I've been so long. You must be starving. Go and have a break, and I'll see you back here in an hour to talk to the journalist. OK?'

The Customer

Four days later, after a busy day in the gallery, Vic was restocking hand-painted cards in the small rack on the counter with her back to the door when she was startled by a slow, molasses-like, southern American drawl behind her.

'I'm not interested in those ropey old cover illustrations in the window, y'all, but where can I buy those interesting-sounding detective books, honey child?'

Startled, Vic spun around and not only felt the blood rushing to her cheeks but a million butterflies start to have a party in her stomach.

'Jerico?'

'Queen Victoria.' He doffed his smart white fedora with its fetching black band at her.

'What are you doing here?'

'I could ask you the same. Being honest, I didn't know you'd be here.' Jerico faltered; his voice went quieter. 'But I really hoped that you would be.'

Vic managed to stop herself from saying 'Aww' out loud as

the handsome one continued: 'The newspaper article omitted that bit. So that's quite the bonus all round, isn't it?' He grinned.

'I didn't know it had gone national?' Vic looked confused.

'Not yet, no.' Jerico smiled. 'A friend of mine lives in Hove, and he told me. And, well, if anyone is going to buy prints of my book covers, it had to be me, surely.' He pulled out a wallet which was crammed full of cash. 'Two hundred and fifty each for the covers, is that right?'

'But you've already got the originals?' Vic queried.

Jerico ignored her. 'And I want the abstract, too; it's incredible. I had no clue you painted like that.'

'Nor did I, until recently,' Vic flustered. 'And I'm sure I can speak to Danny – he's the owner here – and get you a discount.'

'Queen V, when you recognise your true worth, you'll no longer offer others a bargain on your brilliance.' Jerico reached for his wallet.

Vic felt her eyes well. 'Aw. That's so lovely.'

'I take it cash is OK.'

Before Vic had time to answer, Jerico started laying out fifty-pound notes on the counter. 'You can surely afford to buy me an ice cream now?'

'I haven't been on Brighton pier for years,' Jerico said, carrying on licking the vanilla-stacked 99, with its scrummy Cadbury's Flake stuffed inside, that Vic had insisted they both get.

'I love it here.' She tapped the bench they were sitting on. 'This has replaced my thinking bench on the river in Windsor.'

'I think everyone should have a special place where they take time out to think. Especially out in the natural world – that's where I get my thoughts straight, for sure.' Jerico laid his head back to take in the last of the evening rays.

'Do you have a special place, then?' Vic asked.

'If I tell you that, then not only will it not be special anymore, but Mr Pigeons may have to kill you.'

'Fair,' Vic answered, carrying on licking her ice cream. 'Mr Cool.' After a pause, she said, 'It's been bugging me. I've just realised who you remind me of in that hat: Mr Cool.'

'Clever you! Of course, Mr Cool, one of the Vettriano paintings in the book I gave you. I actually have that very print up in my study.'

'Yes! You have the same hat, and it looks as if the couple are on a pier. Not sure I could rock the pink polka-dot number the woman is wearing in it, though.'

'Oh, I think you'd give it a good go, but then again, she does look quite demure.'

'Oi,' Vic laughed. A beat passed. 'Without being too nosy, what exactly is it that you do, Jerico? Because that's quite a bit of cash you just shelled out.'

'Maybe Mr Pigeons has been more successful than I've made out.'

Vic laughed. 'Really?'

'Well, they do say don't judge a book by its cover.'

'You cheeky...' She poked him gently in his side.

'I'm teasing you. My father was a very successful banker. He and my mother have sadly both gone now. They would have loved you.' His voice cracked slightly. 'Mum had me late, and they passed within a year of each other. Mum couldn't live without the silly old bugger.' He shook his head and smiled. 'They left me and my sister our old family riverside home in Bray. I bought sis out with the liquid inheritance, so I choose to write and help other people now. I'm very blessed.'

Vic squeezed his hand. 'They broke the mould with you, that's for sure. But in such a good way.'

They sat in silence for a minute, taking in the buzz of this iconic entertainment zone and the twinkling ocean in front of them. Shouts from four lads playing ball on the beach travelled on the soft breeze. But Vic's mind was far from quiet. Should she mention the kiss? Should she apologise for not responding to him? Should she tell him about Nate… and also, why did she feel nigh on euphoric that this man had come to the gallery to buy her prints?

'So, what's going on for you then, Queen V?' Jerico reached the end of his cone and licked his lips. 'You can, of course, tell me to bugger off if you want to.'

Vic reached for a tissue in her bag to wipe her now sticky fingers, then went for it. 'I'm sorry I didn't answer any of your messages. I guess I felt a little awkward after, well… our picnic.' She closed her eyes for a second. Why couldn't she just tell him? Say it out loud. That she really liked him, but she was HIV-positive and didn't want to feel not only embarrassed, but also scared of what he may think of her. Also, that she felt even worse because she didn't know him well enough yet to gauge his reaction – whether he might run away. In fact, all she wanted to do at this very moment was to take his handsome face in her hands and kiss it right off.

'It's OK. Maybe I overstepped the mark,' Jerico said, without embarrassment. 'I mean, you'd just told me you'd split from your fella, and there's me sticking a kiss on you without warning.'

Vic felt relieved at this get-out-of-jail-free card. 'You didn't overstep the mark. I enjoyed our time very much, but…'

'Ooh, don't you just hate it when that little b-word springs up? No wonder it rhymes with cut.' Jerico was doing his best to hide his disappointment, but Victoria wasn't fooled. 'You don't have to say any more. I get it.'

'I need to find my way, Jerico. With what I want to do with my career, too. I'd worked in Ray's office for ten years. I was frustrated with myself, more than with Nate – that's my ex. Who now wants me back, as it happens.' Victoria couldn't seem to shut herself up. Perhaps if she kept talking, she could convince herself that she had no feelings for this amazing man in front of her.

'We are grown-ups, we kissed, we move on.' Jerico looked out over the sea, the tops of the waves twinkling in the still-warm evening sunshine. 'So are you staying down here as well as working here, then?' He turned to Vic.

'Yes. I've said I'd help Danny out during the summer. I love being by the sea. Like you said, the joy of being close to nature is really helping me clear my head, and I'm sharing his apartment above the gallery on a work-for-rent basis.'

'Wow, that's a good deal.'

'He's a good friend,' Vic added, really hoping that the Danny chat would be over soon, but alas, no.

'Sounds like it. How do you know him? Gallery-owner-meets-artist sounds like a match made in heaven.'

'He's a new friend, or yes, I would have muscled in long ago.' Vic took a sharp intake of breath as she got ready to slightly distort the truth. 'We met at my mate Mandy's hen weekend last year. I adore his boyfriend, too.'

Jerico's shoulders dropped at her last comment. 'Well, I'm glad you are starting to find your way.' He lifted Vic's hand to his lips. The brush of his kiss against her skin was softer than a whisper, yet it reverberated through her entire being like a thunderclap.

Her breath hitched in her throat. 'You love a kiss, don't you?' was all she could muster in reply.

Jerico looked right at her. 'I've always thought that if the eyes are the windows to the soul, then a kiss is surely the key to open it.'

Vic's memory bank flashed to their picnic at the riverbank. The butterflies were back. Because even without that first kiss, she was beginning to realise just how important this eccentric, clever, funny, empathetic and charismatic man was to her.

Vic verbalised her thoughts, 'Maybe it's time I cleaned the lock out then, eh?'

Jerico reached for the large, carefully wrapped parcel containing his new purchases. 'On that note...' he slipped into Scots for a second, 'I really must awa'.' Then back to posh southern. 'I'm having dinner with my friend in Hove.' He grasped the large package to his chest. 'And thank you for these. They are as extraordinary as the woman who painted them.'

'You're too kind.' Vic's voice wobbled slightly.

'Nobody can ever be *too* kind, Queen Victoria.' His voice lowered slightly as he tried to be casual. 'So, are you... are you contemplating going back to your ex?'

Vic thought for a second. 'At this moment, I'm not ruling anything in or out.'

Jerico coughed loudly to clear his throat of emotion. 'Can you please just assure Mr Pigeons that whatever happens, you will continue to illustrate his adventures?'

Vic smiled. 'You can, of course, reliably inform Mr Pigeons that that is a given.'

The Father

Two days later, Vic greeted a smiling Joti at Brighton train station, both wearing flowing summer dresses and flip-flops.

'Look at you, all summery and gorgeous.' Vic kissed her friend on the cheek.

'I'm making the most of the sunshine *and* being by the sea.' Joti grinned as, on cue, a seagull squawked overhead. 'It's so good to see you, Vicki.'

Vic smiled to herself: it was too late for correction. To Joti Adams-Johnson-now-Turner, she would always be Vicki, and that was just fine.

They were soon sitting in a café overlooking the shingle beach, with long glasses of orange juice and lemonade in front of them. It being Sunday, the beach and pier were rammed with day trippers and locals alike, making for a buzzy, fun atmosphere.

'Your text sounded very ominous.' Vic took a sip of her fruity drink and, hoping that she'd got the right end of the stick, asked tentatively, 'I'm guessing you've spoken to Jake?'

Joti took a big glug of her drink. 'I don't know how to thank you enough, but what a shocker!'

'I know, and I'm sorry I didn't say anything to you. I just didn't feel it was my place to. I really hope you understand that.' Vic looked awkward for a second. 'You could do a whole lot worse than Jake Turner, though. Tell me what happened. He must have been so overwhelmed. Actually, the pair of you must have been.'

'Totally. He had to want to come to me and, well, without you telling him about my letter, I would never have found him. I mean, Jake, in Windsor, of no real fixed abode. It would have been like trying to find a needle in a houseboat.' They both laughed. 'Honestly, a scene from *EastEnders* couldn't have been more dramatic.' Joti was wide-eyed.

Vic shook her head, agog. 'I can't even imagine.'

'He showed me a photo of them together. They looked so happy and in love.'

'So terribly sad, that you lost her so young,' Vic said softly.

'Yes.' Joti sighed. 'I'm not sure if it's worse that I didn't know her, and I have nothing at all to miss about her, or the fact that I never got to know her and now she will never get to share my life with me. It was so nice for Jake to be able to relay everything about her personality when she was a young woman.'

'Isn't he just the coolest and sweetest person?'

Vic nodded. 'He really is.'

'Not unlike you,' Joti added.

Vic blushed. 'Oh stop it.'

'I mean it. You are such a solid woman, and I'm so glad that I've met you.' Joti put her hand on her new friend's. 'I feel such an affinity with you in such a short space of time.'

'Despite Chandler pooing on your lawn and me being a moody bitch when we first met?' Vic gave an awkward giggle.

'You were struggling with your mum. I get it.'

And that was before I found out I had HIV, Vic thought, but she couldn't tell Joti – not yet – even though Joti was a nurse and probably wouldn't blink an eye. But defintely not until she had told her mum and brother – and she wasn't sure when that would be.

'What I can't quite get my head around is how *you* know Jake, though,' Joti said.

'Basically, Mum and Dad were unhappy, and one day, Mum tells me, she was walking along the river, he was on the deck of his boat and they started chatting. She tells me he was a great confidant and friend. I have fond memories of me and Albie playing on his boat whilst Mum and he would talk and laugh together. We would also sometimes go for walks with him on the Brocas – that's the large meadow on the Eton side of the river – with whichever dogs were around at the time.'

'Sounds idyllic. I have had two fathers all my life – how mad is that.' Joti drained her glass.

'Beats having half a one, like me and Albie did growing up.'

'Aww. Saying that, *Mister* Adams – my, umm, other dad – was always so busy with his work, he was an absent party a lot of the time, too.'

'Ah, OK. Did you get on with your stepmother?'

'Yes. I knew no different. She was always very lovely to me. Never had children of her own so I never felt like I wasn't number one.'

'That's good, then. And dare I ask how Albie is?' Vic gave a wry smile. 'Or should I say, you and Albie?'

'He's all right.' Joti couldn't keep the grin off her face.

'I'm not saying anything else about my dear brother, except that in there somewhere is a heart of gold.' Vic swirled the ice around in her glass.

'I'm not proud of the fact he was living with someone when, well... it happened... And I wouldn't have carried on if he had stayed with her. It's just the feeling was strong and...'

Vic closed her eyes as her thoughts sprang to Jerico. 'You

don't have to explain. And I would love it to all work out for you both. But I might have to remind you that it wasn't long ago that you were saying – and I quote: "If I never have a man again, it will be too soon."'

Joti laughed. 'At the moment, it's amazing. Albie is amazing. And after finding out about what happened with my mum and Jake, well, I intend to live in the moment.'

'Yes, your parents' sad love story is worthy of a film,' Vic said wistfully.

'It really is.' Joti took off her sunglasses and turned her face up to the strong lunchtime rays. 'Jake said something odd as I was leaving, though.'

'Go on.'

'He said that he had always dreamt of having a family, and it was like a miracle that they were now living right next to each other.'

Vic frowned. 'Did you tell him you were seeing Albie, by any chance?'

'No. We didn't get down to any detail, really.'

Vic sat upright in her seat. 'Fuck!'

'What is it?' Joti looked alarmed at Vic's reaction.

Barry Sharpe's insinuations of Albie not being his suddenly echoed around Vic's mind as if they were yesterday.

'I take it you have slept with my brother?'

'Err... umm... what sort of question is that... Why?'

'Fuck!' Vic reached for her phone and, realising it was out of battery, leapt up. 'I have to call Mum.'

Joti screwed her face up. 'You're being odd. What is it?'

'Wait there – I won't be long.'

Victoria started running towards the main road. Then, as if she was in some kind of weird dream sequence, to the sound of an incessant bike bell, a scream, then a thud, she hit the pavement with force and went out like a light.

. . .

She woke up in a hospital bed to five pairs of worry-filled eyes staring down at her. Thinking she was in the midst of some terrible nightmare, or even that she may be dead, she shut her eyes again. Why on earth would her mum, brother, Joti, Orla and Mandy all be here with her? And why was she here in the first place?

'You had an accident,' Joti said calmly. 'A cyclist knocked you down, but you're OK.'

'Oh, my darling' – Kath Sharpe squeezed her daughter's hand – 'Albie scared the life out of me when he told me you were in hospital.'

'I'm not dying, am I? I don't feel like I'm dying. Saying that, what does that even feel like? Did I bleed a lot?' Vic suddenly panicked. 'And if I'm not dying, why are you all here?'

'No. You bled hardly at all,' Joti added gently. 'You were knocked right out, luckily, with just a bump on your head and a few bruises, but nothing broken. They're keeping you in tonight in case of concussion.'

'And we are all here,' Albie interjected, 'because I didn't give Joti a chance to explain what had happened. You know what I'm like: the minute she said you were in hospital, I immediately hung up, called everyone, bundled Mum in my van and got on the motorway.'

Vic put her hand to where a manageable pain in her head was coming from. It was tightly bandaged. 'The painkillers must be strong,' she said woozily.

'We were worried that it was something else.' Orla grimaced as she said it. Mandy poked her in the ribs. 'You know – just something else connected to something else.'

'The HIV, you mean,' Albie said boldly.

Victoria took a sharp intake of breath at her brother's unexpected revelation.

'HIV?' Joti questioned. 'Oh, Vic, bless you.'

'Yes, that awful virus thing she's got,' Kath Sharpe repeated,

causing Victoria's face to screw up in futher confusion and
shock at how her family knew. Tears started to run slowly down
her mother's face. 'I'm so worried about you dying, darling,
about this awful thing inside of you. When Albie told me, I
didn't know what to do. He clearly knew you didn't want
anyone to know, so we've been looking out for you, darling. I
even researched it at the library and got a leaflet for a drop-in
centre in Slough and popped it on my doormat for you to find.'

Vic couldn't believe what she was hearing. She eased
herself to sitting with tears in her eyes. 'Oh, Mum, you did all
that for me?'

'I promise you, my darling, I am here for you every step of
the way.'

'I'm not going to die, Mum. Not if I can help it. I am being
regularly monitored in a top London hospital and as soon as I
need to, I will start on drugs that will keep me alive. I promise.'

Joti spoke up. 'Vic's right. The treatments are getting better
every day. There is so much research around HIV and it's not
the death sentence it once was – or just a "gay virus".' She
bracketed the words. 'We all need to spread the awareness and
not be frightened of it, like so many people seem to be.'

'I want to know everything,' Albie added. 'So we can
support you. OK?'

Everybody nodded. Orla added, 'We all feel that way. The
more we understand, the more we can be there for you.'

Vic looked at her brother. 'How did you find out?'

'I listened to every word you said to that copper that night I
was in trouble. It broke my heart so bad but I valued your
privacy. I love you, sis. And, well, it was a gamble telling the old
dear.' He looked at Kath. 'But it paid off. Mum, we're so proud
of you for keeping sober for this long.' Tears began to fall down
his cheeks, too.

Vic shook her head. 'Jesus Christ, will you all stop being so
maudlin? I've had a bump on the head, which people may say I

needed anyway, to knock some sense into me.' Orla was the only one to laugh. 'But I feel so loved and blessed that you've all come to me like this.'

'Why wouldn't we?' Mandy asked. 'We love you so much.'

'Did you let Danny know?' Vic looked at Joti.

'Yes, I got the number of the gallery from Directory Enquiries and phoned him whilst you were out.' Joti looked at her phone to see how much battery she had left. 'He sends his love and said to give him a progress report when you're ready.'

'He sounds lovely, Vic. Is there a chance of romance?' Kath's face brightened.

'No, Mum. We are just good friends.' Vic put her hand to her elbow that was now feeling sore. 'Is the cyclist who hit me OK?'

'Yes, she's fine. She was mortified, but I ensured her it wasn't her fault, and she gave me her number to call her later, too,' Joti added. 'What I want to know is, why did you shoot off so fast?'

'I'm not sure,' Vic lied, as the memory of Joti's words about Jake flashed through her mind. She let out a little groan. 'Thanks so much for coming, all of you, but do you mind if I have five minutes with Mum before you all head off? I'm suddenly feeling really quite tired.'

Orla stood up. 'Actually, I think me and Mand will head off now. It's Sunday and the roads out of here will get busy later. I've got an early start tomorrow.'

'Yes, and I need to wee all the time, now I'm due to drop. And I can't be doing it on the hard shoulder in my condition,' Mandy added.

'No, you fecking can't.' Orla kept her face straight. 'Not on my watch, anyway.'

'Too much information,' Albie laughed, assisting the heavily pregnant woman up from her chair.

'And too many visitors.' A jovial nurse popped her head around the curtain.

'They are going. Sorry,' Vic piped up, sticking her tongue out childishly as the nurse walked away.

'Thanks so much for coming, and I'll call you when I'm back at the flat. OK?' Vic blew her girls a kiss.

Joti smiled. 'I can see it from both sides now – about visitors, I mean.'

'I'll wait with Joti in the café whilst you talk to Mum.' Albie stood up, taking Joti's hand and squeezing it. 'I can give you a lift home too, babe, if that works.'

She squeezed it back, lovingly. 'Do you want anything, Vic?'

'No. I'm all right, thanks.'

Vic looked at her mum, who was clearly a different woman from the woman of six months ago. Her skin was brighter, her hair dried beautifully in its neat new style. She had dropped at least a stone. But more importantly than all these *new* positives, she was back to her old self.

'What is it, love?' Kath Sharpe took her daughter's hand.

'Firstly, I am so proud of you, Mum, and I can't believe you got sober for me.' Vic's voice cracked.

'I did it for all of us – myself included.' Kath sniffed loudly. 'I wasn't happy. For years and years. And now I have a purpose. Which is not only you, might I add – or Albie.'

'Jake, too,' Vic replied knowingly.

Kath suddenly looked at peace. 'Yes, Jake, too.'

'Mum.' Kath nodded at her daughter. 'I need to ask you something serious.'

'Go on, love.'

'Is Albie Jake's son?'

Kath let out a little laugh, and then looked to the ceiling for a second. She took a deep breath and faced her daughter. 'No. Your father always thought that – and, as you know, cruelly let it be known to the world. Well, our little world, anyway. Thankfully, our Albie was too young to understand. But he's a chip off the old block all right, your brother.' Kath paused. 'In fact, you're so much more like Jake in temperament and, well, if you look closely, his eyes and nose are pretty similar to yours too.'

'No!' Victoria's eyes widened. 'No way! Why didn't either of you tell me?'

'When you were young, I wanted your dad to keep providing for us, and when he left when Albie was a baby, again, I didn't want to tell you, and for you to blurt it out to your dad – or anyone else, for that matter. As much as I felt I had got one up on your philandering father, I wasn't proud of myself and didn't want you to suffer for that, either.'

'But you could have told me when I became an adult, at eighteen?' Vic shook her head in disbelief. Why hadn't she seen the resemblance? Thinking on it, it all began to make sense. How much Jake had looked out for them all. How he had never moved from his Windsor mooring. How much he had cared for her recently in her hour of need. He was clearly a good man. And how sad, Vic thought, that her mum had kept this huge secret all to herself.

Kath sniffed. 'I felt it had gone on too long and I was scared you'd be angry with me and maybe not want me in your life. I'm so sorry.'

'Oh, Mum, that would never happen. It's OK, really. I get it.' Vic squeezed her mum's hand lovingly. 'But what I don't understand is why you never got together with Jake?'

'He was still in love with Malini. I wasn't ever going to be his second best; I'd had enough of that with your father. We've stayed the best of friends. And well, now I am sober, I intend to spend a lot more time with him, and him me. So why are you asking now if Albie is Jake's son? Is it something to do with your diagnosis?'

'No, Mum,' Vic replied patiently. 'Has Jake told you anything recently about Malini?'

Kath's face dropped. 'No. I've been busy, but what about her? She's not bloody well turned up, has she, Vic?'

'No, quite the opposite. Jake found out that she died many years ago and, well... the reason it was important to know about Albie... is that Joti is his daughter, too – and she is sleeping with your son.'

'Heavens alive!' Kath's mouth fell open. 'And lodger, my arse!' She started to laugh.

'Yeah. Joti told me something that Jake had said which made me think Albie might be his son, and as my bloody battery had gone on my phone, I was racing across the road to get back to the gallery to call you... and then my lights went out.'

'Oh, love, but thank God he's not. And Vic, that means you have a half-sister, too, in Joti!'

Vic swallowed. 'This is just too much!' She shook her head and sighed loudly. 'I may need another whack on the head to get my head around the fact that my father is not who I thought he was, and I now also have another sibling. I've always wanted a sister. How crazy is that?'

'And you promise me that you're not angry, Vic? For not telling you, I mean.'

Vic's face softened. 'No, Mum. More shocked than angry, but we all do what we must do when the time is right, I guess. I haven't missed out on Jake, really. He's been more of a father to me...' She hesitated. '... than Dad ever was.'

'Yes, he has.' Kath sniffed.

'How long has he known I'm his?' Vic reached for the water cup on the cabinet next to her and took a small sip.

'From the minute I did.'

'I can't believe you stayed with Dad, then.'

'Like I said, I wanted stability and Jake was still so full of loss and yearning.'

'But Jake is rich – surely he would have helped you financially too?'

'I directly refused, darling. I'd made my bed. I chose to stay with your father.'

Vic nodded. 'Did you tell Jake about my HIV?'

Kath wriggled in her seat. 'I was scared, darling.'

'It's fine. I think we know he can keep a big secret already, don't we, Mum?'

Kath put her hand on top of her daughter's. 'I love you and Albie with all my heart. You know that, don't you? I always have and I always will.' Tears pricked her eyes.

'Mum, it's OK.'

'It's not, though, really, is it? I've been a terrible mother a lot of the time. And for that, I am truly sorry.'

Vic felt suddenly awash with contentment and love. 'What's important is that you are here now.' She smiled. 'All present and correct…'

Kath's bottom lip wobbled. 'Does Albie know?' Vic said quietly.

'Now I know he's with Joti, I need to speak with Jake and do this in the right order.'

Vic began to well up. 'Oh, Mum, it's so good to have *you* back.'

Kath kissed her daughter on the forehead.

Albie poked his head around the curtain. 'You ready, Mum? We'd better get going. Is that OK, sis?'

'Get in here, you.' Kath reached for the magazine that Joti had left on Vic's side cupboard, rolled it up and jumped up to hit Albie on the bottom with it. 'You little sod, you could have just told me about your antics, you know.'

Albie grinned the grin that had allowed him to get away with everything and anything whilst he was growing up and beyond. 'And what fun would there have been in that, Mother?'

The Three Musketeers

August 2006

'Oh my God, just look at his ickle fingers.' Mandy's newborn gripped his tiny little digits around Orla's. 'What age is he now?'

'Six weeks tomorrow.'

'Aw. And all that hair. He's the spit of his father,' Vic added.

'Poor little mite.' Mandy laughed. 'Talking of fathers, have you seen Jake since you found out?'

'I'm actually going for dinner with him on the boat tonight. Mum thought it was important we speak face to face, without her there.' Vic took a sip of the tea Mandy had just placed in front of her.

'Look at Kath, taking charge,' Mandy said, impressed.

'I know. Great, isn't it?' Vic went over to look in the pram placed at the end of the long kitchen table. 'So Julian, you say? Has he got a middle name?'

'Yes, Julian Winkler Taylor.'

Orla and Victoria were open-mouthed. 'Mandy Taylor, what haven't you told us?' Vic cried.

Mandy laughed. 'I started at that school twelve years ago, and met Steve two years after that. Don't think you were the first to feel the headmaster's cane, Orla O'Malley.'

'You dark old horse,' Vic laughed.

'Less of the "old", thanks,' Mandy chipped in.

'Ew! Not sure I like the idea of sloppy seconds.' Orla screwed her face up.

'Just look at your faces. Of course I didn't. You know me – I was born with a vanilla pod in my mouth,' Mandy added, carrying on washing up their lunch plates and glasses. Vic and Orla couldn't stop laughing.

'Saying that, I really did fancy Mr Winkler. I may have to look him up.' Orla reached for a biscuit from the tin that was in the middle of the kitchen table. 'I've just set up one of those new Twitter accounts. Maybe he's on there.'

'Well, you could do a lot worse, and at least he's divorced now, I believe,' Mandy replied sincerely. 'And for the record, it's Alexander. Julian Alexander Taylor.'

'Ooh, I do like that,' Vic said.

'Very posh,' Orla echoed.

'I know what I meant to ask.' Mandy wiped her hands on her apron. 'Was Danny OK about you coming back to stay at your mum's?'

'Totally fine. I intended to be in Brighton just for the summer, anyway. I know it's only mid-August but I had to meet this little one and I felt ready to come home. He's happy to keep selling my prints, and I insisted he now takes twenty per cent commision on each one. I must start working on some new stuff, but my head hasn't been in it since I've been back.'

'He's such a lovely bloke,' Mandy added. 'And you'll get there with your art, when you're ready.'

'Thanks, Mand. And about Danny – despite all, I'm happy

he's in my life, and I can relax now he's got someone in to cover days off and holidays. He would work seven days a week before he met his fella. And he said I can go down whenever I want to. I'm really lucky there.'

'Good to hear that his relationship is still going strong, too.' Orla flicked the kettle on.

'Yes.' Vic sighed. 'Just need to sort myself out now.'

'Yes, what *is* happening with Nate? I'm slightly confused,' Orla added.

'Yes, and what about Jerico, the author guy?' Mandy added. 'He sounded lovely.'

Vic groaned. 'I don't know *what* about anything. I'm so confused about relationships and how I should actually act or be. It's like I don't know how to feel anymore. It's been so nice to hang out with Danny and just not even have to think about it for a while. I've pushed everything to a vault in the back of my mind. What I do know is that I really like Jerico, but I'm too scared to tell him about my HIV in case he doesn't deal with it, and I'm not missing Nate as much as he is missing me, but he is still hounding me to go and see him.'

Orla took a sip of tea. 'Oh, Vic. In my opinion, you should just come out with it to Jerico. At least you'll know one way or the other.'

'That sounds so easy in principle.' Vic blew out a big breath. 'Nate has given me an ultimatum. Says there's waiting and then there's waiting. He's been so patient with me. He's invited me to the Lakes this weekend to talk face to face. It's only fair, I think.' She looked troubled.

'Yes.' Mandy furtively checked in the pram to see if the baby was sleeping. 'It's no good on the phone. You do need to see him, Vic.'

Orla nodded her agreement.

'I really do.' Vic sighed. 'Here's hoping I come away with some kind of closure.'

The Father

Vic could hear the music of Simon & Garfunkel playing as she approached *Lazy Daze*. The distinguished-looking white-haired and bearded Jake Turner was sitting in his usual chair outside his beloved narrowboat, making the most of the last rays of the August day. He was drinking a can of ginger beer and as he caught sight of Vic, he put out his cigarette and, singing softly along to the lyrics of 'Bridge Over Troubled Water', he stood up, then lowered his hand to help her up on deck.

'Hello,' Vic said softly, noticing their identical eye colour, which she had never thought twice about before. And yes, his nose was quite an ordinary-looking one, with a gentle curve, just like hers, but she'd never picked up on that either.

'Hello, Victoria. Shall we go inside?'

They sat opposite each other on the matching armchairs, Norman asleep at their feet.

'Your mum made us a lasagne so I didn't have to fiddle about with food and we could just talk. How are you feeling about all this?'

'That Mum only ever makes lasagne when I'm around because she knows it's my favourite.' Vic smirked.

Jake remained silent.

'Sorry, I feel a bit nervous. I will always know you as Jake. Call you Jake, I mean.'

'Of course.' Jake nodded.

'I'm not angry or sad. Actually, I don't really know how I feel. After getting HIV, which I know Mum told you about – well, nothing fazes me, really – not even a newly discovered parent.' Vic laughed.

'Always a rainbow,' Jake added with a smile.

'And you can understand why I didn't tell you about that. I nearly did when you told me your devastating news about your parents. Shit, that means my grandparents.' Vic's face fell. 'I've just realised that it was *my* grandparents who died in the fire. We have so much to talk about. I need to find out who I am, where I come from. And so much more about you. The fantastic thing, though, Jake, is that I like you. I like you a lot. You've always been there for me, Mum and Albie, and for that I will be forever grateful.'

'The reason I stayed put in this very mooring spot was for you and your mother. I hope, now, that I'm building my friendship with her, so she can accept more from me.'

'If you mean financially, she doesn't need to. I've never seen her so happy in her whole life. As devastating as it is for you about Malini, it's allowed Mum to love you. Because she never wanted to be second best in your life and was always worried that she would fall for you and you would abandon her.'

Jake looked forlorn. 'She never said that to me.'

'I'm my mother's daughter – we clearly have a problem with stating how we feel.' Vic smirked, again.

Jake got up, went to the kitchen and put the lasagne in the oven to warm. He came back to Vic with three sets of cutlery, which he laid down on the coffee table in front of her.

'Somebody joining us?' Vic enquired.

Suddenly, Norman was awake and running outside, and then Vic noticed someone getting onto the boat. Jake went forward to greet their dinner guest with a kiss on each cheek.

Joti grinned as she caught sight of Vic. 'Hello, sis.' Tears started running down Joti's pretty face.

'Hello.' Vic was smiling through her tears now too.

'Dad was right in his letter about me not being lonely,' Joti blubbed. 'I've got a whole new family here now, and honestly, Vic, I can't tell you how happy I am that we're related. I've always wanted a sister and I could do so much worse than you.'

'Me, too,' Vic laughed. 'That nosy old tosser of a neighour of ours is going to have a field day when he tries to work this one out!'

'What? That we share the same dad, I'm half Sri Lankan and now I'm living with your brother!'

Jake looked to the window. 'There he goes, sprinting to the Windsor and Eton Express offices without his trainers on.' They all laughed.

'Oh, yeah.' Joti started picking at the bowl of crisps Jake had put down in front of them. 'Not sure if I told you this.' She started laughing to herself. 'After the RSPCA incident, I took Chandler out under cover of darkness and got him to shit on the old bugger's front lawn.'

'Oh my God, that's hilarious.' Vic shook with laughter.

Jake looked on with pride and amusement as his two daughters joyously conversed.

'Well, you taught me everything I know on that front,' Joti sniggered.

'Although my actions were completely indefensible,' Vic added.

'I forgive you.' Joti grinned and added, 'Well, you better sit down... Dad – as I've got something else to tell you both.'

'Dad. Wow.' Vic faltered, still finding it hard to believe that

she and Joti shared the same father. 'And what now?' she
exclaimed. 'I'm not sure if I'm ready for any more surprises.'

Joti pulled a black-and-white shiny-looking piece of paper
out of her bag and put it in front of her face.

'You're pregnant?' Vic gasped.

Jake went in to look closer. 'And there's two of them!'

'You're pregnant with twins?!' Tears started to run down
Vic's face. 'And they are my brother's, I take it?'

'Yes,' Joti gasped. 'I'm not that much of a harlot, and I know
I've only known him for five minutes, but when you know you
know, and I'm not getting any younger, and he was up for it, so
we started practising and it happened a lot quicker than we
both thought.'

'I'm so happy for you both.' Vic took a deep breath, meaning
what she said but not denying the pain she also felt at realising
that, despite the fact that she had found peace with the decision
to not have children, she would never feel this joy herself.

Joti squeezed her hand knowingly. 'I have to say, when I
told him it was twins, Albie did nearly faint, but as you know,
my divorce settlement was good and my dad – my other dad,
that is – also left me a tidy penny. And I now have a toy boy
who is good at DIY, so it's a win-win really, all around. I love my
job and will probably go back, plus Albie can choose his hours if
he wants to work. It will be a perfect arrangement.'

Jake kissed Joti on her head. 'Congratulations to you both.'

'I think Albie will actually make a really good father,' Vic
added, blowing her nose.

'And you, dear sister, will make an amazing auntie.'

'Oh my God, yes.' Vic's face lit up. 'Auntie Victoria. I'm
going to be an auntie.' She laughed.

'We can share – one each, if you like,' Joti went on. 'I'm
going to need all the help I can get.'

'Have you told Mum? About the babies, I mean.' Vic stood
up to help Jake.

'We just did. She was over the moon. In fact, so emotional that Albie is going to stay with her and have dinner whilst I am here.'

'A new daughter, new sisters *and* new grandbabies in the family.' Jake went to the kitchen. 'We must celebrate. I have some fizzy cordial somewhere.'

THIRTY-THREE
LAKE DISTRICT

The Goodbye

Victoria had a thing for buffet cars on trains – found it the next-best thing to airline food, which she had always loved, too. She would always finish every scrap of whatever meal was served to her, and was even partial to the small packets of plastic cheese and the fake cream on puddings. Nate would, of course, critique and criticise everything but ended up eating it anyway.

As it was mid-morning, she had decided on a flapjack and a cup of tea for starters. Turning on her iPod and playing Pink's 'I'm Not Dead' through her headphones, she moved her legs as far over from the teenage girl in the window seat next to her as she could. And as the train flew out of Euston Station away from London, she felt immediately soothed by the sight of fields and countryside flashing by.

As the journey progressed, the lyrics of the song began to resonate. Pink sang that she wasn't scared anymore – that she was just changing – and that was so true of Victoria now. The eight months since diagnosis had allowed her to educate herself fully and realise that if she did everything she was told, she *wasn't* looking at a death sentence. Dr Anna at the hospital was not only a complete expert in her field whom Vic trusted literally with her life, but she had also kept everything real, allaying Vic's fears, making her realise that life was worth living and that she could live a long life. The minute she did need to go on the required drug programme, the doctor had also assured her that she would support her all the way through that, too.

Vic had already cut down on her drinking, plus ensured that she got regular exercise now. Through the summer this had consisted of walking or running along the Brighton seafront, and just being in that natural environment had invigorated her. Bizarrely, she felt healthier than she ever had before. She also now had a mum who was present, a more settled brother, a half-sister, was going to be an auntie, and had the type of father she had always dreamt of, not to mention two of the best best friends a girl could ever have. All of which enabled her to feel mentally well and able to face the world, knowing that there was a whole bundle of love behind her. Not that it wasn't there before – she had just been too mentally cluttered to see it.

Meeting Danny had also opened up her life to the dreams she wanted to follow. And being able to work flexibly for Ray was all she had needed to allow her creativity to shine for itself – and for herself, too. Being separated from a long-term relationship had also allowed her time to think and just be.

Although she loved being in a relationship, not being needed had been quite refreshing, too. Getting up at whatever time she wanted, eating when she wanted, even going to bed when she wanted, and essentially being in control of her every move without considering someone else, had been completely liberating.

However, love was love, and even if you tried to hide from it, it was always there. It would stay and fight. Just like Nate had done.

He had seemed so sincere when he had come to see her in

Windsor, and his communication since had been solid. But the stronger she was getting in her head post-diagnosis, the more she was beginning to think that maybe she shouldn't just be with someone through fear. That would be settling – and Victoria Sharpe wasn't a woman for settling!

Her kiss with Jerico had been a while ago now, but it had shaken her to her core. Granted, she hadn't known the man long, but his actions had been pretty amazing too. The Vettriano book had made her feel like he did know her. But she actually knew a lot more about him than he knew about her, now. He had loved his parents and had a sister. He lived in Bray and wrote amusing books about a detective called Mr Pigeons. He had also loved his now-dead dog, Fat Frank. She shook her head to try and stop her ridiculous overthinking, but her butterfly mind was in full flight.

Ray's mum's wise words – *don't settle for the one you can live with, wait for the one you can't live without* – finally resonated with her. She also thought back to Ray's simple question about whether Jerico made her laugh. She smiled to herself at just the thought of him. She certainly felt alive with that man. He kept her on her toes with his wit and wisdom. At forty, he was older than Nate, too, and she had enjoyed that new level of maturity.

But most importantly, Jerico Flint looked at her with diamonds in his eyes, without a glimmer of zirconium in sight.

Vic began to echo Pink's poignant chorus aloud, not caring who in the busy carriage heard.

As the taxi made its way from the station to Nate's new abode, she reached inside her purse and pulled out a strip of passport-type photos of them both, which they had had taken the week they first met. Cheekily poking tongues out in the way new lovers do, kissing, canoodling and basically having fun. She had looked so carefree then. He, so handsome. She remembered they'd spent a day in London wandering along the Embankment, drinking and chatting and laughing, experiencing the joy of those first heady days of meeting someone new. Someone you knew was going to be in your life for more than a moment.

She hadn't had the heart to take it out after it had been there in her purse for so many years. But looking at it now, all she could feel was sadness.

The taxi driver was super-friendly and chatted away to her as they wound their way through the narrow roads with their backdrop of craggy mountain tops and rolling green hills. But quaint stone cottages and sheep grazing peacefully didn't make Vic feel in any way relaxed.

A long field-lined drive eventually led to a rose-covered cottage with a bright blue front door and a delighted-looking Nate running towards her. Vic felt pained, as she could see that he was beaming with happiness.

'Sharpie!' he shouted as she opened the car door. Then, after paying the taxi driver, he got her weekend case out of the boot.

As they reached the front door, Nate put the case down, threw his long arms around her and held her tight. 'God, I've missed you so much, lovely one. It's so good to see you. Come on, let's get you inside.' He laughed and led her by the hand.

'This place is beautiful. It's like a cottage I've dreamt about owning. All that's missing is a white picket fence and chickens running around.' Vic's enthusiasm belied her feelings of dread.

'I told you – I really have lucked out here.' It was the first time that Vic had ever seen Nate proud. The kitchen was rustic and not as small as she had imagined it might be from the outside. He flicked on the kettle. 'Coffee? Tea? Me?' He laughed.

'Tea, please.' Vic tried frantically to form the words in her mind that would make sense, that would cause the least hurt.

But just as it had done so many times before, procrastination had suddenly become her middle name, and she allowed Nate to run with his excitement.

'The main man, my boss, is away for the whole week, so I've got today and the whole weekend to myself. I've got so much planned – or we can just stay and chill out here. Up to you. There's an amazing pool house up at the main house that we can use. There's also a croquet lawn, which could be fun.'

'You playing croquet?' Vic laughed. 'You've changed. Anyway, I want to see this place; give me a show round.' She jumped up and ran first into a cosy lounge, with a large flatscreen TV, dusky-pink corner sofa and a coffee table carved into an elephant shape. A standard lamp with a carved monkey on its pole stood in the corner and expensive abstract art graced the walls.

'Wow, those paintings.' Vic was open-mouthed.

'I knew you'd love those. Sir James – that's the guy who owns this place – he's travelled extensively. You should see the main house. It's out of this world.'

'A "Sir", no less – listen to you!'

Nate gave her one of the lopsided smiles that used to make her feel funny inside, but now knowing what she was about to say to him, all she could feel was a growing panic. He took her by the hand and led her to a closed door. He put his right hand over her eyes, and with a loud 'Ta da,' pushed open the door with his left and dropped his hand from her face.

'Oh, Nate, I can't believe it!' Vic felt like she might be sick as she took in the easel and a table that he had just placed a pot of paint and a brush on. Light streamed in from two large skylights.

'A little studio for you,' Nate announced proudly. 'If you want to be here, that is,' he added quietly. 'I didn't buy much because I don't know what you use and stuff...'

'It's perfect.' Vic's voice cracked. 'Thank you.'

'Now I'm in your good books, quick, let me show you where the action takes place... I mean, will take place.'

Vic slowly began following him up the narrow staircase. She stopped on the second step, took the deepest of breaths, then said in a voice that even she didn't recognise as her own, 'Nate, stop. I can't do this. We need to talk.'

They sat across the kitchen table with cups of tea in hand. Nate looked grey. 'You don't want to come here, do you?'

Vic said nothing.

'If I have to, I will move back to London. We'll make it work.' Nate held panic in his voice.

Vic shook her head. 'Nate, I'm so sorry, it's got nothing to do with moving up here. I don't want to be with you anymore.' Her voice began to crack. 'It is over between us.'

'I've fucked up so many times, I know I have. I'm so sorry, Vic, that I wasn't there in your hour of need. I keep reliving how bloody selfish I was.'

'Like I said before, you were scared. I get it. We've both made mistakes.' Vic took a drink of tea. 'My time apart from you has made me realise I don't want to be with someone I don't love enough, either. You were so adamant about that before, yourself.'

Nate nodded. 'That's fair, but I had time to think and miss you and I figured even if you were only giving me eighty per cent of you, it would be more than most other women I have ever met. You are an incredible woman, Vic. Your energy is infectious.'

Vic felt tears pricking her eyes. 'Oh, Nate. I've been so unfair to you. Keeping you hanging on, because I was too much of a coward to go out in the big wide world with my diagnosis. And, well, when you said you wanted me back, it was a way out of having to worry about that anymore. A compromise. So I didn't have to face the future or have to tell anyone what was wrong with me. I'm so sorry.'

'So, what's changed, then?'

'I'm not scared anymore, Nate. I can do this with HIV, and people will need to love me for who I am.' The words flew out of her mouth from somewhere without thought, so maybe she did actually mean them.

Nate banged his hand on the pine kitchen table and whispered, 'Hallelujah. Halle-bloody-lujah.' Tears began to fall down his face. 'You are beautiful inside and out, Victoria Sharpe. I have been blue in the face trying to get you to realise this, but until you feel it yourself then you never will feel it. And if getting HIV has led you to this place, then bloody hell. If I never see you again, then that's OK because, hopefully, now, despite everything, you realise what's important. Because *you* are important, Vic.'

Vic was crying now too. She had to be honest. 'I'm so sorry, Nate, but I've met someone else. We haven't slept together or anything like that, but... I like him.'

Nate put his hand on top of hers. 'It's OK.' Tears were still streaming down his face. 'With all you've been through, I just want you to be happy. Will he look after you?'

Vic shrugged. 'I haven't told him about my HIV yet so I don't even know if he will want a relationship once he knows.'

'Well, if he needs a reference...' Nate managed one of his lopsided grins, then got up and splashed cold water from the kitchen tap on his face. 'Maybe our relationship had run its course anyway.' He sighed, as he stood leaning against the sink. 'What is it they say? The seven-year itch? We just had ours a year early. Come here, you.'

Nate held out his hand and pulled Vic up out of her chair. Without resistance, she snuggled into his chest as he held her tightly in the way that she loved.

'We had a blast at the start.' Nate sniffed.

Vic nodded her head up and down against his chest, then pulled away and sat back down. 'We had a blast for many years, Nate.' She sighed deeply. 'Will you stay here, do you think?'

'Yes, for the time being.'

'I can see why. It's right up your street, with so many outdoor pursuits on your doorstep.'

'Yes, and now I know that you're not coming, I'll make more of an effort to go out.' Nate smirked. 'And Sir James does have a pretty hot daughter.'

'You're incorrigible.' Vic managed a smile. 'Maybe find one who doesn't mind climbing mountains, this time, eh?' Her voice lifted.

Nate grinned. 'How's the painting going?'

'I've found my calling. I feel so much freer and I really am enjoying it again now.'

Nate beamed. 'That's amazing.'

'And Mum has been sober for months!'

'No way! Go, Kath!'

'And Jake is really my dad, and Joti next door to Mum – you know, the Sri Lankan lady I mentioned – well, she's my half-sister.'

Nate laughed aloud. 'Now you're shitting me.'

'I'm really not.'

'What the fuck!'

'Tell me about it.'

They were silent for what seemed like an age. Then Vic stood up and reached for her handbag on the kitchen side. 'I'm going to go now, Nate.'

His face fell. 'But you've only just got here. Stay for the weekend – for old times' sake.'

'No, Nate. I need to get home.'

'Can we stay in touch, then, please? You know how much I hate goodbyes.'

'Let's just see where life takes us, OK?' Vic, proud of her own strength, sighed deeply.

Nate nodded. 'You know I only wish the best for you.' His voice cracked and he looked away.

'And me, you.' Vic wobbled. 'I need to sort my face. Can you ring me a taxi please?'

Vic went up to the bathroom, used the loo and wiped the black mascara streaks from her face. The taxi was already waiting for her when she came downstairs. Without words, Nate held out his arms out to her and hugged her again, tightly. As she walked towards the taxi, case in hand, she turned around.

'See you when you're older, Nathaniel Carlisle.'

The Drop-in Centre

A few days later, Vic, fresh out of the shower, balanced her mobile against her ear as she looked for a suitable top to put on with her jeans. She could hear her mum laughing downstairs at something on the kitchen radio.

'Mand, it's me. Not a bad time with feeds, is it?'

'No, he's a great sleeper – just like his father. Just got myself a cuppa so it's perfect timing. You OK?'

'Yes. As you know, Nate took it so well that I feel like a great weight has been lifted, to be honest.'

'Good. And dare I ask if you've said anything to Jerico yet?'

'This is why I'm ringing, actually. You know I went to that drop-in centre in Slough months ago?'

'Yep.' Vic could hear Mandy taking a slurp of tea.

'Well, they're have an evening session tonight, all around HIV and relationships. I kind of thought it might help me get my words out in the right way, when I do tell him, but I'm not sure.' Vic let out a growl of frustration as she awkwardly pulled a top over her head, trying not to displace the handset in the process.

'What are you are worried about?' Mandy's kindness shone through, as always.

'It's just, I don't know if I want to talk about anything HIV-related. Especially with a group of strangers.'

'A group of strangers who will understand a whole lot more than most about your situation.'

'I guess.' Vic sighed.

'Go along and see how you feel. Maybe it'll be good to get a different perspective, to understand how others have dealt with all sorts, not just relationships.'

'OK. Thanks, Mand. I just needed your wise reassurance. I'm going to go.'

'Aww, well, good luck, and be sure to fill me in.'

'Will do. Love you, mate.'

'Love you right back.'

Vic checked her phone for messages, then threw it onto the bed. She picked it up again, then cast it back to the duvet. Then, with a shake of her shoulders and a firm 'Just do it,' she slid the handset open and started to text.

> Queen Victoria here. I'm around from 8ish tonight, if you fancied meeting up for a drink?

Jerico's reply was instant.

> Queen V! I'm working until 8. I'll text you a pub in or near to Slough when I find one I like. 8.15 perfect.

Vic screamed, then did a little dance around her bedroom. The drop-in centre was in Slough, so that worked well.

She sat down at her dressing table and began to put her make-up on. With the initial euphoria of the date that she had bravely orchestrated worn off, and realising that tonight's session might not give her all the answers she needed, she began to go over and over in her head what she might say – and, more scarily, how Jerico might react. She cleared her throat and spoke aloud into the mirror.

'So, Jerico, I have something to tell you. I like you. In fact, I haven't been able to stop thinking about you since our kiss by the river. But I am HIV-positive. Which I know sounds scary, but...'

Vic groaned. Why would anyone want to take on someone with HIV, if they had a choice? Maybe it was better not to say anything, and spare him the awkwardness of having to be nice to her so as not to hurt her feelings. And then if he did friend-zone her, which was highly likely, could she just be his friend? Like Orla said, she didn't think she could. On the other hand, the thought of not seeing him again was too much to bear. But she'd want to rip his clothes off all the time, so that wouldn't work either. She groaned again. He might not even want her, anyway. It had been just a kiss, and yes he had come to Brighton, too, and bought all her display paintings, but his friend lived in Hove down the road anyway, so it wasn't actually that much of an effort. Maybe she had just imagined how she thought he felt about her, as a safety net to her sanity and her now-single status.

She picked up her favourite red lipstick. With her upper lip complete, she moved to the lower one, filling in the centre first before blending outwards. She pressed her lips together gently, ensuring the colour was evenly distributed.

With war-paint on, she looked at her reflection and took a deep breath. She felt an unexpected surge of determination. She was ready.

Vic was greeted at the door of Hope Cottage by a very smiley

Chrissie. 'Ah, Victoria, isn't it? Long time no see. It's great to have you back. You doing OK?'

'Yes, yes. You?'

'All good in my stable, thank you for asking.'

Vic beamed back. 'Good, good.'

'Any plans for the long weekend?'

'No, I'm just going with the flow,' Vic said with little enthusiasm, realising that small talk really wasn't her thing and half-wishing she hadn't bothered to come. 'So, what's on the agenda for tonight, then, Chrissie?'

'"Agenda" makes it sound dead posh.' The support worker's dirty laugh was infectious. 'It's really not. People turn up around now. My Doug will put some tea, coffee and biscuits in the dining room and then I'll kick off the session. Not sure if you're aware, but we have a counsellor coming tonight, to talk about HIV and relationships.'

'Yes, I did know about that part. That's why... why I thought I'd come tonight.' Vic suddenly felt anxious. 'I'm a bit nervous actually.'

Chrissie put her hand on Vic's shoulder. 'You've got this, kid. And we've all got your back here, whenever you need us. You're not on your own.'

'What time are they arriving, then?'

'He'll join us all around seven for an hour max. Then once you've had a chat amongst yourselves, then you're free to stay, go, do whatever you please.'

'How many are you expecting?'

'As we advertise ourselves as a drop-in centre, we never know. It's the Wednesday before a Bank Holiday weekend, and I'm not sure if that will affect numbers. Might do, but you'll be able to ask more questions yourself if that's the case. Be a real shame if the turnout is poor, as the boss upstairs says this fella is dead good and you're the only one here at the moment.'

Vic walked into the empty dining room, looked out to the

sparse garden area, and took a deep breath. She'd encouraged Orla to get a counsellor and she still hadn't done it herself. Maybe if this guy were as effective as Chrissie implied, then she could ask if she could see him privately. And this would be a decent way to suss someone out, in a group setting. Reading up on counsellors, Vic had learnt that it was important to feel an affinity with the person who was going to delve right into your soul and out again.

She was just checking her phone for messages when a short, stocky, good-looking blond guy walked in. His long, black paint-spattered shorts showed off tanned muscular legs.

'Hello,' Vic said nervously. 'I'm Victoria.'

'All right.' The man nodded. 'I'm Cole. 'Scuse the work clothes, I'm working on a site down the road this week and went to the pub before I came here. I haven't seen you in here before, have I? Never forget a pretty face, me.'

'No, first time.'

'And before you ask, Victoria, I'm not gay.'

Wow, Vic thought, not quite expecting this level of direct-ness from a stranger. 'Er, I wasn't going to.'

The painter continued without filter. 'You on meds yet, then?'

'No. I only found out in December.'

'It's a shock, innit? But that does wear off.'

'Are you on meds, then?' Getting with the lingo, Vic took in the young lad in front of her. He must be late twenties, she assumed, with a textured crop hairstyle that faded out to his ears. He had a cheeky face – not unlike Albie's, she thought.

'Yeah, just started and – touch wood' – he rubbed his hand on the table – 'I'm feeling OK, so far.'

'So do you come here often?' Vic cringed at what she'd just said.

'Ha! Yes. Slough's greatest pick-up joint. We all come in positive, at least.'

Vic laughed. 'Jesus, I do so need a relationship coach.'

'I disagree. What you doing later, love?'

They both then started laughing. Vic shook her head. 'Now wouldn't that be just too easy, but I've got a lot going on at the moment.'

'Haven't we all, princess? Joking aside, this place is great – has been a lifeline for me when I felt I couldn't go on.'

'Oh, Cole, I'm sorry you've felt that way.'

'Par for the course with all this shit, isn't it?'

'So have you told anyone?' Vic was genuinely concerned.

'It's not really good pub banter, is it?' Cole suddenly looked quite sad. 'Can you imagine?' He pretended to hold a drink in the air. '"All right, boys, so, I was on a lads' holiday, there was this girl, she was hot. I fucked her bareback and now I've got a virus that could kill me if I don't take medicine all my life. And you probably all think you can catch it by sharing a pint with me." No, thanks. I'm not putting myself through it. What if they couldn't cope with it?' His voice tailed off. 'It'd be shit.'

'You might be surprised.' The level of irony around Victoria's own similar worries about Jerico suddenly hit her.

'I don't want to take the chance. Not everyone is willing to be educated. Don't tell me you haven't had minutes of feeling unclean or unlovable,' Cole asked, sounding far wiser than his years.

Vic sighed deeply. 'Yeah, yes, I have, and one of my friends did freak out... but she came around. I've realised that people who care about you, care about *you*. What about your family?'

'Nah. I can't. I don't wanna upset my old woman or my sisters. I'm so grateful for this place. Means I can talk about it openly and not feel ashamed.'

'We shouldn't feel ashamed. We *all* have sex. It just annoys me that the stigma is so rife.' Vic smiled at Doug as he brought in a flask of tea and coffee and some biscuits and put them in the middle of the table.

'You really are a newbie, aren't you?' Cole reached for a biscuit, shoved it in in one go, then spoke, sending crumbs flying everywhere. 'I'd rather keep in my bubble. I find it easier that way. Sorry, I'm starving – should've eaten at the pub.'

Doug popped his head back through. 'I can make you a sandwich, lad, if you want one? Got some ham in the fridge.'

'Wicked, mate. Yes, please.'

Doug looked at Vic. 'You all right for food, lass?'

'Yes, yes, thanks.' Vic nodded, thinking it really was quite like a family here.

Cole grabbed another biscuit. 'Anyway, I say, ignore the naysayers. Which is quite ironic considering I don't tell anyone. But I'm a bloke and I have needs. Hence me being here tonight. I've been hiding behind this diagnosis for too long. It's time to get myself out there, but I want to do right by the women I meet, without scaring the shit out of them when I tell them.'

'Aww,' Vic said aloud, without meaning to. 'Well done, and I hear you, I really do.' She poured herself a mug of tea. 'Do you want one?'

'Coffee, please. I've only had a pint but best not to smell of it in front of the shrink.'

Cole's mobile rang. 'I need to take this – see you in a minute.' He winked and pushed open the double doors out to the garden before Vic had a chance to pour his drink and give it to him.

Chrissie appeared. 'All right, Vic. Looks like this could be it: just me, you and our Cole. He's a good lad, that one.' The savvy support worker waved at Cole, who was sitting outside on the bench seat chatting to someone animatedly. Checking her watch, she beckoned him to head in.

'Hey, Chrissie, how you doing?' he said as he came back into the room.

'Happy to see you, lad. You all right? Told your mum yet?'

Cole shook his head. 'Why do I need to do that when I've

got you here, hey?' He then grinned. Vic could tell the obvious
bond between them.

'I held off telling my mum, too, but she already knew.' Vic
smiled.

Chrissie nodded. 'We know everything, us mums. And even
if my lad came home and said he'd robbed the vicarage, I'd still
have to help him. Like lionesses, we are. Whatever the
situation.'

'Give over, the pair of you. You're ganging up on me now.'
Cole poured himself a coffee and then started to devour the
sandwich that Doug had just put down on the table. The front-
door buzzer rang.

'Right. Take a seat, you two – that must be our man. I'll
have a quick chat and bring him through.'

Cole looked at Victoria. 'You're not my type, but you won't
have trouble finding anyone. You're beautiful, darlin'.'

Vic shook her head in amusement. 'I'll allow the compli-
ment – thank you.'

As Chrissie walked in followed by the counsellor, Vic's
smile was abruptly knocked off her face and her jaw dropped
open in absolute shock and astonishment.

'So, I explained to Jerico that it's just you two tonight, but
he's happy to be here and chat, as he's given up his time
anyway.'

Jerico Flint's emerald-green eyes locked onto Victoria's as he
sat down opposite her, and, as she looked into his soul, her
bottom lip started to wobble. Shooting up onto her feet, she
rushed through the open doors into the garden.

She was standing in the garden with her head in her hands
when she heard him follow her out there and felt his arm rest
around her shoulders.

'I knew there had to be a reason. I mean, who turns down
the advances of an extremely handsome and debonaire best-

selling author?' Jerico's voice was calm and measured, even as he joked.

Vic couldn't even look at him. 'I couldn't tell you.'

'I understand.' Jerico squeezed her shoulder. 'But now I know what we're dealing with here, I couldn't be happier.'

'Happy?'

'Yes, because now I understand.'

'And now you can walk away without getting involved.' Vic's throat expressed a funny little anguished squeak.

'*Au contraire*, Queen V, *au contraire*. That would be like me walking away from a lifetime of sunshine.'

Vic bit her lip. 'That is possibly the most beautiful thing anyone has ever said to me in my life.'

'It's true,' Jerico replied gently. 'I haven't stopped thinking about you from the moment we kissed.'

Vic cleared her throat. 'I've got so much to say to you, but this is not the time or the place. There's no way I can stay for this session.'

Jerico turned and stuck his thumb up to a concerned-looking Chrissie, who was now standing outside the double doors.

'It's fine. We'll talk later. Head to Bray for 8.30. I'll text you the details.'

'And everything really is OK?' Vic's voice shook.

'We get one shot at this thing called life, Queen V, and we are in effect only here for a long weekend, so all I can say is we might as well enjoy it. How much money have you got on you?'

'What sort of question is that?' Vic looked perplexed. 'What do you mean?'

Without reply, she followed him back down the garden.

Jerico greeted Chrissie and Cole with a smile. 'I was just explaining to the young lady here that the cost of not following your heart is spending the rest of your life wishing you had. So, you have some place to go now, don't you?' Jerico raised his eyes.

Without the words to reply, Victoria returned his look with one of awe.

'Are you OK, love?' the Liverpudlian questioned as she unlocked the front door to let Vic out.

'Never better. And you were right, Chrissie – he *is* dead good.'

'See, I told you to trust in the timing of your life.' The support worker winked and shut the door behind her.

The Beginning

Vic's heart was beating out of her chest when Albie dropped her in the public car park in the stunning Berkshire riverside village of Bray. She waved her brother off, then checked the text message that Jerico had just sent her. He had instructed that, from the car park, she should head in the direction of the river down to Ferry Lane. Here she would see The Waterside Inn on her left and in front of her a single bench looking out to the Thames.

Bless Albie for collecting her from the drop-in centre, then waiting at home for her to get ready and bring her to Jerico's suggested meeting spot. She had rushed inside and quickly changed into her favourite powder-blue halter-neck summer dress, which she knew accentuated her eyes. To keep herself cool, she had tied her hair back from her face in a low ponytail, which cascaded down her back like a silky chestnut wave. She had even put on sandals with a little bit of sparkle on them. A light, smoky eye and a smudge of lip gloss over her red lipstick had finished her look.

The evening sun, low and still warm, beckoned Vic towards the riverside and through the picturesque village she'd often passed but had never visited. Her pace slowed as she took in the beauty of the water glistening in front of her. After the past few months of waiting for this moment, the tension in her shoulders eased, her breath deepened and the soothing murmur of boats on the river provided a balm to her butterfly mind.

A few metres ahead, a family of swans glided near the riverbank. And further across the water, she could make out the most sumptuous riverside homes.

And then she saw him with his back to her, sitting on the bench. His raven-black hair was tied back in a neat ponytail and poked out beneath a stylish sunhat. He, too, had changed – into a gaudily patterned short-sleeved shirt and the long beige shorts he had worn in Windsor the day of *the kiss*.

Vic was within a few paces of him when she started to tiptoe. Then, gliding down slowly she sat at the opposite end of the bench to him, saying nothing. A gentle breeze stirred the pages of the book he was reading. He loudly snapped it shut, and turned to face her, making her jump out of her skin. His soulful eyes were twinkling with amusement and kindness as he smiled warmly at her.

'Queen Victoria! Fancy seeing you here.'

'In your special place, you mean?' she replied, grinning from ear to ear.

'Like I said, if I tell you that, then it won't be special, and Mr Pigeons may have to kill you.' Jerico's face remained straight. Vic ripped at the gold embossed wrapping paper and when she saw what was inside, her whole face lit up. 'You spoil me with your Vettriano bounty.' She let out a little squeal. 'And Ae Fond Kiss, I love this print SO much.' She looked intently at the simple but poignant painting of a couple about to kiss intimately under the mistletoe.

'I kind of thought you would,' Jerico offered, moving along

to join her at her end of the bench. 'Are you going to open this then?' He retrieved a small envelope that had been thrown to the floor in haste.

Vic opened it to find a card with the same beautiful calligraphy that she had so joyfully come across in the Christmas present he had given her.

Kiss me again and let's get these souls dancing, shall we?

Yours, hopefully
Jerico Pigeons
X

'Pigeons!' Vic squealed.

He put his finger to her lips to shush her, then gently putting the painting down beside her as their eyes met. A palpable tension. A magnetic pull. A comfortable silence between them until Victoria whispered, 'Kiss me again, Mr Pigeons.'

EPILOGUE
SAINT LUCIA

Mr Pigeons and the Perilous Pitons

April 2010

'Remember when we were sat in that Brighton café in the freezing cold and Mandy insisted we have our hen weekends in the Caribbean?' Victoria sucked through the straw of her pineapple-garnished cocktail.

'Yes,' Orla laughed. 'And just look at us now, sitting in a beach-front bar, drinking rum punch. Trust you to go one better, Sharpie, and actually be getting married in St Lucia, too.'

'Might be you next.' Mandy prodded her friend gently in the ribs.

Orla turned her nose up. 'I don't think my Greg will do it again.'

'Hmm, *my* Greg, eh?' Mandy laughed. 'He'll always be Mr Winkler to us.'

Orla couldn't help but grin. 'Shut up, the pair of you.'

Mandy put her hand to her tummy. 'So annoyed I can't have a drink.'

Vic laughed. 'Well, you will keep getting up the duff.'

'Tell me about it. But forty was always my cut-off age and now this is a girl, I have to stop at three or Steve will actually kill me. It's such a joy that his parents have taken the boys for the week.'

Vic kissed her friend on the cheek. 'I love it. It makes up for all those I couldn't have.'

Mandy welled up. 'Oh, mate.'

'I'm fine, honestly. I am the naughtiest auntie to those two gorgeous nieces of mine, and you know how much we love our dogs.' Vic took another drink. 'I really couldn't be happier.'

'Aww. If you're happy, we're happy.' Mandy grinned.

'And also, please can I request not to be a godmother for this one? It's costing me a flipping fortune.'

'And don't you be fecking looking at me with godmother vibes in your eyes. I've just about learnt to look after meself,' Orla added, causing them all to burst into laughter.

'What a difference five years makes, eh?' Mandy said wistfully.

'Yes, indeedy.' Orla put her head to the sun. 'I meant to ask you earlier, Vic: how are you feeling on your new medication?'

'So far so good, thanks. I remember, after that fateful Brighton night, all I could think about for months was my HIV. But now it's only when I take the tablets and go for my regular checks that I have to think about it at all.'

'I'm so proud of you, mate.' Mandy welled up again. 'You've handled it all so well.'

'Thanks to having friends like you, that's why. Stop, *I'm* getting teary now.'

'Oh, quit all this emotional shenanigans, the lot of you, and raise your glasses for a toast.'

Vic and Mandy did as they were told.

'*One for all and all for one,*' Orla declared.

'*One for all and all for one,*' they all repeated.

Orla stood up and shimmied her shoulders. 'Now come on, hens – let's get clucking!'

Victoria could feel the whole wedding party – consisting of Kath and Jake; Albie, Joti and their twin girls; Mandy and Steve; Orla and Mr Winkler; Ray and Marcus; Danny and Philip; and Gina, Jerico's sister – willing her to get her vows right as the jovial vicar commenced the declarations.

Then, with the words 'You may kiss the bride' and a resounding cheer from the congregation, Mr and Mrs Pigeons began to write their very own love story.

June 2024

Victoria opened her eyes and kissed her husband softly on the lips. 'Happy anniversary, Mr Pigeons.'

'Right back at you, Mrs Pigeons.'

'Fourteen years – how did that happen?' Vic propped herself up onto her elbow and looked at her handsome beau.

'I don't know, but I'm so glad that I married a rich and famous artist.' He kissed her nose. 'Right. Breakfast in bed for my little butterfly, and even better news is that, as it's Sunday, not only am I going to spoil you rotten, but we have a day off from your gallery.'

Jerico got out of bed, stretched noisily and opened the French windows at the end of the long, elegant room. The mesmerising sound of river birds, the swish of trees and a gentle breeze filtered in.

Then the tranquillity was broken by the sound of loud barking and panicked scrabbling against the bedroom door.

'Oh God, here they come, the household cavalry.' Jerico tutted as he opened the bedroom door and two lively mongrels came barrelling in, leapt onto the bed and proceeded to cover

Victoria with wet doggy kisses. 'Monica, Fat Frank the Second, get off your mother – that's my job!'

Victoria laughed loudly. 'Maybe having a dysfunctional family isn't so bad after all.'

Jerico stood in the doorway in all his glorious nakedness. 'My darling girl, I wouldn't have it any other way.'

A LETTER FROM THE AUTHOR

Don't miss out on all my news!

A huge thank you for taking the time to read *How Do I Tell You?* I hope you loved Victoria's journey as much as I felt proud to be writing it. If you want to join other readers in hearing all about my new releases and other writerly goings on, please do sign up to my mailing list here:

If you want to join other readers in hearing all about my new releases, you can sign up for my newsletter:

www.stormpublishing.co/nicola-may

And if you want to keep up to date with all my other publications and other writerly goings on, you can sign up to my mailing list:

www.nicolamay.com

Your review is like gold dust!

If you could also spare a few moments to leave a review that would be hugely appreciated. Even a short review can make all the difference in encouraging a reader to discover my books for the first time. Thank you so much!

Why I wrote this story

Since a close friend shared her HIV diagnosis with me in 2006, I have witnessed her ongoing resilience, courage, and vulnerability, as well as the stigma and misunderstanding surrounding her condition. Although I've long felt the need to contribute to the conversation about women and HIV, the moment never seemed right. With treatments now life-changingly effective and continually improving, but with 53%(i) of people living with HIV worldwide being women and girls, and women accounting for one third(ii) of those with the virus in the UK, I believe it's time to open up this important discussion.

Thanks again for being part of this amazing journey with me and I hope you'll stay in touch – I have so many more stories and ideas to entertain you with!

Nicola May

www.nicolamay.com

 facebook.com/NicolaMayAuthor

 x.com/nicolamay1

 instagram.com/author_nicola

ACKNOWLEDGMENTS

With special thanks to:

My cherished friend Kia, my rock and the inspiration for this book. To Richard Germain for his heartfelt advice and for introducing me to the indomitable Sarah Macadam at Thames Valley Positive Support (TVPS). For the generosity of time and support from Stephan Gampenrieder and Marianne Holt at Terrence Higgins Trust. To Georgia Clark for linking me up with retired HIV nurse extraordinaire Jan Wischhusen. Not forgetting my exceptional editors, and my beautiful sister, Fiona Powell, for offering their skilful and wise insights throughout. As always, big, huge love to the rest of my wonderful family and friends. Last and by no means least to Stanley the Cat, who I'm convinced will start miaowing in swear words soon.

BE KIND. BE AWARE. BE INFORMED

(i)(online source) 'What share of the population living with HIV are women?'. Our World in Data (2024). Data adapted from UNAIDS (via World Bank)

(ii) (online source) 'A Terrence Higgins Trust and Sophia Forum Report: Women and HIV Invisible No Longer' (2024)

For HIV Support and Information

Information on Thames Valley Positive Support (TVPS), high-lighting the services that they offer, plus their donations page can be found here: www.tvps.org.uk/donate

Information on Terrence Higgins Trust and their donations page can be found at: donate.tht.org.uk

As with all charities, even the smallest of donations would be extremely welcome.

Printed in Great Britain
by Amazon

56440352R00169